DANGEROUS
Beauty

Books by Melissa Koslin

Never Miss
Dangerous Beauty

DANGEROUS
Beauty

A NOVEL

MELISSA KOSLIN

Revell

a division of Baker Publishing Group
Grand Rapids, Michigan

© 2022 by Melissa Kosciuszko

Published by Revell
a division of Baker Publishing Group
PO Box 6287, Grand Rapids, MI 49516-6287
www.revellbooks.com

Library of Congress Cataloging-in-Publication Data
Names: Koslin, Melissa, 1979– author.
Title: Dangerous beauty / Melissa Koslin.
Description: Grand Rapids, MI : Revell, a division of Baker Publishing Group, [2022]
Identifiers: LCCN 2021053964 | ISBN 9780800740177 (paperback) | ISBN
    9780800742263 (casebound) | ISBN 9781493438877 (ebook)
Subjects: GSAFD: Romantic suspense fiction.
Classification: LCC PS3611.O749175 D36 2022 | DDC 813/.6—dc23
LC record available at https://lccn.loc.gov/2021053964

This book is a work of fiction. Names, characters, places, and incidents are the product of the author's imagination or are used fictitiously. Any resemblance to actual events, locales, or persons, living or dead, is coincidental.

Baker Publishing Group publications use paper produced from sustainable forestry practices and post-consumer waste whenever possible.

22 23 24 25 26 27 28   7 6 5 4 3 2 1

For Ethan and Elliana.
We wish we could have known you.

For Elizabeth.
We can't wait to welcome you into the world.

Chapter ONE

She ran.

She'd finally orchestrated an opportunity, and she'd run.

Twigs snapped under her bare feet. She hardly felt the pain. It was the sound that rattled through her. *They'll hear. They'll find me.*

She ran faster.

Branches reached out and scraped her skin.

She slipped on some wet leaves but managed to stay on her feet.

She couldn't breathe, but she kept going.

To her left, she could hear cars. It didn't sound like a freeway, but maybe a rural highway. *Should I try to hitchhike?* But the thought of getting into a car with another stranger was too much. She needed to get as far away as quickly as she could, but she wasn't getting into a car with anyone. Logically, she knew the likelihood of finding someone as bad as those she was running from was remote, but logic wasn't forefront for her. Right now was flight mode. Survival.

Darkness started to close around her like a cage.

Go deeper into the woods and stay there tonight? She thought about rest, that she needed to stop and sleep at some point, but she couldn't get her legs to stop running. She'd run miles already.

She'd probably collapse before finding enough control to get herself to stop.

Lights in the distance.

Flight mode subsided slightly. Her survival instincts screamed at her to stay away from people, but she knew she couldn't stay out here in the woods the rest of her life, however long that ended up being. If she were back home, she'd have a fighting chance, but she didn't know this area, what kinds of animals were native, which plants were edible. As she slowed her pace, she realized how cold it was.

She approached the edge of the woods and peered around a tree to the source of the lights—a truck stop. There were so many gas pumps she couldn't count them. There were big semitrucks with their rumbling engines that made her nerves feel like lit matches. They sounded just like the truck she'd been thrown into back home, the one that had taken her over the border to this country. That was actually better than what she'd been living through the last several days. On the truck, there had been many women. They'd had one another for warmth, for comfort.

She hid behind the tree. Since when had that nightmare on the truck morphed into a positive memory? They'd lost a few of the women—a couple of them just didn't wake up, and one had suffered a heart attack, she was fairly certain. But she was almost thankful they'd been taken early. It was a better fate.

The chill seeped into her bones, and she wrapped her arms around herself.

She looked over at the truck stop—warmth, a restroom where she could wash. She dearly wished she had some money. She hadn't eaten in two days. And she couldn't steal; her parents had raised her to be honorable, even when it was difficult, especially when it was difficult. But maybe she could find some food in a garbage can.

Carefully, she analyzed the area, identified all entrances and exits, watched the people. They looked so different here. But they didn't appear to be particularly threatening.

She stood straight, took a breath, and pulled her fingers through her long, black hair. Hopefully her appearance didn't draw too much attention. As she walked across the grass, she tried to wipe the dirt off her feet. All while watching every person, every vehicle.

She moved quickly across the asphalt and into the store. It was huge. There were cases and cases of cold drinks, shelves of food, even two different fast-food restaurants. She made herself ignore the bottles of water so close and headed straight for the ladies' restroom. Mercifully, it was empty. She turned on a faucet, washed her hands, and drank. She filled her cupped hands over and over. Then she washed her face, her hands, her arms. She glanced at the door and decided to risk washing her lower half as well. She lifted her dress and rapidly washed. Maybe she could blend in, disappear, if she was clean enough. She was drying off her feet with rough paper towels when the door opened. She watched the middle-aged woman peripherally but didn't make eye contact.

The woman said something. She thought maybe the woman was asking if she was okay, but with the woman's American accent and how flustered she felt, she wasn't sure. When she looked up, the woman was staring at her, at the bruises on her arms and legs.

She stood, walked into a stall, and locked it.

The woman paused but then used the restroom, washed her hands, and left.

She stood there in the stall and stared at a sticker on the back of the door, written in both English and Spanish. "Human trafficking. Do you need help?"

◦ ▦ ◦

Meric parked and got out of his car. He glanced down at the other entrance before walking inside the store. As he passed the

9

counter, he overheard a middle-aged woman telling the cashier, "I asked her if she was okay, but she just locked herself in a stall. She looked pretty battered."

Meric turned and headed for the hall that led to the restrooms. He stopped outside the ladies' room.

■ ▓ ■

She waited long enough that the woman should be done in the store and back in her car, walked out of the stall, ignoring her image in the mirror, and headed for the door.

She peeked into the hall before slipping out the door.

A strong hand grabbed her arm.

Rage roared through her. She yanked at her arm, but before she could hit the man or scream, he demanded, "Be quiet." It took her a second to realize he'd said it in Spanish, not English. Though he had dark hair and eyes, his skin was too fair—she didn't think he was Mexican, even though his accent was perfect. He lowered his voice, not calming, just quiet. "They're outside."

"Who are you? Let me go." She was sure he wasn't with the men who'd been holding her. He was fairly young like them, probably thirties, but far too well-dressed and polished in his black suit.

She struggled to free her arm.

"I'm not going to hurt you," he said. "They have both entrances covered. You need to call the police."

"I can take care of myself. Let me go."

"This country is different. The police will help."

"No, they won't." She yanked at her arm again, but he was so strong, and she was weak from lack of food, almost no sleep, and all the running.

He held both of her arms and shifted closer. "Stop and think. I know what you've been through, but you need to slow down and think. You have to accept help."

She stopped struggling but glared up at him. He was tall with broad shoulders and strong hands, but she refused to feel intimidated. "You have no idea what I've been through."

"They kidnapped you—out of Mexico, based on your accent. They've abused you and plan to sell you. Am I getting it right?"

"How do you know that? Who are you?"

"Someone who pays attention and who happened to stop for a bottle of water at exactly the right time and place," he said. "If you don't call the police, I will. But you're going to have to tell them your story."

For some reason, tears pricked the backs of her eyes. She hadn't cried at all since they'd taken her—cursed and screamed and fought, but not cried. Why did the tears want to come now?

As he looked at her, his expression changed—something in his eyes. There was a coldness to him that covered him like a sheet of ice, but in his eyes, there was something else. Fury, but also pain.

"Stay here," he said.

Then he walked away. He told the cashier something as he walked by. One of the words sounded like *policia*. He spoke too quickly for her to catch any other words. Was he telling the cashier to call the police?

She shifted to the end of the hall and watched him through the window.

He grabbed a man standing by the door, slammed him up against the glass, face toward her, and looked at her. She realized he was waiting for her to confirm it was one of the men who'd been keeping her prisoner. It was the shorter one with receding blond hair, though he was only maybe late twenties. He called himself Carl.

As she looked at Carl, rage flamed up in her chest.

The polished man seemed to understand her expression. He turned Carl around, even as Carl struggled, and punched him square in the face. Blood splattered against the window, and Carl crumpled to the ground.

Then he burst with speed she wouldn't have guessed a man in

such fine clothes capable of and caught another man, who'd been running away from the other entrance to the store. He caught him halfway across the parking lot, put him in a headlock from behind, and dragged him back to the window.

She walked out from the hall to get a better look. She recognized Josh's face, the face that tormented her nightmares. She made eye contact with the polished man and nodded.

He released the headlock, threw Josh against the glass, and punched him just as hard as he had Carl. Josh slumped to the ground.

The man walked back inside. "Is that all of them?"

She barely got the word out. "Yes."

He turned to the cashier and said something. She heard the word that sounded like *policia* again.

The cashier stammered a response.

The man grumbled "useless" under his breath in Spanish. Then he took a cell phone out of his inside jacket pocket and dialed three numbers.

As she stood there, she realized the entire store had stopped and was staring at both her and the man who'd just knocked out two young, able-bodied men.

He had a short conversation on the phone, hung up, and went back outside to stand over his victims.

She was too shocked to move. Was she really free?

She couldn't stand to be stared at any longer and went outside. "You shouldn't leave," the polished man said.

There were just as many people staring out here, but it didn't feel so bad. Maybe because there was one person here who understood her language. "I don't know . . ."

"I understand you don't know what to think yet. That's a reasonable reaction. But you need to stay here and tell the police what happened."

She realized she'd placed herself with him blocking her view of Josh. Just the thought of looking at him made her want to run.

"If you don't tell the police, they'll be released and will be free to do the same thing to someone else."

A thought struck her. "And they'll arrest you for assaulting them."

"Probably." He didn't seem terribly concerned about that.

But she was. "I'm staying."

"That's brave of you." He said it matter-of-factly, as if not intending to give a compliment, simply stating a truth. He glanced over at Carl, who was still unconscious like Josh.

"Who are you?" she asked. "What's your name?"

"Meric."

A couple of women standing by a parked car whispered to each other.

He glanced at the women and back to her. "May I ask your name?"

She hesitated. "Liliana."

He looked down at Josh and then back to her. There was that something in his eyes again. "Thank you for letting me help you."

"You didn't exactly get permission."

She thought the corner of his mouth twitched just slightly.

The sound of sirens made her jump. A few seconds later, two police cars pulled into the lot.

"I'll stay," Meric said. "You won't be alone."

She'd almost forgotten what it felt like to feel comforted. Everything was suddenly alien.

Meric motioned to the police officers, and they both walked over to him. One of them asked something. She tried to remember the English her mother had taught her. She'd thought her English was decent, but she'd only ever spoken it with her mother, who'd had a distinctly Mexican accent—the American accent was difficult to understand. And being dropped into a foreign country under these circumstances made it harder to focus on a different language.

"Español?" Meric asked.

They both nodded.

"I'm Meric Toledan"—both the officers' expressions flickered with recognition—"and this is Liliana. She was being trafficked by these two men." Meric nodded toward Josh and Carl.

"Is that correct, miss?" one officer asked with a heavy American English accent.

The other officer checked on Josh and then walked over to Carl, surely making certain they were just knocked out.

"Yes, sir." She glanced at Meric then back to the officer. "The cartel took me from my home in Mexico and brought me and about twenty other women across the border in a truck. Then these two men paid them and took me. They said something about a buyer. I think they're middlemen."

"Do you know where the other women are?"

Her shoulders slumped. "No, sir. I've been with these two men for several days. I have no idea where the other women were taken. I don't know why they separated me."

The other officer, after talking into his radio, came back over.

"Because you brought a higher price," Meric said.

Her brows twitched together in confusion.

"Exceptional beauty brings a higher price."

"And how are you involved, Mr. Toledan?" one of the officers asked. The way the officer addressed him sounded like he knew who Meric was, and did she catch a hint of suspicion?

She spoke up. "He saved me. He saw what was happening, and he saved me."

The officer addressed Meric. "How did you know what was happening? Do you know these men? Are you involved?"

Liliana's voice hardened. "He's not involved with them. He risked his own safety to help me."

"Thank you, miss," the officer said and then turned back to Meric. "How did you know what was happening?"

Meric's tone and manner was unemotional. "I overheard a woman telling the cashier about a young lady in the restroom looking scared and battered. I'd already noticed the men standing at both entrances. I waited for Liliana to come out and confirm my suspicions."

The clerk had come outside. She apparently spoke Spanish. "That's right, Officer. This man parked and came inside well after the other two men arrived. He didn't interact with them, not until after he'd spoken to her." She indicated Liliana. "I can pull the security camera footage for you."

"Please do. Thank you." The officer seemed mostly appeased.

The officers asked Liliana several more questions. Inside, she was upset. Now that she didn't need her rage to fuel her and help her survive, she was on the verge of breaking down. While they questioned her, two more officers arrived and an ambulance. The EMTs checked on Josh and Carl, while the officers watched over them.

She answered another question, and her voice shook.

Meric shifted closer and murmured, "You're safe now."

She nodded once, barely a movement.

He hesitated, and then he turned to the officers. "What's going to happen to her? Where will she go?"

"She's undocumented, so we'll have to call ICE. She'll likely be kept here while the courts work out what happens with these two." He indicated Josh and Carl, who were now being loaded onto gurneys. "After that, I assume she'll go back home."

"I can't go back." It popped out of her mouth before she could stop it.

"You don't want to go back to Mexico?" Meric asked.

"I can't . . . My parents and my sister are gone. If I go back, they'll just take me again." She kept looking at Meric, and more of her story spilled from her lips. "They tried to take me once before, but my father fought them off. The next time, they came prepared." She had no idea why she'd been targeted, but she'd seen far too much—there was no way the cartel would let her live.

"They killed your family," Meric said.

15

She nodded. And finally, a tear escaped and fell down her cheek. Meric turned to the officers. "She needs asylum."

"She can certainly request it." Then he added in an apologetic tone, "But asylum is usually for those who fear persecution from their government, typically due to race, religion, or political opinion or activism. In this case, the government of Mexico isn't trying to harm her. They should technically be the ones to protect her." The officer turned to Liliana. "I'm very sorry."

Meric looked at Liliana. She felt like his gaze was boring into her. Men had always looked at her, but with him, it felt different. She should be scared of him—he was cold and distant, and she had the impression he was used to being in command. But she wasn't scared of him. Maybe she wasn't thinking clearly. Maybe she was too overwhelmed.

Meric asked the officers, "May I speak to her for a moment?"

"We need to question the witnesses. Stay here." The officers headed in different directions and began taking statements from people in the parking lot and inside the store.

Meric took off his suit jacket and wrapped it around Liliana's shoulders. "You must be cold."

The jacket held his warmth, and the scent was slightly musky— not cologne, maybe just the scent of his soap mixed with his body chemistry. The fabric was thick and soft, nicer than she'd ever felt in her life.

"Do you think you can trust me?" he asked her.

She didn't know how to respond to that.

"If you get sent back to Mexico," he said, "do you have any other family? Anyplace you can go that would be safe?"

She felt uncomfortable telling him all this. She had the feeling he was trying to do something to help her even more. He'd done enough. "They're dead." She paused to control her voice. "I don't have any money. They took the little my parents had."

"The cartels are powerful in Mexico. You think they'll still target you."

"I don't know what will happen when I'm not delivered to the buyer." She paused. "I . . . There's a leader near where we lived. He . . . he tried to buy me from my father. When that didn't work . . ."

"They're not going to let you go," he said. "You're valuable, you've angered and embarrassed them, and you've seen too much." He looked at her in that intense way of his. "You can't go back."

"I think I have to."

"Applying for an employment green card won't work. I've sponsored several employees, and I don't think I can get any more pushed through at the moment." He paused. "There's a way I can keep you here. But you'd have to trust me."

She waited.

"You'd have to marry me."

"No, you can't do that," Liliana said.

"That's the only way to keep you in the country and out of a detention facility. The system is so overtaxed, there just aren't a lot of places for illegal immigrants to stay, and I don't know how safe the facilities would be for you. If we get married, I can take care of you. Unfortunately, there aren't a lot of options."

Too many thoughts swirled through her mind like a tornado.

He glanced over at the officers and lowered his voice. "I would make sure you're safe, fed, clean, comfortable. That's it."

She tried to catch her thoughts long enough to organize them, like trying to catch a feather in the wind.

One of the officers came back over. "We're wrapping up."

"Where are those two men being taken?" Meric asked.

"Hospital. They need medical attention." He looked at Liliana and added, "They'll be under guard."

"Thank you, sir."

"We'll need to take you with us now," the officer said to her.

Meric lightly touched her arm. The gesture was simple. Nothing, really. But she could feel his touch, his kindness, seeping through the jacket he'd wrapped around her. "Yes," she said to him.

Meric turned to the officer. "We're getting married. As I'm sure you're aware, I'm a citizen. If we're married, she may come home with me, correct? She'll still be available for questioning and testimony."

The officer hesitated, as if shocked. Then he said, "I'm not sure how much red tape will be involved."

"I can take care of that. I simply ask that you not take her while I get things arranged."

"It's late. Government offices are closed. And isn't there a waiting period—"

"I believe you realize who I am," Meric said.

The officer nodded. He glanced at the other officers on the scene. "I'll keep her here for more questioning, but I can't do that for long."

"I don't need long." Meric turned to Liliana. "Will you please hand me my cell phone? It's in the inside breast pocket."

She fished it out and handed it to him.

"Thank you." He pressed a button, waited for the person on the other end to pick up, which was only a few seconds, and proceeded to have a conversation in English. She understood bits and pieces. Apparently, he knew a judge and some other kind of official—senator?—who could help get past any waiting periods or other restrictions.

He paused his conversation and asked her, "What's your last name?"

"Vela."

He also asked which area of Mexico she was from and her parents' names.

He ended the call and told the officer, "Within an hour."

"Are you sure?" Liliana asked.

"Yes." Then he glanced down at her bare feet. He asked the officer, "May I take her inside? She's cold, and she needs something to eat and drink."

"Of course." The officer stepped forward and held the door.

Inside, Meric bought her a bottle of water, which she drank straight down. Then he bought her a bottle of Gatorade. He also bought her an apple and a banana, as well as a pair of sandals that were on a display rack by the door. "I'm sorry they're not warmer," he said.

She kept thanking him for every little thing. She realized the food and shoes were probably nothing to him, but for her, they felt like blessings from God.

They sat on a bench just outside one of the fast-food restaurants. They barely spoke, but she somehow felt calm. Calmer than she'd felt in months, since the cartel first started showing interest in her.

Eventually, his phone rang. He talked in English and then ended the call. He addressed the officer. "You have a courthouse in town. The judge is on his way there to perform the ceremony. The paperwork is ready."

The officer raised his eyebrows. Then he said, "I'll need to take her there. You can follow."

Meric asked Liliana, "Are you all right with that?"

She nodded.

A few minutes later, she sat in the back seat of the police car. She kept looking out the rear window at Meric following in his shiny black car. She kept waiting for him to turn off on a side street and leave her. But he followed all the way to the small courthouse.

They walked into the building, followed by the officer. He said he'd be the witness to the marriage, but Liliana had the feeling he wanted to see if it actually happened. Obviously, Meric was someone of note—perhaps because he was wealthy. But was there more to it than simply that? She wondered if Meric was pushing the limits of the law by marrying her just to keep her safe—maybe the officer was trying to help her by letting the marriage happen?

The judge and a clerk were waiting for them. Meric helped her understand the paperwork, which was in English.

Then they walked into the judge's chambers, followed by the officer.

Meric appeared composed and impassive, as if this were a business transaction. He spoke to the judge in English and then told Liliana, "He doesn't speak Spanish. I'll translate."

She nodded.

As the judge spoke, Meric murmured the translation. His voice was just as cool, no hint of emotion or hesitation. Liliana, however, jittered with emotion. She wasn't entirely sure what she was feeling, but she felt a lot of it. Or maybe it was too many different feelings that got confused in one big, tangled ball. But she didn't show anything on her face.

Meric translated the vows and told her she needed to say, "I do." She repeated the words.

The judge asked something.

"He's asking if I have a ring," Meric said. "I'll buy one later."

She nodded. She didn't think it was a good idea to point out blatantly, in front of the officer who spoke Spanish, that it wasn't a real marriage so they didn't need rings.

Meric answered the judge, and the judge said more in English. "I pronounce you husband and wife," Meric translated. "You may kiss the bride."

Meric looked at her. She could see on his face he would not kiss her, wouldn't even consider asking that. But she wanted to make sure they did this correctly. Could someone say they weren't really married if they didn't kiss? She lifted onto her toes.

"You don't have to," Meric murmured.

She brushed her lips against his, barely a touch. She'd expected revulsion at that kind of touch with a man, but that wasn't what washed through her. She didn't understand what it was, but it wasn't revulsion.

Meric looked at her for several seconds.

She broke the silence by asking, "What now?"

The officer standing behind her answered. "You're free to go, but please be available for further questions."

She nodded.

Meric took a card out of his wallet and handed it to the officer. "Thank you." Then he said to Liliana, "Are you ready?"

She didn't really know if she was, but she nodded.

He led her outside and to his car. He held the door for her. She sat and waited for him to walk around to the driver's side. The car had tinted windows, black leather seats that felt like butter, and controls that looked like a spaceship.

He didn't use a key to turn on the car but just pressed a button. He drove for a while, and they didn't talk.

She felt like her emotions hadn't quite caught up to reality. She tried to wrap her mind around everything that'd happened. As she finally fully realized she no longer had to fight, no longer had to focus everything within her on survival, thoughts of her family took over. She tried to push the memories out, but images kept flashing. Her father standing in front of her and her mother and sister, protecting them, and then him being shot in the head. Her sister's scream. Her mother's sobs.

Meric drove through the downtown of a large city.

Liliana dug her dirty fingernails into the side of her leg.

He pulled into a parking garage next to a huge building of steel and glass. The lights of the city sparkled off the windows.

He parked in a spot right next to a glass door leading to a lobby with elevators.

He looked over at Liliana. "Are you all right?"

"Fine." She fumbled with the fancy door handle and stood from the car.

He stood as well and led her to the lobby.

In the elevator, he pressed the button for the top floor.

The images of her family kept flashing through her mind. How her mother had tried to protect her daughters and had been beaten. The men had discussed taking her mother and her sister as well.

"Liliana."

They'd tortured her mother, and in the end, they'd decided she was too old and broke her neck. The sound of it—

22

"Liliana. It's all right."

She realized Meric was talking. *It's Meric, not those other men.* He rested his hands on her arms. "Liliana."

She pulled away and squished herself into the corner of the elevator.

"I'm sorry."

She shook her head, and she realized tears were running down her cheeks.

The elevator stopped, and the doors opened, not to a hallway but straight into an apartment.

When she didn't move, Meric said, "Please come inside. You can rest."

She forced her legs to work and walked off the elevator.

Her sister's screams echoed in her head. Her sweet little sister, only twelve years old.

"It's my fault." It took her a second to realize the words had come from her own mouth.

"Nothing that happened is your fault."

"They killed them because of me."

His voice was hard. "None of it is your fault." He shifted closer and caught her gaze. "Do you hear me? Nothing."

"If I'd have just gone with them—"

"They would've killed them anyway. Those men are inhuman garbage." A string of curses flowed from his lips, almost poetically. "Do you understand me, Liliana?"

She kept looking at him, at the barely controlled rage in his eyes.

She felt her expression crumple, and a sob bubbled from her chest. But she kept looking at him.

"You're safe. Do you understand?"

The tears wouldn't stop.

"Do you believe me?" he asked.

Still meeting his eyes, she nodded.

Then her strength left her all at once, like a dying battery, and she fell to her knees. He knelt, stayed with her, but didn't touch her again.

His voice softened, so gentle she almost couldn't believe it was him. "You can grieve now. You don't have to be strong anymore."

She sobbed again and curled forward.

She wasn't sure how long she cried, but he stayed there with her on the floor. He didn't talk anymore, didn't touch her, but stayed.

⬛ ⬛ ⬛

Liliana woke to sunlight. She bolted upright and looked around. She was in a bed covered in sheets and blankets softer than a newborn baby's hair. One wall of the room was all windows that looked out over a city far below. The room was huge, bigger than her family's entire house.

It took her a few seconds to remember where she was. She was at Meric's home, right? Or had that all been a dream?

Maybe this was the buyer's house.

Maybe she was still a prisoner.

She slid out from under the covers and looked around. The furniture was modern but comfortable—a couch and chair, a desk, some bookshelves. She happened to notice one of the titles . . . in Spanish. One of the closet doors was open. Inside hung several outfits, all with the tags on.

Despair threatened to overwhelm her. It had to be the buyer's home. Meric hadn't had time to set up a room like this for her, nor would he have any reason to. But the buyer, he could be the kind to want to dress her up like a doll.

But then she looked more closely at the clothes—nothing fancy and certainly not skimpy. There were jeans and long-sleeved T-shirts, one dress that was long and flowy.

She decided to venture out of the room. She cracked the door and peered out. It opened to a huge living space, furnished in the same modern whites and grays as the bedroom. Two of the walls were made of windows, which let the morning light

24

splash across the space and made the few glass vases and décor pieces sparkle.

She walked out slowly. Past the living room was a large dining area and then a kitchen. To the left was an entry area with white marble tile leading to the elevator.

The sound of a man's voice made her stop.

Cautiously, she moved past the dining room. Some part of her contemplated getting on the elevator and running. But as she moved closer to the sound of the voice, she realized it was Meric's.

On the other side of the entrance area were open double doors. She looked inside and saw Meric standing at the window, talking on his cell phone. With how quickly he spoke and some of the terms he used, it was hard to understand his English, but his tone was very direct.

This room had similar furnishings, but it looked like it was actually used, unlike the rest of the place. On the desk sat a couple of computer monitors and a tablet, and on the credenza was a stack of file folders. The desk chair was pushed to one side, obviously long abandoned.

He turned and saw her, said one clipped sentence into the phone, and ended the call. His shirt was rumpled, the top two buttons undone, and his sleeves rolled up, and his jaw line was shadowed with stubble. Had he not slept?

"Good morning," he said. She hadn't noticed his eyes before, how dark they were.

"Hello."

"I hope you didn't mind that I carried you to bed."

"Did I . . ." Details of her breakdown from the night before were slowly coming back, though she refused to let her memories take her over like that again. "Did I fall asleep on the floor?"

"It was the end of a long journey. You were exhausted."

End? She wasn't sure about that.

"Did you sleep all right?" His tone was different from when

he'd been on the phone, or was it just the language change that made him sound different?

"I wasn't sure where I was."

"I'm sorry about that. But I wasn't about to leave you on the floor all night."

"Where did the clothes come from? Is that someone else's room?"

"I had one of my employees buy a few things so you'd have something clean to wear. There are also some items in your bathroom so you can bathe. Of course, when you're up to it, you can go buy whatever products or clothes you want."

"I don't have any money, but I'll pay you back when I can."

"I don't want money, Liliana." He turned and dropped his phone onto the desk.

Had she offended him?

She stepped back, about to leave the room, but then she asked, "Did you not sleep?"

He glanced over at her and then back out the window.

She took a couple of steps into the room and noticed a newspaper on the desk. One of the headlines on the front page had his name in it. "What's that?"

He looked over. "A bunch of morons talking to themselves."

"But that's your name. Why are you in the newspaper? On the front page."

He sighed. "I'm sure you noticed a certain reaction to my name yesterday. Apparently, several people at the gas station recognized me, and the press dug from here. I'm not the most popular figure."

"Why do people know who you are?"

"Money tends to do that." He sighed again and faced her properly. "I'm sorry, Liliana. I'm not frustrated with you." He moved toward the door. "You should have breakfast."

She followed him out to the kitchen.

"I had some groceries delivered as well, but I'm not sure what they brought." He opened the refrigerator. "What do you like?"

"How many employees do you have?"

"Enough to get the work done."

"What kind of work?"

He set a gallon of orange juice on the counter. "In simple terms, I buy companies that are struggling and reorganize them."

"Does that make you unpopular?"

"Reorganization often means plenty of firings. That's part of the problem."

"Part of the problem?"

He turned back toward the refrigerator. "Do you like eggs?"

She allowed him to change the subject. "I can make them." She took the carton of eggs out of his hands.

"I wasn't hinting for you to cook."

"I know." She looked at the fancy stove and tried to figure out how to turn on a burner. "You don't even buy your own food. I doubt you're very good at cooking it."

The corner of his mouth just slightly twitched. He didn't show much emotion in general, but she liked that the tiny amount she did see was genuine. She would much rather that than fake.

He had to look in two different cabinets before pulling out a pan, but at least he knew where the glasses were. He poured them each orange juice. She wished he had some spices; all he had was salt and pepper. She did the best she could.

"Do you want anything else?" he asked. "I'm sure there's some sausage or bacon in the freezer."

"I think I should go slowly." She scooped the eggs onto the plates he'd set on the counter.

"Until you get used to eating again," he surmised. "How long had it been since you'd eaten before the fruit you had at the truck stop?"

She focused on what she was doing and didn't look at him. "A couple of days." She didn't want to talk too much about any of that. She felt like she was asking for pity if she did. She didn't want pity.

She set his plate on the kitchen island next to him. The delicate plate clinked on the shiny white marble countertop.

"You're strong," he said.

She looked up at him.

"You'll learn pretty quickly that I don't do pity or even sympathy very well. But I'm very good at recognizing a strong mind." He opened a drawer, took out two forks, and handed her one.

She leaned against the opposite counter and ate her eggs slowly. She felt full so quickly.

A different male voice made her jump, and she realized it was coming from a small screen sitting on the counter. There was a man in some sort of uniform, speaking in English. She recognized the words "Mr. Toledan" but most of the rest was gibberish to her. She wished people would speak more slowly.

Meric pressed a button under the screen and replied, and then the screen went black again.

"I need to meet with someone quickly," Meric said.

"Of course." She realized he was a very busy person. She wasn't sure why he wasn't at his office—she assumed he had one somewhere—but then maybe it was the weekend? She had no idea.

"I need to get a bath," she said. "I'm sure I don't smell wonderful." She rinsed her plate, left it in the sink—intent on cleaning it properly later—and headed back to the bedroom in which she'd woken. She heard the elevator ding as she closed the door.

There was a big bathroom off the bedroom. She found soaps and shampoos and lotions, and then she tried to figure out how to turn on the shower. It looked complicated but was simple once she figured it out. That seemed to be the theme of this place.

While the water warmed up, she decided she wanted more to drink. She didn't think she'd ever not be thirsty again. She walked back out toward the kitchen. She heard Meric talking with another man in his office. When she realized they were speaking Spanish, she instinctively paused.

"It's next month," Meric said.

"Should I coordinate with Agent Bando?" the other man asked.

Agent?

"No," Meric said. "I'll deal with Bando myself."

With a jolt, Liliana realized she had no idea who Meric really was.

Chapter THREE

How could I have allowed myself to be so relaxed around a man I don't know? Liliana went back into the bedroom and locked the door. She should've escaped down the elevator. Why'd she come back here? She cracked the door and listened. Meric's voice sounded closer—she guessed he was done with his meeting and was showing the other man out.

She closed and locked the door again.

Options. She needed to figure out her options. If she went back to Mexico, she'd almost certainly be caught again, and she couldn't let herself think about what they'd do to her this time. But she couldn't just leave here either. The marriage was the only thing letting her stay in America. If she left, surely he'd divorce her, and then she'd be illegal and she'd get deported back to Mexico and be back to square one. What other options were there?

English, she needed to improve her English and then do what she could to understand the American immigration system. She walked over to the wall of bookshelves, hoping to find something that might help. After looking over a few shelves, she found a Spanish/English dictionary. She sat on the edge of the bed and opened the book.

But then she paused and looked out the windows, allowed her thoughts to catch up.

Meric had been unendingly kind. He'd risked being arrested

for assaulting Carl and Josh. He'd *married* her just to help her, a total stranger. And last night, he'd had the perfect opportunity to take advantage of her, and he hadn't. He hadn't even touched her. She wasn't being fair to him. She didn't have the right to listen to his private conversations, and she had no way of knowing what the conversation was about anyway.

She set aside the dictionary, took a deep breath, stood, and walked into the bathroom.

Not knowing much about him, wondering if he had secrets, still bothered her, but she would not allow herself to judge him on snippets of conversations, not when he'd been nothing but good to her.

She did know one thing—she couldn't take advantage of his generosity for long. She had to find a way to free him. As she thought about it, though, it wasn't about freeing him—it was about freeing herself. She didn't feel comfortable here. But then, would she ever feel comfortable anywhere again?

Probably not.

As she stepped out of the shower and glanced at the door to make sure it was still locked, she forced all these thoughts out of her head. She couldn't dwell on them or else she wouldn't survive.

After saying a silent prayer of thanks for shampoo and soap and the clean jeans and long-sleeved T-shirt, she walked out into the living area. She continually watched every corner, a habit that would not stop anytime soon, she was sure.

She washed, dried, and put the dishes back in the cabinet.

"You don't need to do that." Meric stood in his office doorway.

Liliana nodded as she wiped out the sink.

"There's a dishwasher, and I have someone who cleans three days a week."

"You obviously don't use your kitchen." Liliana rinsed out the paper towel and draped it on the edge of the sink before she turned to face him. "And I doubt you use your living or dining rooms either. Why do you have someone cleaning three days a week?"

He'd been walking toward her and stopped. Something in his expression changed, seemed colder. Or maybe . . . just hidden behind that sheet of ice.

Finally, she asked, "Is something wrong?"

"No." He walked away, down the hall between the kitchen and office, which she assumed led to his bedroom.

■ ▩ ▣

Meric closed his bedroom door and went into the bathroom. *What have I gotten myself into?* He'd known, even as he was doing it, that the whole thing was rash. Which was not like him. But her situation had reminded him so much of—

Get it together. You're better than this.

He turned on the sink, let the cold water fall over his hands, and pulled his fingers through his hair. He looked at himself in the mirror as water trickled down from his hairline.

He could get through this.

He had to.

There was no other choice.

■ ▩ ▣

Liliana retreated to her room, sat in the desk chair, and resumed reading the Spanish/English dictionary. She sat there for a long time. It made her feel a little more confident to understand more English, more than just a simple vocabulary, though she wasn't sure about pronunciation of certain words. She could see them in her head but wasn't sure how to say them.

It was late afternoon by the time she came back out of the bedroom. She'd started trying to read one of the books on the shelf, one written in English. Sentence structure wasn't too hard to understand, but she'd spent half the time looking up words. Though it was tedious and difficult, she hadn't wanted to stop.

But she told herself not to ignore her hunger, not if she wanted to get her strength back.

The living space was deserted. She had a feeling that was normal.

She paused at the kitchen. Should she find food for herself or go find Meric?

"You can have anything you want in the kitchen." Meric had come out of his office. His tone wasn't cold so much as detached, like he was only half there. Preoccupied with work?

"I'd like to make you something. What do you like?" She started toward the refrigerator but then paused. "What day of the week is it?"

"Tuesday." He remained several feet away.

"I assume you have an office somewhere. Why aren't you there?"

"I'm not about to leave you alone on your first day in this new situation." Then he added, "And the papers would have a field day."

"Why?"

"Tyrant Meric Toledan won't even give his bride a honeymoon."

"What did that story in the newspaper say about you, anyway? You never said."

"Nothing worth caring about."

She waited for a better answer.

"I don't remember the details."

"Do you mind if I look at it?" She headed toward his office. He stepped back as she passed him. She picked up the newspaper, which was still on his desk, and came back to the kitchen. Her afternoon of English study was paying off. She was able to understand more of the words.

"Can you read that?" he asked.

"My mother taught me English basics—she cleaned house for an American and learned the language pretty well. And there was a Spanish/English dictionary on the bookshelf. I'm trying to learn more words."

"Reading is probably easier than listening and speaking."

"If people would just slow down when they talk." She looked down at the paper. "I think I understand some of this. Why does this say . . . Does that mean trapped?"

His voice returned to that aloof tone. "As for what happened at the gas station, the police are not releasing that information, that trafficking was involved, not until they complete the investigation into Josh and Carl. The press is making up stories. They theorize that I used your position as a new immigrant to take advantage of you. Perhaps that I brought a beautiful naïve young woman here for the purpose of trapping and controlling her."

"You're right—a bunch of morons talking to themselves." She folded the paper.

"How much English do you understand?"

"If I concentrate, I can pick up most words, but the accent sounds weird and people talk too fast." Then she added, "And I don't know how to pronounce some words properly. Would you help me with that?"

He hesitated.

"You don't have to if you're busy."

"You should eat. Have anything in the refrigerator or pantry." Then he said the same thing in English, but slower.

"You sound different when you speak English." She opened the refrigerator.

"The languages are very different—romance language versus Germanic."

She wasn't sure it was just that. She looked through the kitchen and found enough to make a decent salad. She made him one as well. She asked him some questions on where to find things, though he seemed to guess about some of it, and every time he answered, he said it in both languages.

By the time they were done eating, she'd tried speaking a few simple sentences in English. It felt harsh on her tongue, but he said she'd done very well.

She hoped maybe he would keep her company for a little while. Just so she could practice some more. But after thanking her for the meal and helping put the dishes in the dishwasher, he retreated to his office and closed the doors.

But less than a minute later, he came back out, phone to his ear. "Thank you for letting me know immediately." He ended the call.

"Is something wrong?" Liliana asked.

"Carl Walsh made bail. He's been released."

Her heart pounded so hard it hurt. "What do you mean he's been released? How could they release him?"

"He has a clean record up until now. The judge allowed bail, and apparently he has a cousin willing to put up the funds. I'm sorry." Then he added in a stronger tone, "You're still safe here."

Liliana turned and looked out the expansive windows.

His voice was gentler. "Are you all right?"

"Yes." She didn't have a choice but to be all right.

❖

"What do you mean you lost her?" the buyer roared into the phone. "How do two grown men *lose* one small young woman?"

On the other end of the line, Carl spluttered. "She—she knocked me down, and . . . The door was locked—I don't know how she got out."

He immediately understood. "I *explicitly* said no sampling. What did you think you were doing?!"

"We didn't, I promise. She's still the virgin you paid for. I swear."

"Virgin but not untouched. I said *unspoiled*. That means she's mine—not for the likes of two little swine like you. Do you think I went through all this trouble and expense so *you* and that baboon friend of yours could have your jollies on my dime?"

"We didn't—"

His voice went deadly quiet. "What did I say would happen if my instructions were not followed?"

Carl was silent.

"You can run, but I will catch you."

Carl's end of the call went dead.

Chapter FOUR

"I'll be fine here alone," Liliana assured. He hadn't gone to work yesterday, and she figured he needed to go. She didn't want to hold him back.

Meric continued to look at her with concern.

Liliana held her shoulders straight and chin high. "I don't need babysat."

"That's not what I meant," Meric said.

She calmed her tone. "I meant you don't need to worry about me." But then maybe he was a little worried about leaving her, a stranger, in his home. "I'd like to use the day to keep working on my English. If I want to stay here, I need to speak the language more fluently. I'll just be in my room all day studying, not the best company." Hopefully that set his mind at ease, whatever his concerns.

"All right." To her surprise, he took a few steps closer to her. He'd been keeping his distance from her, though she wasn't sure if it was to put her at ease or for some other reason. He held something out to her. "Call me if you need anything."

She took the cell phone out of his hand. It was basically just a black screen with casing. She didn't want to admit she had no idea how to use it.

Out of his breast pocket, he took his own phone, which looked to be the exact same kind as the one in her hand. He showed her how to get the screen to come on and how to pull up the phone application, where she saw his name on the screen. "My number is already saved," he said.

She nodded.

He turned and walked toward the entryway. He pressed the button for the elevator. "Call if you need anything."

She nodded again and headed back to her room. A few seconds later, she heard the elevator ding and the doors slide open and then closed again.

And suddenly, she felt the aloneness acutely. She'd rarely been alone in her entire life. The feeling made her remember even more vividly that her family was all gone. She'd better get used to this feeling.

She sat at the desk and dove into the dictionary. Meric had given her a notebook and pencil to help with her studying. She found writing to be very helpful in aiding her memory. Writing hadn't mattered much at home. She'd worked any job she could to help earn income for her family, and it certainly didn't require writing. Her aspiration had been to someday find a job cleaning for a wealthy family, like her mother. Her mother had to stay on-site most days because it was too far to travel every day, which had been hard on her little sister. Liliana had hoped perhaps in the next few years her sister would be old enough and could stay with her mother sometimes and help, like Liliana had done on occasion.

Liliana forced her thoughts away from her family and refocused on her work.

Hours passed.

It was early afternoon when Liliana finally looked at the clock on the bedside table and realized lunchtime had come and gone. She reminded herself again that she needed to build her strength, stretched her cramped neck and back, and stood.

She was halfway through the living space when the elevator dinged. *Isn't it too early for Meric to be home?*

When the doors opened, it wasn't Meric who stepped off the elevator.

"Oh, hello, miss." A middle-aged woman in jeans and a T-shirt stopped short at seeing Liliana.

Liliana realized she'd spoken in English—and Liliana had understood.

"I'm sorry to startle you," the woman continued. "You must be Mrs. Toledan. I saw the story in the paper." Liliana didn't understand all the words, but enough to put it together using context. The woman said something else, but Liliana couldn't quite catch it.

"*Español?*" Liliana asked. The woman looked to be Latina—perhaps she spoke Spanish?

The woman smiled. "*Sí.*"

Liliana continued in Spanish. "Are you here to see Meric?"

"No, ma'am. I know he's at the office. I like to clean when he's away so I don't disturb him."

"Oh. He said he has someone clean three days a week."

The woman started toward the hall past the kitchen. "Not that it needs much."

Liliana followed.

"I'm Teresa, by the way. Don't mind me. I'll be in and out as quickly as I can."

"Don't rush on account of me. Can I get you something to drink?"

Teresa smiled. "No, thank you, ma'am."

Being called "ma'am" felt strange and wrong.

Teresa opened the first door on the right. Liliana hadn't been down this hall at all—she'd assumed it held just Meric's room, but this room had a washing machine, dryer, mop and bucket, vacuum cleaner, and shelves lined with cleaners.

"So, this is where the cleaning supplies are," Liliana said. "There's nothing under the kitchen sink."

"I'll be quick," Teresa said.

Liliana realized Teresa was trying to excuse herself from Liliana's company, and then it hit her that she saw Liliana as the lady of the house. Liliana paused awkwardly in the doorway.

Teresa took the vacuum cleaner from its spot in the corner and slipped past Liliana out to the living room. The vacuum buzzed to life a few seconds later.

Liliana grabbed a rag and glass cleaner from the shelf. She'd looked out the windows last evening and had touched the glass. She'd tried to wipe her handprint with her sleeve, but it hadn't come off quite perfectly. She started with that spot and continued cleaning the rest of the windows.

Teresa turned off the vacuum. "I'll get that, ma'am."

"I used to help my mother. I'm good at getting the streaks." Though there weren't many on the mostly spotless windows.

Teresa stood there for a few seconds, but then resumed vacuuming. She finished the area rug before Liliana finished with half the windows. Teresa started toward the room Liliana was using.

"It's okay, you don't need to do that room," Liliana said.

"It's no trouble."

"You don't need to do that room," she said again. She would see Liliana wasn't sharing Meric's room—would she tell anyone that the marriage wasn't real?

Teresa continued toward the room, and Liliana followed, trying to think of a way to stop her. Teresa walked inside and looked at the desk. Thankfully, Liliana had made the bed meticulously this morning, and it didn't look slept in.

"I'm using it as a place to study," Liliana said. "I'm trying to learn English."

Teresa smiled. "I'm glad it's finally getting some use."

"I don't think he gets a lot of houseguests."

"Never. He had it set up so nice, it's a shame she never got to enjoy it."

"Who never got to enjoy it?"

Teresa hesitated. "Mr. Toledan's mother. He made this room for her."

"Oh. Is she coming back soon?"

Teresa's voice quieted. "She passed when he was a teenager."

"I'm so sorry for him," Liliana said. "I wonder why he made a room for her if she's been gone so long." Then she thought she shouldn't say such things and advertise how little she knew him.

"He doesn't talk to me about it, of course, but he did mention when I started that I should keep this room perfect. I've picked up bits and pieces over time, and from what I've gathered, he'd promised to give her a nice home someday."

And he hadn't let her passing stop him from fulfilling that promise. A gentle smile curved Liliana's lips.

"Don't listen to the papers," Teresa said. "They make him out to be evil because it sells. He doesn't make it easy to see, and sometimes I don't think he believes it himself, but he's a very good person."

"I know," Liliana said.

Teresa smiled. "I'm sure you do." She turned on the vacuum and started on the rug in the seating area.

Liliana went into the bathroom and quickly threw the shampoo and such under the sink. Hopefully Teresa wouldn't look under there. She went back out to the living space and continued cleaning the windows. A little while later, Teresa came back out of the bedroom.

"You know I'll get that," Teresa said. Then she added, "I like to make sure this place is perfect."

Liliana stopped and looked over.

"I owe Mr. Toledan a lot. I like to make sure I do a good job for him."

Liliana realized why Teresa seemed to be a little annoyed at her cleaning. It wasn't out of misplaced respect for Liliana—it was because Teresa liked to be the one to take care of these things for him, out of some kind of appreciation.

"Why do you owe him?" Liliana asked.

"He's sponsoring my green card."

"So you can stay here?" Meric had mentioned something about

that the evening they'd met, that he couldn't get another one pushed through right now.

"He gives me employment so I can live here." Teresa continued back to the laundry room.

Liliana put the rag and glass cleaner away and went back to her desk. She tried to focus on her work, but a question nagged at her, something she wanted to ask Teresa.

Finally, she let herself get up and go find Teresa. She was in Meric's office dusting.

"How well do you know Meric?" Liliana asked.

"Probably about as well as anyone." Then she added, "Except you, of course."

Liliana could feel Teresa's curiosity about the sudden marriage, though she was sure she'd never actually ask anything.

"Have you ever met anyone he's dated?" Liliana asked.

"Never. I don't think he's ever been very active in the dating scene."

Liliana wasn't sure what to make of that. He was extremely attractive and wealthy—surely a coveted catch. But then maybe he wasn't interested in a partnership but just flings.

"Has he ever come on to you?" The question popped out before Liliana could think of a better way to phrase it.

Teresa stopped and faced Liliana squarely. "Never." Then she added, "I meant it when I said he's a good person."

Liliana smiled. "Of course he is. I didn't phrase that right. I meant you're very pretty, that's all." Which was true, though she was older than Meric by probably ten years.

"Thank you, ma'am." Teresa went back to dusting.

Liliana retreated to the kitchen and tried to find something to eat.

After cleaning Meric's bedroom, Teresa put everything away and headed toward the elevator.

Liliana was looking through the cupboards. "Is there a Latin grocery around here?"

"Turn right out of the building, down the block on the left. There's a grocery store with a decent Latin section."

"Thank you. I want to make Meric some flautas or maybe tamales, but he doesn't have much to work with in this kitchen." It was the truth; plus, she wanted to convey some kind of feeling toward Meric in front of Teresa, not let her suspect she didn't really even know him.

Teresa smiled. "I'm sure he'd like that." She pressed the button for the elevator. "Have a nice day."

"You too."

When the doors to the elevator closed, Liliana took a relieved breath. But then that feeling of aloneness returned. She ignored it and found something small to eat.

She was back at her desk when the elevator dinged again. She stood by her door, ready to lock it. The fact that people could come straight into the apartment set her on edge. Though she was sure Meric had some kind of security measures in place, she had no idea what they were.

"Liliana?" It was Meric's voice.

She walked out of the room as Meric set a small bag on the kitchen counter. She stood on the other side of the island.

He took a small box out of the bag and set it in front of her.

"What's this?"

"I told you I'd get you a ring."

"Right." People would certainly wonder why if they noticed she didn't have a wedding band. She opened the box. It wasn't just a simple gold band. She slid the box back across the counter. "I think they gave you the wrong one."

He slid the box back to her. "People would question if I didn't give you a nice diamond."

She picked it up and looked at the contents more closely. There was a white gold ring with a large rectangular diamond, as well as a band lined in small diamonds. The stones and metal shimmered in the light.

"Do you like them?" he asked. "I can get you something else if you prefer."

"I've never seen anything so beautiful." She looked up to catch that slight crook of his mouth, and a distinct smile in his eyes. It was the closest to a proper smile she'd seen from him. "Thank you."

"You're welcome." Then he added, "Put them on. I guessed your size."

She put the band on first and then the big diamond. "Perfect fit." She was impressed he'd estimated so accurately.

As he folded the small bag, she noticed he wore a plain white gold band. Something knotted in her stomach. Maybe she was nervous to be wearing something so expensive. She reminded herself she'd give the rings back to him soon enough, when she could solve her immigration status and release him from this marriage.

She made a simple dinner, though he protested that he'd planned to have something delivered, and they sat at the glass dining table to eat. He chose a chair at the other end of the table from her.

"How are you today?" he asked.

"I studied. I'm getting better, I think."

He paused. "But how are you feeling?"

She didn't answer.

His voice was quieter. "You're not dealing with it. You need to deal with it so you can heal."

She kept her gaze on her plate. "I don't have that luxury."

"That's what I'm trying to do for you, Liliana. Give you that time."

"I'm fine."

Several seconds passed before he responded. "I don't think you are."

She didn't respond. The meal continued in silence.

He was almost done eating when his phone rang. He excused himself and went into his office.

Liliana stood, walked over to the kitchen sink, and rinsed her plate. She turned off the water and noticed Meric's voice was aggressive, not his usual level tone. She understood his English pretty well, again using context to fill in the blanks. "My relationship status is none of your concern." There was another word in there that she assumed was a curse. "You would do well to remember I am not one of your underlings. If you think someone else can do what I'm doing, go work with them. Otherwise, keep out of my business."

Chapter FIVE

A scream ripped Meric from sleep. He pulled his Glock from its holster on the side of his nightstand and sprinted out of his room. This floor was locked out of the elevator this time of night, so he rationally knew no one was in the apartment. But Liliana's scream flung him into an intense protection mode.

Another scream.

He ran through the empty, dark apartment and to her room. He tried the handle and was surprised—and unnerved—that it wasn't locked. She'd have it locked, wouldn't she? Had someone found a way in? He rushed inside.

She was lying in bed, and no one else was in the room.

At the sight of her tangled blankets, disheveled hair, and glistening skin, he realized she was having a nightmare.

She covered her head with her arms as if fending off a beating.

He rushed over and set his gun on the nightstand. He wanted to comfort her, but if he woke her, would seeing him here just terrify her more?

"No!" she screamed and then wrapped her arms around herself, covering her chest and across her hips.

And he realized what kind of dream she was having, what she was fighting against. They'd done more than beat her. They had, in the very least, sexually molested her.

But how could he of all people comfort her?

"Don't touch me!" Her tone was strong, aggressive, but he could hear terror under her anger.

And he saw the black bruises on her arms.

She kicked and writhed so much that her nightgown rode up, and he saw on her beautiful skin more bruises—her legs, her stomach, her back. Rage flashed through him at the thought of her having to fight off those scum, how hard they'd hit and grabbed her to cause bruises that dark.

"No!" she roared.

He dropped to his knees and whispered, "Liliana."

She writhed.

"You're safe," he whispered. "You don't have to fight anymore."

She screamed.

He continued to whisper, but it turned hard, "I won't let anyone hurt you like that again. I'll beat them like I did when we met."

He reached out to touch her cheek but stopped. "I will destroy anyone who tries to touch you again."

She whimpered, but at least it wasn't a scream.

His tone softened. "You're safe."

She flailed.

"You're safe. I'm here. I'll protect you."

A tear escaped the corner of her eye.

"You don't have to fight anymore. Grieve. Heal."

She turned her face into her pillow, and her shoulders shook with tears. She stopped writhing.

"Breathe," he whispered. "You're safe."

She continued to cry but didn't wake.

"*Papá*," she whimpered.

He had no idea how to try to offer comfort about her family. He couldn't bring them back.

"I'm sorry, Liliana."

She shifted her hand on the mattress, closer to him.

He could see the calluses from a hard life of labor, but her hands were also gentle, delicate. They made him think how soothing it would be to be touched by her. When he'd held her hand that one time, he'd felt calmer somehow.

"You're safe," he whispered again. "I promise."

Finally, her crying calmed, and she lay still.

He stayed there on his knees, watching her beautiful face.

But then he made himself stand, pick up his gun, and walk out of her room.

Liliana woke early, showered, and went out to make Meric breakfast. He continued to protest when she cooked for him, but he also ate everything she made.

"Here," he said after they'd finished breakfast. He held a handful of cash out to her. "You may not be comfortable walking around outside yet, but there are shops and restaurants downstairs. I thought you might like to do something other than study."

"No, thank you."

He set the money on the kitchen island. "I know it looks like a lot, but it's not. And we need to keep up appearances."

She glanced at the money.

"My work is very successful," he said. "I will never spend everything I have."

She was starting to be able to see through his cool exterior. It would make him happy if she took the money without complaint. He liked to do things for others. Maybe because his mother had died too early for him to do much for her.

"All right. Thank you."

He also set a card on the counter. "Scan this in the elevator, and it'll give you access to this floor."

She nodded.

"Call me if you need anything." He pressed the button for the elevator.

When he was gone, she left the money where it was on the counter and went back to her room to resume studying.

A couple of hours later, the elevator dinged.

Her heart thudded in her chest. *Maybe it's Teresa again.* But she'd just been here yesterday; why would she come two days in a row?

She stood to lock the door. But then she decided she didn't want to be trapped in here. She slipped out the door and peeked around the corner. A man in a uniform that looked like some kind of scrubs walked off the elevator.

Liliana's entire body tightened, ready to fight.

Calm down. The man was small and didn't appear to be threatening. He walked from the elevator straight to Meric's room. A minute later, he came back out with a laundry bag.

He's just picking up Meric's laundry.

The man stopped and looked at her. "Do you have anything else to pick up, ma'am?"

She stepped around the corner and forced her voice to sound stronger than she felt. "No, thank you."

He smiled and nodded and then pressed the button for the elevator.

Then he was gone, and she was alone again.

She leaned against the wall and caught her breath.

And then she realized how scared she was for absolutely no reason. She grabbed the phone, key card, and the cash Meric had given her and got on the elevator.

She barely remembered what the elevator looked like from her original ride up. It looked a lot like Meric's apartment—white marble floors and bright white walls covered in molding. She pressed the button for the main floor. It was a long ride down. When the doors finally opened, she walked out into a large lobby area with wood-paneled walls. A man in a uniform standing at a marble counter greeted her—must be the doorman. She followed the sound of lots of voices through the glass doors and around the corner and found an expansive mall. There were shops and restaurants and people walking to and fro. She'd never seen anything like it.

She almost turned back around and retreated.

The sight of a stunning fountain pulled her forward. It was double her height, and water cascaded down an organic-looking sculpture. Carved out of smooth, glistening white granite, it looked like an ancient, gnarled tree trunk covered in vines that lashed out here and there. The sound of trickling water reminded her of the little brook back home.

She shoved those memories away and looked around. She'd been to the market innumerable times, of course, but this was something entirely different. Perhaps like the fancy shopping mall she'd heard about in Monterrey. Curious, she walked around. But she also remained cautious of those near her and steered clear of men.

She passed a jewelry store with glittering stones and metal. Then she glanced at her own large diamond and band of sparkling smaller stones. They looked odd on her hand. And yet she'd grown used to the feel of them on her finger so quickly.

The next several shops were all clothes. The mannequins in flowy dresses and stylish accessories, plus all the well-dressed people bustling around her, made her glance down at her own outfit—just jeans and another long-sleeved shirt. Though she now very much preferred this simple outfit that covered so well, her mother had made her lovely dresses when she was little. She'd made wonders out of scraps of pretty fabric.

Again, she pushed the memories away.

She didn't go into any of the shops, but she looked in all the windows. Eventually, she came across a directory for the building. She was thankful she'd been working so hard on her English. She didn't understand all the words, especially the big ones like podiatry and chiropractic, but enough to make some sense. The second floor appeared to be all offices—doctors and lawyers and real estate and a few things she didn't understand. The third floor said something about "resident amenities"—a gym, what she was pretty sure was some kind of shared lounge, a game room, something called a sauna, the management office, and a couple of other things she wasn't sure about.

The number of people in this mall was starting to bother her. She decided to explore the third floor. In the elevator, she had to use the key card to get to the third floor—hopefully that meant fewer people would be there.

She walked off into a large open space with carpet with a subtle flowing pattern. Directly in front of her were two wide double doors, which opened into what appeared to be the shared lounge. She could hear voices and decided to bypass that room. She walked slowly around the space.

"Lost?"

She spun around at the sound of a male voice.

There was an older man, probably in his sixties, standing by the door to the stairs. "Sorry. Didn't mean to startle you."

"You didn't," she lied. English felt so weird on her tongue. She knew her accent had to be thick. She meandered back toward the elevator, while trying not to look like she was running away.

"New to the building?" He approached her.

She stopped, still with a good ten feet between them. She didn't want to interact with people, but she did want to practice speaking English. "Yes."

He smiled. "Welcome. Which floor?"

She hesitated. "Top."

He raised his gray brows and glanced at her left hand. "You married Toledan."

"Yes."

"Why would a nice girl like you do something like that?"

She lifted her chin.

"I mean no offense." He offered a smile.

"Maybe not to me, but you do to Meric." Her annoyance seemed to make her English flow a little more easily.

"It appears I've put my foot in my mouth. I do tend to do that. Forgive me." He continued smiling. "Let me show you around?"

He continued without waiting for an answer. "In there is the lounge. Old biddies playing bridge in there now. Boring as all."

An elderly female voice called from the lounge, "Not as boring as an old man obsessed with model cars."

He muttered, "Old but not deaf, apparently."

Liliana couldn't help but grin and headed into the lounge. There were couches on one side of the room and round tables on the other, where four old women sat playing their card game. The man followed her.

One of the women looked up. "Don't let Wilmer bother you. He likes flirting with pretty girls."

One of the other women added, "Now that he's old enough to get away with it."

All four women laughed.

"Benefits of age, ladies," Wilmer said.

Liliana chatted for a few minutes with the ladies, pleased that she was able to follow the conversation. They seemed nice, and being immersed in the language helped her get used to it.

They didn't push too much about her marriage, though she could see shock and disapproval, and maybe even pity, in their faces, no matter how much they tried to hide it.

In the elevator, she thought about the mall and all the fancy amenities in this building. Her past and world were very different from Meric's. Her family had lived in one of the poorest areas in Mexico. Surely, he'd grown up rich and privileged. She'd move on as quickly as she could and free him to find someone who suited him better. But at that thought, something quivered unpleasantly inside her. *Just nerves at the idea of being completely alone, that's all.*

The elevator doors opened, but Liliana paused at the sight of a young man standing at the kitchen island.

The young man looked over at Liliana and smiled. "You must be the new Mrs. Toledan."

She stayed on the elevator and held the doors open. "Can I help you with something?"

"I'm so sorry. I guess you're not used to seeing some strange person in your house. I'm Alfred, Mr. Toledan's assistant. I just came to grab a file." He held up a manila folder. "And then I got distracted by an email that needs a quick response." He turned back to the tablet on the marble counter.

She reminded herself that no one Meric didn't trust would have access to this home and stepped off the elevator. Besides, Alfred did not in the slightest remind her of Josh or Carl, though he looked about the same age. His clothes were perfect, not just well-ironed and professional, but stylish and precisely tailored to fit his slender form. And his dark blond hair wasn't the standard male cut with nothing but a neat combing after a shower, like Meric's, but slightly more edgy, flawlessly styled with product.

"I'll be out of your hair in a second," Alfred said as he typed on the tablet's screen.

Liliana didn't understand what he meant by "out of your hair," but based on his tone and body language, she assumed it was something about wanting to hurry. "No rush." She walked around the island and to the refrigerator. "Would you like something to drink?"

He stopped typing and smiled over at her. "I'm used to this place being empty as a tomb."

"It does have a . . ." She paused to think of the word. "Sedate feeling about it."

"Funny you can't say the same thing about Mr. Toledan." He laughed a little and resumed typing.

"He does seem brusque when he's on work calls." *Brusque* was the right word, wasn't it? She'd just learned it this morning.

Alfred laughed again. "People are so scared of him."

She set a bottle of water on the counter next to his tablet. "But you're not?"

He continued typing—she was impressed he could do that while holding a conversation. "I see more than most people."

She waited for him to stop typing.

He tapped an icon on the screen, and the tablet made a sound. "He's not exactly a warm personality, granted. But I understand why you chose to trust him."

She wanted to ask him what he meant but couldn't very well if she wanted to keep up the act that the marriage was real.

He leaned his hip on the counter, facing her. "I arranged the paperwork for the marriage."

So, he already knew the marriage was unusual, at the very least. She wasn't sure how to respond.

"I guess the media doesn't have much to go on," Alfred said. "He doesn't do interviews, doesn't give them the slightest insight."

"They still shouldn't make things up."

"They cover themselves with phrases like 'according to sources.'"

"Doesn't make it right."

He smiled a little and picked up his tablet. "Yep, you get it." He slid the tablet into a small leather satchel.

"Was that . . . an interview?"

"Gotta make sure the boss is protected." He rolled his eyes, still smiling. "Not that he needs it. Watches his back quite well on his own, but still my job, you know?"

She decided she liked Alfred. "How long have you worked for him?"

"Oh, goodness. Six years now."

"So, right after college?" she guessed.

"Didn't go to college. I fell into this job backward. He bought a small company I was working for."

"You were the assistant to the owner of that company?"

"I was the dishwasher. It was a small chain of restaurants."

She raised her eyebrows.

"Mr. Toledan came into the restaurant I was working at, started asking the manager all these questions. Manager didn't have a clue, so I showed him everything. I guess he was impressed I knew all the numbers. Offered me a position at his office on the spot."

"He told me he's good at spotting a strong mind. Looks like he was right."

He pressed his hand to his chest, fingers splayed. "How flattering."

"So you like working for him?"

"Well, he's cold, calculating, and harsh. Ridiculously smart and freaking shrewd. Does *not* do pity—if he fires you, it's for a good reason, and he's *not* going to feel bad about it. But he's also one of the kindest people I've ever met. Weird combination. Takes some getting used to."

"That seems a little . . ." She couldn't think of the right word.

"Contradictory? Odd that he can be both those things at the same time."

"Yes."

He shrugged. "Seems that way at first. Until you understand him."

"And you do?"

"As well as anyone's going to, probably. I think part of the reason he's the way he is is because he's self-made, you know? He never had anything handed to him."

So he hadn't grown up rich and spoiled. She supposed that seemed to align better with the Meric she knew—the little she knew. "And so he doesn't hand anything to anyone else."

"He expects people to work for what they get, and he has zero use for anyone who doesn't."

A little pang of guilt settled on her shoulders.

"Well," he said as he threw the strap of his bag across his body and picked up the bottle of water, "congratulations."

She lowered her brows in confusion.

"On the marriage."

"Of course. Thank you."

He walked over to the elevator and pressed the button. Then he looked back. "It's still so weird. Mr. Toledan married. Never thought that would happen."

She hesitated, wanting to ask why but not sure if she should.

"Thanks for the water." The elevator doors opened, and Alfred stepped in.

She set the cash Meric had given her on the counter.

Then she looked through the kitchen to find something nice to make him for dinner. There was plenty of food, just not much of what she was used to. She wanted to make him something delicious. She eventually decided on something acceptable though not terribly exciting.

While she prepped the vegetables, the silence of the place started to get to her.

She found the TV remote control hidden in a decorative box on the glass coffee table. It took her a minute to figure out how to work it. She flipped through a few channels and settled on what appeared to be a local talk show about life in the Houston area. She focused on the language, happy she understood, for the most part, although it was admittedly getting exhausting. The last segment of the show was about baking and walked through a recipe for a pie. It was easier to understand because she could watch what they were doing as they spoke. Liliana realized Meric had all the ingredients. She wrote down the recipe and started on it so it would be finished and cooled by the time he was done with dinner.

While she was taking the pie out of the oven, the news came on. The top story made her stop and stare at the TV.

"The victim is identified as Joshua McConnell. He was found dead in his cell early this morning. The police are not releasing much information at this time but have confirmed they suspect foul play and are investigating accordingly." A picture flashed across the screen.

Josh. Carl's partner, the man who'd helped hold her captive. The man who'd . . . beaten her so thoroughly when she'd fought against his molestation. The bruises from his fists still hurt enough that she had a hard time sleeping.

She didn't know what to think, how to feel.

She hated to admit to herself that relief was a large portion of what mixed around inside the blender that was her head. *Dear God, I'm sorry.* And then came more fear and anxiety. Who would have killed him? Who would have taken the risk to kill him while he was in police custody, and who could have possibly gotten to him in there? Carl? That might make sense—Josh knew everything and could possibly turn on Carl, especially if he knew Carl had gotten out on bail. And maybe someone like Carl knew other criminals in jail who might be willing to commit murder? If Carl was capable of killing his trusted partner, would he come after her next?

* * *

The buyer sat in his favorite chair by the expansive windows and snapped the newspaper open. He loved the smell of a real newspaper and refused to read it on a tablet or computer. It wouldn't be the same.

He read all the news and shook his head at so much of the stupidity in the world around him.

Then he browsed the rest of the paper.

When he came to an article about Meric Toledan, he stopped. Married? Why would someone like him marry?

He continued reading. "'The young woman, Liliana Toledan née Vela, is an immigrant from southern Mexico.'"

Liliana Vela.

His chair toppled backward as he stood and roared unintelligibly. Rage shook through him, and heat enveloped his body until he thought he would combust. Thoughts of strangling Toledan and then the girl overwhelmed his mind. He could see the fear and then the life slowly extinguishing from their eyes.

He paused, as a new plan slowly formed in his brain.

His lips curved into a smile.

Chapter
SEVEN

The cell phone Meric had given her started ringing. She looked at it sitting on the counter. The screen displayed his name.

She picked up the phone and answered. "Meric?"

He spoke in Spanish, that same level tone that was oddly comforting. "I just heard some news."

"I saw it on the TV." She was thankful to be able to speak Spanish after muddling through English all day, especially right now when she didn't think she could focus on it so well.

"Are you all right?"

She had no idea how to answer that. She wanted to say she was fine, but the lie was too big for her to pull off.

"I'm almost home."

Relief so strong she wanted to cry flooded through her. But then she admonished herself—she was perfectly able to handle this, all of it, on her own. She truly did know that, knew she could find a way to live through anything that came at her as long as she had her faith, but still, she couldn't deny she wanted Meric to be here.

She focused on keeping her voice level. "Do you think Carl could've done it?"

"I think that's one of two very likely possibilities."

"He's probably still in the area."

Meric paused, as if understanding what she wasn't saying.

"Even if he was stupid enough to try to come for you, there is no way he could get to you. You're safe."

She was quiet, not sure what else to say. But he didn't end the call.

The elevator dinged.

"Is that you already?" she asked. "On the elevator?"

The doors opened. Without thinking, she picked up the knife she'd been using for the vegetables.

Meric stepped off the elevator.

She set the phone down and resumed chopping.

Meric came straight to her and touched her shaking hand, barely the brush of his fingertips. The sensation shot up her arm.

She looked up at him. His expression was his normal impassive. Except his eyes. There was softness in his eyes. "Are you all right?"

She turned back to the vegetables and nodded.

He removed his hand and stepped back several feet. "We're looking for Carl. I have people on it."

"Why?"

His voice was quiet. "You'd feel better if you knew where he was."

She didn't argue.

They stood there in silence for several minutes, just the clacking of the knife against the cutting board and the droning of the weatherman on the TV.

Meric took off his black suit jacket and draped it on the back of a dining chair. Then he pulled off his tie, added it to the jacket, and loosened his top couple of shirt buttons. She looked up and happened to notice how well his bicep filled out his shirt sleeve.

She turned back to the vegetables. Her mind felt even more like a blender. Why would she even notice such a thing? How could she possibly find any man attractive? Not that she blamed every man for the actions of a few, but she couldn't imagine willingly having a relationship with any man.

And yet, she felt better when Meric was around.

"Do you like cooking?"

So engrossed in her own thoughts, she almost didn't catch what he'd said. She shrugged.

"Then why do you insist on cooking so much?" he asked.

"That's generally what one does when they're hungry." Then she added, "I explored the building today. I looked around the mall and the amenity floor, met a few of your older neighbors."

He was quiet, but she could feel his gaze on her.

Finally, he said, "Alfred said he met you."

"He was very nice."

"He told me about your conversation."

"He stopped to answer an email before returning to the office." She didn't want him to think Alfred had been irresponsible.

He paused again. "Alfred is pretty much free to take as much time as he wants whenever he wants."

"Good. He seems like a good worker."

"He is. Extremely intelligent and efficient." Then he added, "He told me you asked a little about me and how I run my business."

She looked up. Would he be mad?

"I'll keep saying this until you believe me," he said. "I don't expect anything from you. You are not my employee. You don't owe me anything; you don't need to *earn* your way here. I've done what I've done because it's the right thing to do. If you enjoy cooking, then do as much of it as you want. But do not do it because you think you owe me anything. And the same goes for cleaning and anything else you can think of in that pretty head of yours." He turned, grabbed his jacket and tie, and walked down the hall.

She wasn't sure what to make of his abrupt departure. He seemed frustrated, but she had the feeling there was more to it than just her wanting to earn her own way.

She kept glancing at the clock, waiting for him to come back out.

Just as she started to wonder if he would stay in his room all evening, he walked out while talking on the phone in English. "Cancel any other services," he was saying. "I can bring the laundry to the office. They can pick it up out of my car."

Laundry—Liliana knew that English word well from her mother. She paused in the middle of moving sautéed vegetables from the pan to a plate. She mouthed "no" at Meric.

"Hold on the arrangements. I'll talk to Liliana first." He ended the call.

"Why are you making changes?" she asked in Spanish.

"Because you're uncomfortable with strangers randomly coming in and out of the apartment. I'm sorry I didn't consider that before."

"I'm sure you trust them if you let them in here."

"But you don't have any reason to. I want you not only to be safe—I want you to feel safe."

"But I don't want you lugging your laundry around."

"Why?"

She didn't respond.

"So, I can't take my own laundry to my car, but you can clean all the windows in the place?"

"How'd you know that?"

"Answer the question, Liliana."

She huffed and continued plating dinner.

"Sounds like I win."

She fought back a smirk as she set a plate down on the island for him.

He was looking at her closely. "Yes, I can see I've won."

"You're too confident."

"Usually people call me arrogant."

"Maybe that's what you are." She took her own plate over to the table.

"Perhaps so." He took his plate and sat in his usual chair at the other end of the table from her. "And perhaps it's justified."

She tried to stifle a laugh and didn't entirely succeed.

"All right," she said, between bites. "I propose this: Teresa keeps her normal schedule. She takes this job personally, and I think it would bother her if she didn't get to keep this place as perfect as she does. You're allowed to take your laundry in your car. Anything else, you send Alfred and tell me when he's coming. Deal?"

"I'm *allowed* to take *my* laundry."

"Yes."

"I propose an amendment."

"What?"

"Your laundry is included with mine. I'd rather you spend your time doing something more interesting—reading, shopping, taking walks. If you want to improve your English, those things will help a lot more than menial labor."

"No. You're lucky I don't do your laundry for you. You do have a washer and dryer."

"I'd have the things removed first."

She set her fork down. "You would actually do it, wouldn't you?"

"Without hesitation."

She sighed, partially a growl.

"Your laundry is included with mine, or else the washer and dryer go away."

She rolled her eyes. "Fine."

"Settled." He stood and picked up his plate. "I feel like I should draw up a contract."

She watched him load dishes into the dishwasher, enjoying the mirth in his eyes. But then she made herself look away.

<hr>

"I think I need to draw up that contract." Meric had just come around the corner into the kitchen. Morning light splashed over him.

Liliana looked up from the fruit she was cutting. "What?"

He nodded toward the fruit.

She refocused on what she was doing. "Maybe this isn't for you." Then she added, "Besides, fruit can hardly be considered a full breakfast."

"True. I'll make some eggs." Instead of brushing past her to get to the refrigerator, he walked around the island. He took four eggs out and set them on the counter. Then he looked in one of the lower cabinets.

She cleared her throat. "Left."

He moved left one cabinet and took out a pot. He glanced at her before putting it in the sink and turning on the faucet. While he waited, he took his phone out of his pocket. He typed something and then tapped the screen a few times.

She stopped and faced him. "You're looking it up."

"Hmm?"

"You're looking up how to boil eggs."

He slipped his phone back into the pocket of his slacks. "What makes you say that?"

She held her hand out. "Show me your phone."

He raised his brows, still with that usual flat expression. No wonder people were scared of him—he didn't let them see who he was, and his natural expression was so cold.

"Well," she said as she took the pot out of the sink, "we both know that's what you were doing."

He took the pot from her, and their hands brushed. He turned away and set the pot on the burner. Just like last evening, the warmth from his touch radiated up her arm. She returned to the fruit.

They were quiet for several minutes.

She gave him a plate with fruit, and he rinsed the soft-boiled eggs in cold water, peeled them, and gave her two. They ate while standing at the island, on opposite ends.

The quiet felt odd for some reason. She didn't want him to leave with the atmosphere like this. She teased, "To not know how to boil eggs, you must have grown up pretty sheltered."

He paused before answering. "She never showed me how to cook. She wanted me to focus on school."

"Your mother."

He walked over to put his plate in the dishwasher and didn't look at her.

She made her voice gentle. "She passed when you were a teenager, right? How old were you?"

He closed the dishwasher with a click. "Sixteen."

"And your father?"

He shook his head, barely a movement, and she understood from his expression that this was not a subject to be broached.

She decided to push just a bit more. "So, you went to—what's it called—foster care?"

"No."

"A relative?"

"She was my only family." Though he answered her, he kept his focus out the window, his expression even more detached than usual.

She hesitated to ask anything further.

He looked at her. "You have the right to know some things about me. I don't want you to feel any more uncomfortable here than you already do."

"I appreciate that."

"But I'm not good at this."

"I understand."

"Does it make you feel more at ease having more information?"

She admitted, "Yes."

He took a breath and refocused on the window. "She died from severe pneumonia. She was too proud to go to the free clinic. By the time I talked her into it, it was too late. The State tried to put me in foster care, but I couldn't pretend to be part of a family. I'd already graduated high school—accelerated program—and my motivation to go to college evaporated."

She quietly asked, "Where did you live?"

"The streets."

Silence.

"So you know," she said.

He turned to her. "I know what?"

"You know what it's like to be terrified and alone."

He met her gaze. "You've been through so much worse."

"But you've felt it, at least to some degree."

Still on the opposite side of the island from her, he faced her fully. "Yes." She felt that he understood what she was saying—that he'd had enough life experience, that he'd lived through enough of his own torture, that he could comprehend her level of pain.

His voice was low. "You're not alone in this."

She only nodded, not able to put into words how much she appreciated that.

He clenched his jaw. "I was alone and young and didn't know much about the streets. I almost died a few times—I was beaten and stabbed. There was one man, early on, who found me . . . attractive. I was able to fight him off. I understand that kind of terror and desperation."

She didn't speak for fear he would hear the tremor in her voice.

His voice hardened. "You are not alone in this."

Quiet.

Finally, he broke eye contact and stepped back.

He went into his office and returned with his suit jacket on, though no tie. He pressed the button for the elevator.

The doors opened.

"Meric," she said.

He paused and looked back.

"Thank you," she said.

He got on the elevator, and the doors closed.

Liliana took a deep breath. She felt relief in a way. He understood—she felt less alone.

She decided to push herself today. She grabbed her things,

including Meric's cash, and headed downstairs. She'd find that grocery store Teresa had told her about.

When she walked outside, her confidence began to falter. She'd never been someplace like this—all concrete and glass, and so many people. Would a grocery store be in a downtown area like this?

She decided to try the cell phone map application. She'd never had a phone like this before and didn't know much about electronics in general, but she managed to figure out how to search for grocery stores. Remembering how to spell "grocery" was the hard part. She turned right and headed down the sidewalk.

So many people around made her extremely uneasy, but she reminded herself the crowd should make her feel safer—no one would try to hurt her with so many witnesses. She hated that this was how she thought now. She couldn't let her curiosity control her gaze. She focused on the people around her, making sure no one got too close, watching each corner.

She managed to find the grocery store in the bottom floor of another big building. Her tension remained high as she meandered through the store, but she managed to find the items she needed. She wanted to make Meric some proper Mexican food—he'd just have to deal with it. She grinned to herself in the line to check out.

Outside, she turned to head back to Meric's building. On the next block, she glanced back.

That man . . . she'd seen him in the store, and now he was walking about thirty yards behind her. It definitely wasn't Carl, and he was much more clean-cut than either Carl or Josh.

At the next corner, she stopped at the crosswalk to wait—and to see if he kept going.

He slowed his pace.

The signal to cross lit up. She started forward with the other people in the group and looked down the street, as if interested in the sights.

The man was following behind her.

Chapter EIGHT

Liliana resisted the urge to call Meric. Maybe the man really was just going this way too. And what did she expect Meric to do? *I'm fine.*

Then flashbacks of that first day being taken from her home took over her mind.

They'd killed her family. And then a large man had wrapped his arms around her and started carrying her out. She'd been too overwhelmed with loss and shock to comprehend what was going on. He'd gotten her to the car before she'd even started fighting. By then, it'd been too late.

That would not happen again.

That instinct her father had called *la pantera* roared through her head. She'd been a calm child—until *la pantera* took over. Someone picked on her sister, tried to cheat her mother at the market—she didn't stand for it.

And this, right here, was different. She was in America now, run by law, not cartels. And there was just the one man.

But she didn't want to lead him back to Meric's building and definitely didn't want to risk getting stuck in an elevator alone with him.

She made it across the street and turned left down the sidewalk, the opposite direction from Meric's building. She slowed her pace, letting other people pass her, separating herself from the bulk of the people.

Then she stopped, turned around, and looked straight at the man.

He stopped, and his eyes widened a bit.

He turned and crossed the street, barely dodging oncoming cars.

Liliana continued down the sidewalk at a much faster pace, and also kept an eye on the man. He turned down a side street and disappeared. Liliana kept moving, while watching her surroundings closely. She probably looked paranoid. Maybe she was. She wasn't sure.

Had the man turned because she'd caught him or because some random woman stopping and staring him down had freaked him out?

She consulted the map application on the phone to be sure she didn't get lost. She headed around the block and then back toward Meric's building, but one street over. Memories of first coming here came back as she saw the parking garage that was attached to the side of the building, where Meric parked his car. For safety reasons, she avoided the parking garage and found a side entrance to the main floor mall.

She forced herself to slow her speed. Just to be safe, she sat on the edge of the fountain for a few minutes to make sure everything and everyone appeared normal. She didn't see the man who had followed her, nor did she see anything that seemed out of place.

The longer she sat there, the calmer she felt. The man had most likely been no one, just a random man walking in the same direction. She decided not to tell Meric.

She went back upstairs and studied for a while and then tried reading a book in English. It was getting easier—she could focus on the story more than remembering what words meant. She stayed in the apartment the rest of the day, and in the late afternoon, she started on dinner. Whenever she thought of how Meric would harass her, and yet still eat everything on his plate, she smiled.

When he walked off the elevator, he growled. Actually growled. She pretended to ignore him.

He went to his room and came back out a few minutes later, changed into jeans and a T-shirt. He leaned against the island and crossed his arms.

She glanced at him and then quickly away. Why was she noticing how he looked, how his arms and chest filled out the thin cotton shirt? Why was she repulsed by any other man but not this one? After what she'd been through with the cartels, the trip across the border, and then with Josh and Carl, she'd been positive she would never see any man as anything other than something to be feared. She hadn't wanted to admit to herself how attractive he was—his strong build, square jaw, angular features, dark intense eyes, plus his confidence. Maybe she was temporarily curious about him because he was white—nothing more than something different. Though she thought she spied some Latino in his eyes—deep brown with dark lashes.

"You went to the store?" he asked.

She nodded but kept her attention on the pan she was cooking on.

"I'm glad you were comfortable enough."

"It wasn't easy," she admitted.

"The most worthwhile things are difficult."

She prepared a plate and handed it to him.

"Thank you. It smells great." He sat at his usual seat at the table.

She took her usual seat at the other end.

"You should buy some clothes," he said. "There are plenty of stores downstairs."

"I have clothes. Thank you for them."

"I had only a few purchased. I didn't know what you'd like. You need at least enough to get through a couple of weeks."

"I'll think about it."

"If you're not comfortable in the crowds, I can have Alfred pick up a few more things."

She didn't want to add more work to Alfred's plate. "I'm sure I can manage."

"Good."

They didn't talk anymore, didn't even look at each other.

Sometimes she wasn't sure what to make of him. One minute he was almost playful, and the next he was silent. But then, she supposed she had the same problem. After he finished everything on his plate and put it in the dishwasher, he went down the hall. She took her time finishing and then sat there at the table, staring out the windows.

When Meric didn't come back, she went to her room and tried reading some more. What she needed to start focusing on was immigration laws, how to free Meric. There wasn't a computer in this room, not that she knew how to use one, but she thought maybe she could use the phone he'd given her. She found the internet application and started searching and taking notes. She had to look up a lot of words, and the language pattern was harder, thicker than basic conversational speech.

It was late by the time she lay down in bed. Like usual, she prayed silently over and over to keep the memories and the fear at bay long enough so she could fall asleep.

But they always came in her dreams no matter what she did.

She woke to the sound of screams. She wasn't sure if they were from her memory or from her own mouth. She stared at the dark ceiling, trying to grasp reality. There'd been another voice too, male, but soft and kind. It'd helped soften her terror.

Then she noticed something next to the bed.

A man.

Kneeling next to the bed in the dark.

She scrambled back, away from him.

"I'm sorry. I didn't mean to scare you." It was Meric. The lights of the city coming in through the windows were just enough for her to recognize his face, though her tears made his features blur.

She couldn't control her breathing.

"You screamed." His voice was muted, soft. "I came to make sure you're all right." He stood. "I'm sorry." He started for the door.

The voice, the one that'd helped soften the terror of the dream, it was his. He'd been speaking to her, calming her?

"Don't go," she whispered.

He paused at the door, his back to her.

She realized he wore no shirt, just pajama bottoms. His lack of clothes, his thick and strong arms and shoulders, should scare her, but nothing about him scared her. All she could think of was that he'd been so concerned about her he'd run over to her room without thinking about his attire.

He turned to face her but didn't move closer. "I'm sorry."

Tears silently fell down her cheeks.

"You're safe," he said.

"Don't go."

He walked back over and knelt beside the bed.

She lay down facing him.

"You're safe here, I promise," he murmured.

Another tear fell and absorbed into the soft pillowcase.

"I'll stay as long as you need," he said. "I'll do anything you need, anything to make it just a little better."

More quiet tears came, but for a different reason now.

"You can sleep," he said.

She kept watching him.

"You're safe. You can close your eyes." Then he added almost inaudibly, "I promise I won't hurt you."

"I know," she whispered. She slid her hand over the sheets, closer to him.

He hesitated as he met her eyes, reading her. Was he deciding if she was okay with him touching her? Or if he was okay with it?

Another silent tear fell down her cheek.

With the gentlest touch, he held just her fingers.

She felt her body finally relax, and she closed her eyes.

Chapter
NINE

Meric rinsed his razor in the sink with a quiet swish.

All he could keep thinking was, *It was a mistake.* He'd over-stepped—gone in her room without being invited. What had he been thinking?

But she hadn't seemed upset. She'd even asked him to stay. And he had. Stayed the rest of the night and hadn't left until morning when she'd started to stir. Then he'd left quickly, for fear he'd scare her again. Perhaps she hadn't been fully awake when she'd asked him to stay. Perhaps she wouldn't even remember.

He wasn't sure what to think.

Except that he needed to be more careful. Not just for her sake, but for his.

He ran the razor over his jaw one more time and swished it in the water. He set the razor in the medicine cabinet and emptied the sink.

Then he rested his hands on the counter and glared at his reflection. *Get your head straight.*

He pushed away from the counter and walked away from the mirror.

Once he was showered and dressed, he considered leaving. Escaping. But it was still very early, and he needed to make sure she was all right. He walked out to the kitchen. He looked around to find something he was able to cook. *Cook* was probably too strong a word—*prepare* was more accurate. Toast and more fruit. She'd seemed to like the fruit.

He felt the need to fill the quiet, or maybe distract himself, so he turned on the TV. He rarely actually watched it. It was there for background noise and occasionally news, though those were usually one and the same.

Liliana woke feeling a little strange and oddly calm. It took her a few seconds to remember why.

Then she heard voices. The TV. Meric was up already. Instead of showering and dressing, she found a cardigan to put over her white cotton nightgown.

She walked out into the living room and saw him at the kitchen island cutting up fruit. "Is this retribution?"

He looked up but then back down at what he was doing. There was that coldness of his again. Sometimes she felt like it was less barrier and more puzzle.

She stood on the other side of the island. He was wearing a T-shirt and jeans, and she remembered it was Saturday. She focused on his face and didn't let her gaze linger anywhere else. "Not trying eggs today?"

He looked up at her. But then his attention snapped to the TV like the laser sight on a gun.

She turned and watched, understanding the English pretty well. It was some kind of talk show, and a young, very pretty woman with cascades of blonde hair was talking. A tear slowly fell down her cheek. "I thought we were in love. Well, I was, anyway. Maybe I was dazzled by the Meric Toledan name, the money and fame, his good looks, maybe at first. But I fell in love. He'd been so attentive. I see now it was just attentive enough to get me into bed when he wanted it."

"What do you mean, exactly?" the host, a middle-aged woman, asked.

"He just . . ."

The host reached over and squeezed her hand. "It's okay. You're safe here."

The blonde woman nodded. "He would give me gifts. I didn't think he was trying to buy me off at the time. It'd seemed so thoughtful, you know? Like he'd say, 'I saw this in the store window and thought of you.' I thought I was seeing who he really is. I thought all the stories about him were just talk. I know I probably sound naïve."

"Not at all," the host said. "You sound like a woman in love. Like so many others who fall into the trap men like this set. You're the victim."

Liliana hated that word—*victim*. She refused to think of herself like that, as a *victim*. She was a fighter. Even if she lost sometimes, needed help sometimes, she would never stop fighting.

The blonde woman nodded as she looked at her hands fiddling in her lap. "But finding out I was wrong about him wasn't the worst part."

"What was the worst part?" the host asked. "You can trust me."

Liliana wanted to roll her eyes—*trust you and the entire viewing audience.*

"He . . . Well, he . . ." The blonde took a deep breath.

"It's all right. You can say it."

"He found out I was pregnant. And he . . . forced me to have an abortion."

"Forced?"

"He took me there, and well, he kind of stood over me the whole time. I got the point real clearly . . ."

The blonde kept prattling on, but Liliana's attention shifted to Meric. It was as if she could feel rage rolling off him like black fog. He was staring at the TV. Then he took the knife in his hand and hurled it across the room, all the way through the dining and living rooms. It sank directly into the center of the screen, and the TV went dark and quiet.

She tensed, and it felt like all her blood stopped in her veins.

He continued to glare at the black screen.

He glanced at her. "Sorry." He turned to retreat down the hall.

Liliana realized his reaction was more than just anger at lies being told about him, that it had to be related to something deeper. She headed him off before he passed his office.

He stared past her. His expression was blacker than a starless night in the desert.

She spoke gently. "Tell me."

"I'm sorry I scared you." He shifted to walk around, still not looking at her.

"You didn't." That wasn't entirely true, but she would never tell him that.

He glanced at her and then away again.

She noticed his hands were shaking.

She took one of his hands.

He pulled it away and stepped back. "Please."

"Tell me."

"I need to be alone. Please." He was still staring past her.

"You need to talk."

He looked at her, and something in his eyes seemed to calm just a bit. "Please, Liliana. I don't want to upset you."

"You don't upset me."

"I will if I don't calm down."

She moved closer and took his other hand as well, a little surprised at herself. "So, talk to me, and that'll help you calm down."

He looked down at their hands and moved to step back. She held on, wouldn't let him go. Though she knew he could physically force her to let go, she felt sure he would never force her to do anything.

He closed his eyes and took a breath.

"Who's that woman?" Liliana asked.

Quiet.

"Is she an old girlfriend?"

He opened his eyes, this time looking right at her. "I've never seen her before."

Liliana nodded. "That's what I thought."

He lowered his brows slightly in confusion.

"The man she described isn't the Meric I know."

He looked at her for several more seconds and then tried to step back again. She held tight.

"I'm sure this isn't the first time someone has made up stories about you," she said. "Why did this one bother you so much?"

He didn't answer.

"I hope you know," she said, "I would never share our private conversations. You don't know me that well, but—"

"I know you wouldn't."

She squeezed his hands. "Why did this one bother you so much?"

"Abortion."

"You would never do such a thing."

He looked away.

"Meric," she said. "I know you wouldn't do that."

"I could never ask a woman to kill her own child. I can't imagine . . ."

"Does it upset you that someone could think you would do that?"

"I don't care what people think of me."

That seemed to align better with what she knew about him. She kept her voice gentle. "What has you so upset?"

Quiet.

"Meric," she murmured.

Finally, he said, "My mother, she told me once how she couldn't fathom such a thing—killing her own child. I remember how the idea disturbed her."

She waited. There was something more—she could see it in his eyes.

"But she should have." He met her gaze. "She should have aborted me."

"Why . . . Why would you say that?"

He yanked his hands out of her grasp and walked away, down the hall.

Chapter TEN

Liliana let Meric go. She wanted to follow him, make him feel better, but there had to be something more to it all, something he wasn't going to tell her. She stood there for several minutes, trying to think of something she could do.

But she wasn't *really* his wife. She didn't really know him, which was even clearer right now. She had no idea what to do to help him. She sat on a stool at the kitchen island for a long time, hoping he'd come back out.

But he didn't.

She wiped down all the kitchen counters, though they didn't really need it.

He still didn't come.

Finally, she went to her room, showered, and dressed. When she came back out, he was still nowhere in sight, but there was a note on the counter saying that Alfred was seeing to it that the TV was replaced this morning. She realized she'd been hoping maybe he'd spend some time with her today, since it was Saturday. But she reminded herself he didn't owe her anything, and he was obviously the kind of person who didn't care much for socializing.

For some reason, she didn't want to sit here today. She tucked the phone, key card, and cash in her jeans pockets and headed down in the elevator. She'd find a few more pairs of jeans and simple tops, and the clothing debate would be done, without adding more work to Alfred.

"Mrs. Toledan," the doorman greeted.

She forced a smile and walked out of the large lobby.

She'd thought the mall area had been busy the first time she'd come down here. It was a lot worse today. But she didn't let herself go back upstairs.

She stopped at the fountain and scanned the shops within view.

"Liliana?"

She spun around. "Ethel. Hello." It was one of the bridge-playing women.

Ethel smiled at her, and her cheeks crinkled. "You look a bit lost, dear."

"Maybe a little—what's the word?—overwhelmed."

"Stores or the people?"

"Both," she admitted.

Ethel smiled. "What're you looking for?"

"Clothes."

"Lots of those stores here."

"Too many."

"Ah." She nodded. "Come with me."

Liliana followed her to a small restaurant nearby, where they found the other ladies—Tallulah, Florence, and Alma—as well as Wilmer. "We have a little project," Ethel said to the group.

A few minutes later, Ethel was leading the way into a clothing store. The ladies peppered her with questions about what she liked, and Wilmer stood to the side harassing.

"Don't dress the poor girl like an old biddy," Wilmer said.

"She's choosin' her own style," Tallulah said.

Alma brought a shirt over for Liliana to look at. It was a fancy tank top.

"I, um, like to be covered," Liliana said.

Alma gently patted her cheek. "Good Christian girl."

A tiny voice in Liliana's head whispered that she wasn't a good Christian girl anymore. She'd managed to fight off some of it, but they'd still molested her. She was no longer clean. But she stomped on that ugly voice and pushed it out of her head.

"What about this?" Florence yelled from across the store as she held up a pretty cotton shirt with long sleeves.

Wilmer rolled his eyes. "She thinks everyone's as deaf as her."

"If yer havin' such a bad time," Tallulah said, "you can just be gettin' on yer way."

Wilmer ignored her.

Liliana nodded at Florence, and Florence grinned.

"How about some more jeans?" Ethel said.

Liliana nodded. "I like pants better than dresses." She didn't care that much what kind of pants. She just felt more covered, safer in pants. It made her a little sad not to feel comfortable in dresses anymore, especially when she again remembered all the pretty dresses her mother had made for her as a child, the dresses her sister had inherited and looked so pretty in.

She pushed those thoughts away and walked over with Ethel to a wall covered in jeans. She looked at every style, but they all appeared to be rather tight. Maybe they wouldn't be so bad on.

A few minutes later, the ladies went to the dressing area with her, and Wilmer waited outside. She put on a pair of jeans and a top and looked in the mirror.

"Let's see," Florence called.

Liliana pulled back the curtain.

"Oh, how pretty," Alma said.

"You don't look comfortable," Ethel said.

"I wish they weren't so tight," she admitted.

"That seems to be how they make young ladies' pants anymore. But you look lovely, dear."

"She has a figure that can pull off anything," Florence said.

Liliana tried to smile.

"Oh," Alma said, "I saw just the thing. I'll be back." She hurried out of the dressing room and was back a minute later holding what looked like a very short dress, or maybe it was a long shirt?

"I think that's too short for her comfort," Ethel said.

"That's what I thought," Alma agreed. "But might it look cute with the jeans? I've seen other young girls do it. I always thought it looked cute." Alma handed the garment to Liliana.

Liliana closed the curtain and changed. It was fitted to her upper half, but not skin-tight, and flared at the waist. It made her feel more comfortable in the jeans. She opened the curtain.

"Oh, that's lovely," Tallulah said.

Liliana picked several things and headed to check out. She was just starting to understand American currency, but the prices seemed high to her. But then she counted the money Meric had given her, and it barely made a dent. He'd given her a lot of large bills.

She came out of the dressing area. Wilmer was there and wrapped her arm around his as he led her to the cashier. She wanted to jerk away, but she stopped herself.

"Blink three times if you need help escaping," he said. "Don't let these old biddies push you around."

"Yes, please tell us if that old geezer is bothering you," Florence yelled.

Tallulah snickered.

While Liliana checked out, her personal shoppers laughed and bickered.

"That's an awful lot of cash," Wilmer said as they left the store. "That Toledan didn't give you a credit card?"

"I didn't ask."

"You shouldn't have to *ask*. He should be taking care of you."

"He is."

He pressed his lips together. Then he stopped and faced her. "You just tell me if he's not good to you, you hear?"

"Don't badger the poor girl," Tallulah said.

Wilmer kept his focus on Liliana. "I mean that."

"Meric is good to me, I promise."

"All right," he said. "I know you're a smart girl." He didn't sound convinced, but he let it go.

"Have you eaten lunch?" Ethel asked Liliana.

When Liliana said no, Ethel led the group to a smoothie place that also sold sandwiches. They sat together and chatted while they ate. She liked being with them because they felt normal. They had no idea everything that'd happened. And while they bickered with one another, they were nothing but kind to her.

It was midafternoon when Liliana headed for the elevator, several bags in hand. The ladies had decided to go for a walk, and Wilmer said he wanted to go to the cigar store in the mall, which no one else was interested in.

She approached a man standing with his back to the wall reading a newspaper.

Her feet slowed. He looked familiar. She glanced around. Perhaps she'd seen him in the mall? She thought about it and realized she'd seen him walk by the clothing store earlier. He didn't have any bags in his hands, just the newspaper, so he wasn't here to shop. He looked clean, nice haircut, slacks, and a blazer—again, nothing like Josh and Carl.

A thought occurred to her that she hadn't considered before— maybe he was a reporter trying to get dirt on Meric? That seemed more plausible than someone out to harm her, especially after seeing that ridiculous interview this morning. The interview that'd upset Meric so much.

She walked up to him but stayed several feet away. "Who are you?"

He seemed to pause for half a second before looking up. "Excuse me?"

"Who are you?"

"Look, lady, I don't know who you are." He walked away.

She watched him leave, made sure he left, before she went upstairs.

Chapter ELEVEN

Liliana woke with a start, gulping air, as if some outside force had ripped her out of the dream.

She looked over, hoping Meric would be there like last night, but he wasn't.

He hadn't been home all day. He'd texted her to tell her he wouldn't be home for dinner but hadn't told her where he was or when he'd be back. It'd been after ten when she'd heard the elevator and his footsteps down the hall.

And then images from the dream, from her memories, again flooded her mind. During the day, she could mostly control them, but not at night. She felt like her mind was too tired to fight the terror always clawing through her.

Please, Lord, please give me strength.

She prayed over and over, but she couldn't seem to get her mind under control. She couldn't get her breathing to calm, and she realized she was about to hyperventilate.

Before she could consider if it was wise, she got up and walked out of the room, across the dark apartment, and down the hall that led to Meric's room.

She came to what she'd thought was the end of the hall and realized the hall turned. She had no idea what was around the corner, but she was pretty sure the door in front of her was Meric's. She could see a bit of light spilling out at her feet.

The images flashed again, and she swallowed a sob.

She knocked on the door and then turned the knob. "Meric?"

He was sitting up in bed, leaned against the headboard, reading a file. "Liliana. Are you all right?"

A tear fell from her lash line, and she wiped it away. She wasn't sure what she'd been thinking coming here, but she couldn't get herself to walk back out either.

"I can't . . ." she said. "I can't get it out of my head."

He didn't respond.

Another tear fell. "I'm sorry." She turned to leave.

"Liliana."

She stopped but kept her gaze on the floor.

His voice was gentle. "Come here."

She turned back to him.

"Come sit with me."

She walked over and sat next to him on the edge of the bed.

"Do you want to talk about it?" he asked.

She shook her head. "I can't."

Quiet.

She wiped another tear off her cheek.

He set his hand on her shoulder, lightly, barely a touch. "Would it help if . . . Would it be all right if I held you?"

She turned her head to look at him and felt her expression crumple. Then she leaned into him and rested her head on his shoulder. He wrapped his arms around her.

She cried against his warm skin.

He held her tightly, hands carefully on her upper back and her hair. She'd thought she'd never be able to withstand a man's touch, even a friendly touch, ever again, but his hands felt different. Kind, comforting, not asking for anything.

She held herself against him. He felt warm and strong, safe. Her breathing calmed.

They didn't talk.

She lost herself in the feel of him, his quiet hands slowly stroking her hair.

She felt her consciousness leaving her. She barely got the words out. "Thank you."

※ ※ ※

Meric felt the difference in her breathing, the calm steadiness of it, and knew she was asleep. He stopped stroking her silky hair but didn't dare let go of her for fear she would wake.

He closed his eyes and tried not to think, not to feel.

He could feel the curve of her back through the thin fabric of her nightgown, and that brought the image of her standing there in his bedroom doorway, beautiful and unguarded. Then he'd noticed she was crying.

Now she was calm and sleeping peacefully, and his mind and body raged. He was afraid his pounding heart would wake her, but she continued to breathe slowly and deeply.

He looked down at her beautiful face. He'd never seen a beauty so flawless.

Why am I being tortured?

He focused on the peace in her expression. That ever-present fear and anger that he could always see—maybe more sense—was gone. He wished he could give her life back to her—her innocence, the love of her family. But he couldn't.

And he needed to remember he was not the answer.

All he could do was support her, give her the things she needed and space to grieve. And above all else, safety. He needed to keep her safe from the world, and from himself, so she could heal.

※ ※ ※

Light started to filter into the room, and Liliana slowly opened her eyes. She was still with Meric, pressed against him, wrapped in his arms. She was more aware than she'd been last night, perhaps because she'd slept so deeply. His body was against hers, and her hand lay on his bare chest. His skin felt warm.

She moved her gaze away from him and noticed the file on the bed next to him. It was in English, of course. It said something about the next auction and a shipment from South America. It had to be something to do with his business, right? But she'd thought he was more involved with the acquisition and reorganization of businesses, not so much the day-to-day running of them. And what did a product shipment have to do with an auction? If he was bringing in some kind of product made in South America, wouldn't he be selling it in retail outlets, not at an auction?

His low murmur pulled her away from her questions. "Are you awake?"

She sat up, and he took his arms away from her. She felt cold.

"I'm sorry," she said. "I don't know why I—"

"Because you needed comforted and to feel safe." He hesitated, then added, "That's what I want for you."

She stood and walked toward the door. Then she stopped and looked back. "Thank you."

She walked out and closed the door.

She crossed her arms to get her hands to stop shaking and headed for her room. She showered and dressed quickly and went out to the kitchen to make something for breakfast. It was Sunday—maybe he'd stay home today.

He came out a little while later, hair still wet from his shower. She wondered if maybe he'd comment on her new clothes.

She handed him a plate, and he stood at the island to eat. He didn't talk to her, didn't even look at her.

Is he mad at me for coming to him last night?

But he'd been so gentle and kind.

The silence continued. She tried to eat but wasn't hungry anymore.

He put his plate in the dishwasher. "Thank you." He headed for the elevator.

"Are you working today?"

"I have some things I need to do. Don't wait up for me." He

stepped into the elevator. As the doors closed, his tone changed, gentler, like it'd been last night. "Have a nice day, Liliana."

And he was gone.

Liliana cleaned up the kitchen and went to her desk to continue her research, but she couldn't concentrate. She found herself staring out the window rather than being productive.

The sound of a voice coming from the other room broke the silence and made her to jump. "I'm sorry to bother you, Mrs. Toledan." She walked out to the living room and realized the voice was coming from the screen on the kitchen counter. The face of the doorman was on the screen.

She figured out which button to press and asked, "How can I help you?"

"Hello, ma'am. I apologize for disturbing you. I have a Detective Hughes and a Detective Johnson from the Houston Police Department here to see you."

Chapter TWELVE

"Shall I let them up or take down contact information?" the doorman asked.

Liliana figured they were here to follow up on Josh and Carl. "Please let them up. Thank you very much."

"Yes, ma'am." The screen went blank.

A minute or so later, the elevator dinged, and two officers stepped off the elevator. She'd expected uniforms, but they were in suits. They both held up a badge.

The one on the left, who had a gray mustache, said, "Good morning."

"Good morning. Would you like something to drink, officers?"

"I'm *Detective* Hughes," the man with the mustache corrected.

Liliana paused. And then she turned to the other man—much younger, with reddish-blond hair. "And you must be Detective Johnson." She addressed both of them, "How may I help you?"

"Have a seat, ma'am," Hughes said.

"Please." She motioned toward the dining table.

When they didn't sit, she figured maybe they were being polite and waiting for her to sit first. She took the chair Meric usually sat in.

Detective Johnson sat at the other end of the table and took a small notebook out of his breast pocket. Detective Hughes remained standing, on the other side of the table from her.

"Is this about Carl Walsh and Josh McConnell?" she asked. "Do you have any new information?"

"How long have you been married to Meric Toledan?" Hughes asked.

Liliana paused. "Almost a week."

"And *why* did you marry him, a man you presumably barely know?"

She didn't know what "presumably" meant, but she definitely understood his direct and unfriendly tone. "I'm sorry—what is this about?"

"Answer the question."

Liliana wasn't sure how to handle this. She didn't understand what they were after, and she didn't know American law well enough to know what she could and couldn't refuse to answer. All she knew was she'd better not lie to the police.

"I care for Meric very much," she said.

Detective Hughes leaned his hands on the table, and his voice lowered. "Look, we can help you. We just need your cooperation."

"I don't understand what you want."

"Don't play with me. I can't help you unless you cooperate. Why did you marry Toledan? Why did he bring you specifically to live in this penthouse? Why are you unguarded?"

She struggled to catch his quick words, and then understanding snapped into place in Liliana's head. She stood. "You can leave now."

Detective Johnson spoke with sympathy in his voice. "We can help you. We can take you out of here right now—if you give us information on Toledan."

Liliana held her chin high. "There is no reason for me to leave."

Johnson sighed. "Please. Let us help you."

"I don't need help. Meric saved me."

Johnson looked up at Hughes and shook his head as if disappointed.

"I am not an idiot," Liliana said. "Meric has done nothing but show me kindness."

Johnson's tone continued to be gentle, but in a placating way. "That's how he draws you in."

"Please leave." She pointed toward the elevator.

Neither of them moved. "You don't want to do this, Miss Vela," Hughes said.

"It's *Mrs. Toledan*," she corrected. "I'll kindly thank you to leave my husband's home."

"Not *your* home?" Johnson asked.

Anger burned in her throat like alcohol, but she managed not to curse at them. She walked over to the elevator, pressed the button, and when the doors opened, she held them. "Have a nice day, Detectives."

Johnson sighed and tucked his notebook back into his breast pocket. Then he stood. He moved slowly. Liliana's patience was receding like a candle burning down. But did the wick belong to a candle or dynamite?

Hughes got on the elevator, but Johnson stopped and held out a card. "I suggest you hide this somewhere he won't find it."

She snatched it out of his hand, partially to get him moving, and partially because she wanted to make sure she could properly identify them for Meric.

Johnson walked into the elevator, and she let go of the door.

Liliana shook with fury.

She walked into her bedroom, picked up her phone, and called Meric.

He answered before the first ring stopped. "Hello?"

"Two detectives just left."

"Did they give you an update on Josh or Carl?"

"No. They were here because they think you're involved in human trafficking. They offered to get me out if I gave them information on you."

"What did you tell them?"

Why doesn't he sound confused? "Nothing. I made them leave."

"I'm sorry you had to deal with that."

There's something he's not saying. But what? She took a silent breath. "When are you coming home?"

"Not until late." Then he added, "Unless you're not all right."

"I'm fine."

"You don't sound fine."

"I'm just really angry."

He paused. "Why're you angry?"

"What do you mean, 'Why am I angry'? They accused an innocent man of an unspeakable crime. Police officers who should be smarter than that, who should be *protecting* citizens like you. That's why I'm angry."

He was silent.

Realization dawned. "Did you think I'd believe them?"

"You don't really know me."

"I know you literally saved my life and put yourself in danger to do it. I know you'll miss an entire night of sleep just to comfort me. I know you don't even touch me unless you have my express permission. I know you try to spoil me. And you'd do the same thing for anyone."

"Not anyone."

"Anyone who's a decent person."

He didn't respond.

She took another breath, trying to calm her anger. "I'll see you later."

"Don't wait up."

She ended the call and plopped down into her desk chair.

Then she picked up her phone and started another internet search. Next time, if there was a next time, she'd understand her rights, what she did and didn't have to do for the police. Educating herself always helped calm her down, or at least let her feel some sort of control over her circumstances.

Meric didn't come home until late. She lay in bed waiting,

listening for the elevator and the sound of his footsteps. She'd memorized the sound. He didn't come to see her, to say goodnight. She'd known he wouldn't. She tried clearing her mind, like every night. Finally, she tried closing her eyes and remembering what it'd felt like last night—warm and safe and calm.

She dreamt, but she didn't wake screaming.

In the morning, she moved quickly to be able to make sure he ate something for breakfast. And maybe to hear him tease.

When she went out to the kitchen, she noticed his office doors were closed, and she could faintly hear his voice. Why was he on the phone this early? She took a pan out of the cupboard.

He came out a little while later, dressed in his usual simple but tailored suit.

She held out a plate for him.

"I'm sorry. I need to get moving." He pressed the button for the elevator.

"You should eat."

"I'll grab something at work."

She set the plate down on the counter.

As the elevator doors closed, his voice returned to that gentle tone. "Let me know if you need anything."

She stood there for a few seconds.

Then she dumped the food in the trash can. She'd never wasted food in her life, but she had no appetite and didn't want to look at it.

She headed back to her room but couldn't seem to sit still or concentrate. She decided to go to the grocery store again. She was still angry at the officers and needed to work off the frustrated energy, that was all. Walking would be good for her.

It still set her on edge to be out in public, but she knew she needed to get used to it. She grabbed a few things at the store—ingredients she needed for a different dish. Then she waited in line to check out, trying to feel at ease though stuck in the aisle with people in front of and behind her. She didn't let herself fidget and took slow breaths.

What didn't help was seeing Meric's picture on the front page of a tabloid.

Finally, she made it to the cashier and checked out.

She walked quickly back to Meric's apartment. Teresa was there cleaning. Liliana smiled at her and tried to be pleasant while she put her groceries away, but she wasn't in the mood to chat so she went to her room, closed the door, and tried to bury herself in study and research.

Hours passed slowly.

She was about to start on dinner when her phone beeped with a text from Meric: *"Don't wait up."*

She dropped the phone on the desk with a clatter.

She didn't bother making anything for dinner and just ate a piece of bread.

Then she lay in bed and tried to clear her mind, but really, she was listening for the elevator. She debated whether she should call him, make sure he was all right.

It wasn't until two in the morning when the elevator finally dinged.

She quickly got out of bed and went out to the living room.

Meric was standing in front of the open refrigerator guzzling a bottle of water. His hair was disheveled, and . . . there was a rip in the shoulder of his jacket.

"Meric, are you all right?"

He barely glanced in her direction, closed the refrigerator, and headed for the hall. "Fine."

She considered following him, but when he didn't look back, didn't even pause before closing his bedroom door, she turned and went back to her room.

Chapter THIRTEEN

In the morning, Meric was gone so early Liliana missed him completely.

All day, she again had trouble concentrating.

She tried watching the evening news to learn more about this country and this city and test her English. And maybe to distract herself.

There was a story about a car accident where someone died and then something about nursing home abuse. She picked up the remote control to change the channel and find something less unpleasant. But the next news story made her stop.

"Meric Toledan is under investigation. The police aren't releasing any information on the details, but they have acknowledged that an investigation is ongoing. More on that as the story develops." The anchorwoman moved on to a different story, but Liliana didn't pay attention.

She sat there with her phone in her hand, debating. Should she call him? How much was her business? Yes, she was technically his wife, but in name only. But she was living here, financially dependent on him for the moment—that gave her some right to ask questions, didn't it?

Finally, she texted him. "Are you coming home tonight?"

He responded. "Don't wait up."

Frustration clawed up her spine. She texted back. "I need to talk to you."

He didn't respond for a good ten minutes. "I'll be home after 8."

While she waited, she tried to find something on the television to watch, but she was not feeling patient enough to focus on it.

It was almost eight thirty when the elevator finally dinged.

He walked off the elevator and barely glanced over at her before walking into the kitchen. "Have you eaten yet?"

She stood. "There was a story on the news about you."

"Not uncommon." He took a bottle of water out of the refrigerator. Faced away from her, he drank.

She waited for him to be done, to come over and sit with her on the couch.

He threw the empty bottle into the trash. "You haven't eaten dinner. Why?"

"What's going on? Were those detectives just fishing and trying to make a name for themselves, or is the police department really investigating you? Why would they think you're involved in human trafficking?"

"Don't listen to the media—they just want to increase ratings. Why haven't you eaten?"

"What makes you think I haven't eaten?" *And why do you care? Just answer my questions.*

He motioned toward the drawer that held the trash can. "No food waste or even wrappers. You haven't eaten all day, have you?"

"Have you?"

"We're not discussing me."

"I'm trying to, but you keep pushing the topic back to inconsequential things."

"Your health is not inconsequential. You've been through a lot; you need to take care of yourself."

"So do you. You're barely sleeping and probably barely eating. What's going on, Meric?"

He closed the trash can drawer and sighed.

"You look exhausted," she said in a gentler tone. "Come sit down."

He paused. Then he took off his jacket, dropped it on the counter, and walked over. He sat on the other end of the couch. "I'm sorry the news stressed you out. It has nothing to do with you."

"But it has to do with you. I may not really be your wife, but I do care about what's going on with you."

He looked past her, out the expansive windows to the darkened city.

Her tone was soft. "Please talk to me."

He shifted his gaze to her. "It's not true—whatever you saw on TV, whatever those detectives said."

"I know that."

"That's all you need to know."

She shifted closer to him. "Please."

He stood and walked around to the other side of the coffee table. "I think you need to consider why you're pushing this so hard."

"What do you mean?"

"You're focusing on anything else. Because you don't want to deal with what's really upsetting you."

"Seeing an innocent man being attacked is what's upsetting me. You refusing to talk is upsetting me."

His voice lowered. "You need to deal with it, Liliana. You can't heal until you deal with it."

"We're not talking about me."

"You don't have to tell me anything, but you do need to deal with it. The nightmares aren't going to stop until you do."

She stood. "I'm dealing with it fine. I'm moving forward. I'm improving my English and learning about this country and its laws. I'm learning how to integrate. They will *not* win."

His eyes softened. "I know they won't win. Not against you." He took a breath. "But you need to deal with everything that's happened. At least start the process. If you really want to be free."

"I am free. I don't let anyone control me."

"They are controlling you. Your memories will slowly kill you if you don't face them. I've been there; I'm still there sometimes, still fighting to get to the surface and breathe." His voice was raw. "I can't let that happen to you."

Her voice rose. "No one controls me!"

"I want to help you, Liliana—"

"No! I'm a fighter! I won't let them win. They have to kill me first."

He moved around the table toward her, but she shoved him. He took a step back but didn't leave, just stood there looking at her.

"They have to kill me first!" she screamed.

She squeezed her eyes shut, and tears rolled down her cheeks. When she opened her eyes, he was still there, still just looking at her.

"I fought!" she yelled. "I got away. They won't win. I won't let them."

"They hurt you, Liliana. It's not your fault."

"But it is my fault." More tears fell. "They came because of me. They shot my papá. I didn't fight. He fell to the ground, and I . . . I didn't . . . And then Mamá . . ."

"It's not your fault."

She screamed, "They're dead!"

"I'm so sorry. I wish I could . . ."

She rubbed her hands over her face and then yanked them away. She wanted to move, to scream, to fall down. She just wanted it to stop.

"What else, Liliana? Get it out."

She shifted to walk away, escape into her room.

He grabbed her hand. "Get it out."

"You want to hear about it? Is that what you want?"

"I want you to survive it."

"I did. Don't you understand? Those women on the truck, they didn't make it. I tried to help them, but I didn't know what to do. They died." Images flashed through her mind—the blank, dead eyes of Maria. She'd had children, a boy and a girl. She'd just wanted to get back to them. But she was dead. "They wouldn't stop and let us bury them. We moved them, laid them out, tried to show them honor. But then the smell . . . They wouldn't stop." She dragged in a haggard breath. "They wouldn't stop!"

His voice barely made a sound. "And some part of you wishes you could trade places with them, the women who didn't make it."

She shifted to move, to yank away from him, but then she stopped.

"I'm right," he said. "Aren't I?"

She looked away.

"Get it out, Liliana. Yell. Curse. Anything."

She screamed, "No!" She picked a glass up off the coffee table and hurled it. It hit a window mullion and shattered. The sound reverberated through her head.

"They hurt you," he said. "Let yourself be angry."

"I am angry! Don't you understand? I'm nothing but angry." She cursed and screamed. "They touched me. They ripped my clothes off. I fought. I gave Josh a bloody nose."

And then he was right in front of her. "You did fight. And you got away. *You* did that. After everything else you survived, you did that. You're amazing."

Tears fell. She could barely see him through the moisture in her eyes.

He moved closer and gently rested his hands on her cheeks. "And now you're safe. Do you hear me? No one will ever touch you again."

She wrapped her arms around him, pulled herself to his chest.

He held her tightly and whispered, "You're safe. I promise." He stroked her hair with a strong but gentle hand. "I won't let anyone hurt you again." He rested a hand on her cheek, holding her to his chest, and whispered, "I promise."

And then it was silent.

The world felt still. For the first time in so long. She'd broken through and could think past the terror, could imagine a road ahead, no longer stuck in a moment of everlasting fear. And she remembered . . . Sitting on the riverbank with her papá, how he could bring such contentment with nothing but quiet and that smile that twinkled his eyes, the smile he reserved just for his little girls. Her beautiful mamá in the kitchen, talking and laughing, never saying much of anything, but having so much fun. And her sweet little sister, who would follow her around and drive her nuts, and at the same time make her feel so important. The other memories were still there, would always be there, but she could remember how beautiful her family had been without the memories being destroyed by ugliness. This was only the start— she knew she had a long road ahead still, but she finally felt like she might be able to get through a day without feeling like she was dying inside little by little.

She squeezed Meric tighter.

And she registered the feel of him under her hands, his muscular back.

The silence seemed to change, get thicker somehow.

Warmth, from Meric, from herself—it crept through her, slowly rolled in like fog. Something inside her quivered in a way she'd never felt before.

Meric drew his fingers slowly through her hair and down her back. Her skin tingled.

She shifted her hands over his back, held him tighter.

But then Meric pulled her arms off him and walked away. He didn't pause or look back but kept walking and disappeared into his room.

Another tear fell down Liliana's cheek, and she wiped it off as if striking it from existence.

Meric walked out onto the balcony off his bedroom, trying to get as far away from Liliana as possible. Maybe the smells of the city would drive her scent out of his head.

He gripped the railing so hard his arms shook.

He'd been doing so well staying away from her. Why was it so much more difficult with Liliana?

And then it hit him.

He closed his eyes and cursed. He wanted to roar obscenities.

His back slid down against the windows. He sat there on the balcony with his knees bent and his fingers curled into his hair. He didn't know what to do.

Meric didn't come back, didn't explain himself.

Liliana went to her room and sat down at her desk, now able to focus. Something had to change, and she would make it happen.

Chapter FOURTEEN

Meric let himself get up at his normal time. It probably wasn't wise, but he wanted to make sure Liliana was all right after he'd abruptly walked away from her last night. But when he went out to the kitchen, she was nowhere in sight. Then he noticed a note on the counter: *"I've gone out. Will be back later. LV"*

It was good she was going out, feeling more comfortable in her new life and new surroundings. He hoped that maybe she felt better after finally getting it all out last night. These were the thoughts he kept pushing through his mind, anyway.

Festering in the back of his head, so far back that he couldn't reach it, were the initials she'd written—LV. Liliana *Vela*. Not Liliana *Toledan*.

◼ ▩ ◼

Liliana headed through the mall downstairs. Most of the shops weren't open yet, which meant fewer people.

"Liliana!"

She spun around. Some part of her expected to see Meric, but it was Wilmer who walked quickly toward her with a big smile.

"Good morning," Wilmer said.

"Hi, Wilmer. Your lady friends not with you?"

He waved his hand dismissively. "Those aren't my *lady friends*. Too old for me."

"Alma and Ethel might be, but aren't Tallulah and Florence about your age?"

"Pshaw. I'm still in my prime." He beat his chest with his fist. She hadn't really paid attention before, but she realized he wasn't a small man, had probably been quite the athlete in his younger years.

She laughed, though it sounded hollow.

He took her arm and tucked it in his. "I'm looking for a young and lovely lady."

His contact felt like barbed wire in her veins but she managed not to pull away.

"Have breakfast with me," he said. "I'm paying."

"The shops aren't open yet."

He started guiding her to the right. "The smoothie place is."

"I should really get going."

"You deserve to take a break."

She wanted to point out that she didn't have a job, nothing much to take a break from, but then she thought maybe he meant a break from Meric. Her thoughts on Meric were too scattered to discuss. She let Wilmer lead her to the smoothie restaurant.

She ordered orange juice and an apple and let him pay. It seemed to make him happy.

"So, how long have you lived here?" she asked.

"Not long. Thought this might be the place to meet a pretty lady." He grinned. "So, what has you out so early this morning?"

She took a sip of juice as they sat at a table. "I could ask you the same thing."

"Getting into mischief as usual." He looked at her hand. "Well, isn't that quite the rock."

"Meric has good taste."

"I've never faulted the man his taste, that's for sure." He winked. "Is that why you're up and about so early—on an errand for Toledan?"

His attitude toward Meric rubbed her the wrong way, but

then she tried to remember how the media painted him. Without any other evidence, what were people supposed to believe? She wondered why Meric ignored the things people said about him. Why didn't he try to set the record straight? She believed him that most of the time he didn't care, but he did care sometimes. A knife through a TV screen was pretty clear evidence of that.

"Is that it? It's something for Toledan?"

"No," she said. "Well, kind of, I guess. In a—how do you say?—in a round way."

"Roundabout way."

"Right. I'm still learning English expressions."

"You speak it very well. When did you learn?"

"I knew the basics pretty well, and I've been studying since moving here. Meric has helped a lot."

"And you married him just after moving here, right? A few weeks?"

She didn't want to correct his timing and bring attention to the fact that she'd married Meric after just meeting him, only a little more than a week ago. That would cause a whole bunch more questions from Wilmer, and he wasn't afraid to ask them.

Then Wilmer asked, "Wait, you weren't totally fluent until *after* you met Toledan? If your English was only basic, how'd you get to know him well enough to marry him?"

"He speaks Spanish. As fluently as he speaks English."

"Huh." He pursed his lips. "I didn't know that. He doesn't strike me as the type to learn someone else's language. More like the type to force his language on everyone else."

She folded her hands in her lap. "Wilmer, I need you to do me a favor."

"Anything. I want you to know I'm here for anything you need. You have a safety net."

"That right there is what I need—for you to stop speaking poorly of Meric. At least in front of me."

"I wasn't speaking poorly of—"

She tilted her head and gave him a pointed look.

He lifted his hands. "All right, you got me."

"All the stupid things you see on the news, none of it's true."

He pressed his lips together.

"I admit I haven't known him that long, so maybe you'll doubt that I know *none* of it's true. But I do know he's been kind to me. He's never said a harsh word. He's done . . . a lot for me. A lot more than I could've ever expected anyone to do."

"Sounds like there's a good story in there."

She smiled a little. "A story I'm not going to share. But will you trust me on this one thing?"

He smiled, and it made his blue eyes seem even brighter. "Of course. I'll be good, I promise."

"Thank you." She picked up her napkin and wrapped it around the last of her apple.

He picked up her notes, which had been underneath her napkin. "What's this?"

"What I'm doing today." She took it back from him.

"That's a list of jobs. Why're you looking for a job?"

She gave him part of the reason. "Because I take care of myself."

"Does Toledan know? I don't mean this as rude, I promise, but I don't think he's going to like that."

"Meric respects that I take care of myself." He'd seemed so proud of her last night, for how she'd escaped. She tried not to let herself think about how he'd left so abruptly, how he didn't spend time with her anymore.

"Are you sure those are the right kinds of jobs? I don't think he's—You know what, never mind. I'm your friend, and I support you in whatever you do."

She smiled a little. "Thank you, Wilmer."

"If you need a character reference, I'm your man." He picked up the pencil she had sitting on her notes and wrote his phone number in the margin.

They threw away their trash and headed out through the mall area, now starting to come to life with employees arriving.

"I'll see you later." She headed toward the main doors.

"Liliana."

She turned back.

"What did you mean? When you said what you're doing today is for him in a roundabout way?"

"It's a long story. Thank you for breakfast." She walked away.

Out on the sidewalk, she paused to look up a couple of addresses on her phone. One of them was a hotel just down the street. She started in that direction.

She filled out an application at the hotel. She was able to meet the housekeeping manager, who seemed happy she spoke decent English, though her accent was still heavy. She was thankful she'd spent so much time on that.

The next hotel was a couple of miles away. She considered figuring out the bus system but decided she couldn't handle being so close to so many people. She used the map on her phone and walked. She was still working on getting her strength back anyway and being pampered up in Meric's apartment wasn't helping with that.

She went to a couple more hotels and a restaurant before hunger got the better of her. While she stood on the sidewalk near a food truck finishing her chicken wrap, she started to wonder about the businesses Meric owned in this city and which ones they were. She'd decided to use Vela on all her applications, so at least no one would recognize her name. But what if she took a job at a business that Meric owned?

Well, it wasn't as if he'd ever meet the maid in one of his hotels or the waitress at one of his restaurants. And she figured she'd eventually take her work experience, once she had some, to another job in a different city. That way, he'd be completely free of her.

Appetite suddenly gone, she threw away the second half of

her wrap. She would've saved it for later, but she couldn't exactly carry it around in her pocket. She took out her list to decide where to go next.

She felt exhausted, but she kept pushing herself.

Shortly after three o'clock, she walked out of a large and very fancy restaurant. It was oddly situated in what looked like a borderline industrial area. There was an abandoned factory to one side—brick and broken windows. And on the other side was another brick building that'd been converted into condos. The street was narrow, made even worse by the cars parked along each side.

She typed the address of Meric's building into her phone and started in that direction. By the time she got back, it would probably be close to four o'clock. She considered cooking him dinner but then figured he probably wouldn't be home for dinner anyway.

She tried to push thoughts of him out of her head and focus. She was so tired from walking all day, trying to understand and speak English with so many different people, trying to make a good impression, presenting herself as a good employee—all while forcing her mind away from what it continually wanted to go back to.

At the next block, she turned left. She wasn't sure whether or not she liked how empty this street was. She didn't want to be around too many people, but being alone didn't feel safe either. She walked more quickly.

The next block was busier, and she slowed her pace.

She glanced down at the map on her phone to make sure she was on the right road.

A hand grabbed her arm and dragged her into an alley.

Chapter FIFTEEN

Meric stared at his computer screen. He'd read the same document twice and still wasn't comprehending it.

What in the world is wrong with me?

He hadn't been in the best mood all day, granted, but he'd been able to concentrate. Until now.

"Mr. Toledan?" Alfred was standing in his office door.

Meric looked up. "Yes?"

"Mr. Barnes is asking if you have any feedback."

"I need to go through it again." He turned back to his screen.

Alfred hesitated. "Are you feeling all right?"

"Fine, thank you."

Still Alfred paused, and Meric could see his expression peripherally, his confusion and maybe even concern.

"I just need more sleep," Meric said.

Alfred nodded. "Let me know if I can get you anything." He walked away, back to his desk in the outer office.

Meric tried reading the document again, but the words looked like little cinder blocks dotted along the page like some ineptly constructed wall.

■ ▦ ■

Liliana struggled. The man was strong and had her from behind, a hand over her mouth. She tried to bite his hand but couldn't quite get a grasp. She twisted and writhed, but he was so strong.

He dragged her deeper into the alley.

Fear and fury raged inside her, each fighting for dominance.

Then she pushed them both out of the way and grasped rational thought with both hands, like a racecar driver gripping the steering wheel. She'd thought so many times about when the cartel had come to take her, and she'd listed out in her mind what she should have done. *Focus on causing pain. Disorient them.*

She tried to stomp his foot, but he was pulling her along too fast. He was behind her, so she couldn't kick his groin or smash his face with her hand.

Think, Liliana.

Use the same targets but different tools.

She slammed her head back toward his face. She heard a crunching sound, and the man cursed. But he kept dragging her.

She slammed her head back again, and he staggered.

She gained her balance the best she could, reached back, and smashed her fist up toward his groin. He cursed again, breathless.

She stomped his foot and tried to pull away.

He tightened his arms but didn't get as good a hold. She had just enough room to twist and hit her elbow across his chin.

She lunged and managed to pull out of his grasp, but before she could get her balance and run, another man ran toward her down the alley. She prepared herself for another attacker, but he rammed into the man who'd dragged her here. Her attacker slammed into the brick wall. She heard his head smack with a horrible thud that sounded oddly soft against the brick.

The new man turned to her.

But he wasn't new. He was the same man who had followed her from the grocery store.

She stepped toward him, ready to attack.

He put his hands up, palms out. "I'm not here to hurt you."

"Who are you?"

"We need to get out of here. I don't know if there are others or how long he'll stay knocked out."

"Who are you?" she demanded.

"I work for Mr. Toledan."

"What?"

"His security."

She took a step away, but he followed.

"Mr. Toledan said to tell you the first thing he ever said to you was '*Silencio.*'" *Be quiet.* No one would ever guess that was the first thing Meric had ever said to her.

She stopped.

"Please come with me."

"What's going on?"

"I'm going to take you to him. To safety. That's all." Then he added, "Do you have the phone he gave you? Call him. Ask him who Barrett is."

"I'm going back out to the sidewalk first."

He nodded and walked with her.

Back out by the road, Liliana stopped and pressed the button to dial Meric.

He answered before the first ring stopped. "Hello?"

She reverted to Spanish, maybe because he'd answered in Spanish or maybe because it was comforting. "I met someone named Barrett."

He hesitated just half a second. "Please let me talk to him."

"Who is he?"

"Please let me talk to him so I can verify he is who he says."

She handed the phone to the man.

"Sir," Barrett said. "Yes, sir. Situation three." He paused to listen and then lowered his voice. "Three five one lima." He glanced around at their surroundings. "Ten minutes . . . Yes, sir." He handed the phone back to Liliana.

"What's going on?" Liliana demanded.

"Are you all right?" Meric asked over the phone.

"Meric," she demanded.

"Barrett will bring you to me. Will you please go with him?"

"Okay." She looked at Barrett and nodded. He glanced down the alley, surely to make sure her attacker wasn't following them, and then he led her down the sidewalk, quickly.

Liliana looked around to memorize where they were going. "Shouldn't we call the police?"

"I would like to get you out of there."

"Where is he taking me?"

"To my office. Everything's all right."

She held on to her anger, or else she knew her hands would start shaking and her mind wouldn't stay as sharp. "You need to tell me what's going on."

"First, I—"

"No, nothing first. Answer me."

His voice was softer. "I need to see you're safe. Please."

Her anger started to ease, but her hands didn't start shaking, miraculously. She followed Barrett in silence but also kept the phone to her ear.

A few minutes later, they walked into a large four-story office building. It was all glass and white and sleek. Inside, the receptionist nodded, and Barrett continued past her to an elevator. Just as he hit the up button, the doors opened, and there was Alfred on the elevator.

On the phone, Meric said, "Alfred will bring you up to my office."

Alfred smiled and motioned for them to get on the elevator with him.

Liliana wondered how Meric knew they'd just come upon Alfred, but then she noticed a camera in the corner. Was he watching? She was silent, but she didn't hang up.

The elevator doors opened into a small and empty lobby with black carpet, white walls, and a swirly piece of modern art on the wall. Alfred led the way to the one door. He waved a plastic card in front of some kind of scanner on the wall, there was a buzz, and he opened the door.

The space beyond was a sea of cubicles with some offices lining the far walls. The cubicles were all white, as well as the walls, but everything was decorated—one cubicle with colorful charts and graphs, the next with children's artwork, the next with family photos. On the walls were more art pieces—colorful swirls and boxes and circles on canvas.

At the far corner, they came to double doors that led to an outer office. The space looked like Alfred—stylish and just so. Colored file folders neatly arranged, a notepad, nameplate, and shiny pen on the desk, perfectly straight.

"Go on in." Alfred motioned toward the door opposite and then took his seat at his desk.

Inside the next room, Meric stopped pacing and focused on Liliana. "Are you all right?"

"What's going on?" she asked, though her voice wasn't as harsh.

He walked over to her, put his gentle hands on her cheeks, and looked into her eyes deeply, like he could see down the rabbit hole that was her mind.

Several seconds passed.

She felt the calm of his hands sinking into her skin, like a raindrop slowly soaking into cotton.

"Are you all right?" he asked.

"Yes."

"Did he hurt you?"

"I fought him off, and then Barrett knocked him out."

A soft smile slowly curved his lips. "He wasn't prepared for the likes of my Liliana."

Her smile matched his.

"You're sure you're all right?" he asked. "Do you want to go to the doctor?"

"I'm all right." Then she added, "I don't want to go anywhere else unfamiliar today."

"I understand."

Then he glanced over at Barrett, let go of Liliana, and took a step back. Liliana realized they'd continued speaking Spanish, and from the blank look on Barrett's face, she guessed he didn't understand. Or maybe he was trying very hard not to react to their conversation, which had felt oddly intimate.

Meric's tone resumed its usual lack of emotion as he switched back to English and asked Barrett, "Do you have a description of the man?"

"He had his hood up. I didn't stop and take a good look. You'd given direction to put her safety above all other considerations. But I believe he was just a local vagrant. I don't know if he targeted her randomly, or if we have a larger problem."

"What do you mean 'larger problem'?" Liliana asked.

Barrett looked at her and then back to Meric, obviously deferring to Meric to answer or not.

"Are you having me followed?" Liliana asked Meric.

Meric's jaw clenched. "You were never supposed to notice him. I'm sorry."

"Why would you do that?"

"I just wanted to make sure you're safe, all while giving you freedom."

"I'm not exactly free if I have a man following me, am I?"

"You're completely free. He's there only to make sure no one bothers you. No other reason."

"But you're tracking where I'm going."

"No. He has clear instructions not to report to me other than if someone tried to hurt you. You can go anywhere you want, whenever you want. He's nothing but a ghost."

Barrett nodded.

Meric switched to Spanish. "I promise, Liliana."

"Why would you do that?"

"Carl Walsh made bail. I didn't want to take even the slightest risk that he would find you. But I didn't want you to be any more scared than you already were, and I wanted you to feel free. I didn't think having an armed guard would give you either of those things." He ran his hands over his face and then dropped them to his sides. "Maybe I didn't do it right. I don't know."

"It wasn't right for you to have me followed."

Meric paused. "I didn't think of it that way. He was only there when you were in public, never anyplace private." He sighed. "But I see your side. I should have cleared it with you first."

"I guess we can deal with that later." And they would. She switched back to English. "What do you mean 'larger problem'? Do you think Carl is after me?"

"We found him. He's been hiding out—hasn't left the house he's staying in."

"Could he have sent someone else?"

"Carl is the middleman. He's the one who would usually do the legwork, not send someone else to do it. I suppose it's possible he could send someone, but based on what we've learned about him, not terribly likely."

"You've researched him?"

"Of course."

"Why didn't you tell me?"

"I would've told you had we found anything concerning. But like I said, he's done nothing but hide out. He didn't appear to be a threat."

"So, you don't think he was the one to have Josh killed."

"We can't be sure."

"Could that have been something unrelated to anything that's happened? Maybe he angered someone in jail?"

"It's possible."

"But you don't think likely."

"I don't have any evidence one way or the other." Then he admitted, "It doesn't sit right."

She hesitated. "So, it might not really be over. I'm not really free."

Chapter SIXTEEN

Meric held eye contact. "You are free." He shifted closer, and his voice lowered. "If anyone wants to get to you, they have to go through me." His voice lowered even more, threatening. "And that is not easily done."

Fear wrapped around her like vines. Not fear for herself. Fear for Meric. Could she be putting him in danger? But who would put so much effort into getting to her? She was no one, just another woman being traded and sold like trading cards.

Finally, Barrett spoke. "Today might've been just some vagrant trying to take your wallet. Woman apparently alone—it's certainly not unheard of."

Meric glanced at Barrett, and when he spoke to Liliana, his voice was back to normal. "Statistically, that's more likely."

She paused to consider. "I'd like to go back to the apartment." She needed time to think things through.

"Would you like me to take you?" Barrett asked.

Before she could tell him *No, thank you*, Meric said, "I'm headed home anyway."

"Shall I take my usual post?" Barrett asked.

Meric glanced at Liliana but then said, "Yes."

"Yes, sir."

Liliana turned and walked out, and Meric followed.

While passing Alfred, Meric said, "I'm leaving for today. Text me if anything needs attention."

"Will do." Then he added to Liliana, "It was nice to see you again, Mrs. Toledan."

"Bye, Alfred."

Meric and Liliana walked quietly to the elevator and then out to his car parked along the road. He held the door for her. They rode in silence.

He pulled into his space in the garage attached to his building and shifted into park. "Where did you learn to fight?"

She'd been lost in thought and looked over at him. "I read about it."

"You read about it?"

"I looked up the most effective places to hit a man. I found pictures of how best to strike."

"And you were able to remember that and reproduce the strikes under that kind of stress?"

She didn't answer, not sure what he was getting at.

He raised an eyebrow, but then stood from the car. She got out as well.

They walked into the building, and as soon as the elevator doors closed, she asked, "Why didn't you tell me you found Carl? Why didn't you tell me about Barrett?"

He hesitated before answering, his gaze on the shiny stainless-steel doors. Then he faced her. "I should've told you."

She hadn't expected him to acquiesce so easily, so sincerely.

"I wasn't trying to keep you in the dark," he said. "I would've told you had we found anything to worry about. I just wanted to make sure there was nothing out there that could hurt you. Any more than you've already been hurt."

"Would you tell me the details? Anything you've found?"

"Are you sure?"

"I appreciate what you're trying to do, but I handle things better when I have information."

"I suppose I should've seen that." He took a breath. "Carl is staying with an old girlfriend. When his cousin bailed him out, he stayed with him the first night, but then there was some kind of argument. He left and has been at his ex-girlfriend's trailer since. He hasn't left once."

"Do you have someone posted there full-time?"

"Yes."

"That seems excessive." How much could that be costing him? He didn't respond, didn't even give an expression.

"What about Josh? What do you know about him?"

"It was more difficult to get eyes inside the jail. From what we know, he mostly kept to himself, but the information is spotty at best. We do know he didn't have much family to speak of, at least none who haven't disowned him long ago, probably due to his drug use."

"Cocaine." She struggled to block the images from her head, what he'd been like after he got high.

He nodded. "There are too many unknowns to determine who killed him and why. Maybe he made enemies with the wrong person in jail. Maybe someone found out he was involved in trafficking, very possibly including children. Child abusers don't usually fare well in jail. Maybe something from his past came back to haunt him—that list is long."

"What about Barrett?"

"Honestly, I didn't think you'd venture farther than the mall downstairs. I have four men rotating shifts. They keep an eye on things. When you left the building that first time, Barrett hovered in the background. I hadn't told him to follow you, but he decided he wanted to make sure you were all right. I'd instructed him not to tell me where you went or what you did, but he did tell me you seemed nervous to be out alone."

"Did he tell you I saw him?"

"I told him to stay farther back—I'm afraid I wasn't very polite. Obviously, you're more aware than he realized. He's ex-NYPD, usually better at remaining undetected." The corner of his mouth twitched. "Freaked him out when you stopped and stared him in the eye."

"Why didn't you replace him if I'd seen him?"

"If he remained invisible, it wouldn't have mattered." Then he added, "And there are very few people I trust with the job."

The elevator stopped, and the doors opened. They stepped off.

"Is he your own personal security or something?" She set her things on the kitchen island.

"He runs my company's security."

"He runs the whole company's security? Why was he the one you placed downstairs? Isn't that something someone under him would handle?"

"He's the one I trust the most."

She turned and walked over to the refrigerator to get something to drink.

"Wait," he said. "There's something . . ."

She stopped and glanced back.

He came up behind her and lightly touched the back of her hair.

"What's wrong?"

"Did you get knocked down?"

"No. Why?"

"There's blood in your hair. Are you sure you're not hurt?"

"It must be blood from his nose or mouth. He had me from behind. I headbutted him."

"You must've hit him hard."

"As hard as I could." Then she added, "You don't think I seriously hurt him, do you?"

"Would you care?"

"Yes."

"Why?"

She wasn't exactly sure. She moved to open the refrigerator.

"Hold on. I'll clean this out of your hair."

"I'll take a shower in a minute."

"It might be a good idea to keep a sample. Just in case."

She stood still for him, and he dampened a paper towel. He stood behind her. He lightly touched her hair with his left fingertips and ran the paper towel over her head with his right hand. His touch sent tingles over her scalp and down her back.

They were quiet while he slowly and gently cleaned her hair.

He stepped back. "I think that's it. But you should probably shower as well."

She nodded, trying to hang on to the feeling of his fingertips on her hair.

She turned to face him.

He walked away, opened a cabinet, and took out a plastic bag. He put the paper towel inside.

"You knew where the bags were on the first try," she teased. "I'm impressed."

"Just don't ask me where pans or cooking utensils are."

She smiled and headed toward her room.

"Liliana."

She looked back.

"Are you angry? About any of it."

She hesitated. "Please don't hold things back from me."

He nodded.

She went into her room.

* * *

He started toward his office, with the bagged paper towel, but then he noticed the paper she'd left on the counter, a list of some kind. A list of jobs. That was what she'd been out doing today. Trying to find a job.

He walked into his office and closed the door.

She was trying to get away from him. But could he really begrudge her independence, freedom?

He took his cell phone out of his pocket and dialed Alfred.

"Hello, sir," Alfred answered.

"Can you please make a purchase and bring it here?"

Once he was done speaking with Alfred, he sat at his computer and went through some emails. A little while later, Alfred texted that he was on his way up. Meric met him at the elevator, thanked him, and told him to head home, not back to the office. Then Meric walked over to Liliana's door and knocked.

There was a pause before she opened the door, wet hair falling over her shoulders and against her flushed skin.

He focused on just her eyes, nothing else. "I'm sorry to bother you," he said. "I just wanted to give you this." He handed her the tablet, the best one on the market. Then he walked away, back to his office, and closed the door. She liked to feel informed—a good tablet with internet would be helpful with that.

Though there were certain things he had to keep from her.

He unlocked his top desk drawer and took out the burner cell he had in there and dialed.

When his contact on the other end of the line picked up, he said, "It's me."

"Mr. Toledan," the man on the other end of the line said. "What a pleasure it is to hear your voice."

"I don't have time for your inane pleasantries. There's a vagrant in an alley." He gave the general location of the last checked-off location on Liliana's list. Based on the time it'd taken her and Barrett to get to his office, she hadn't been too far from there when she was attacked. "This guy attacked a woman today. She beat him off and left him in the alley unconscious. Find him and make him tell you who hired him, using whatever methods are needed, and report back within a few hours."

Chapter

SEVENTEEN

Meric walked with his hands casually in the pockets of his slacks. He glanced around the room—the paintings with gilded frames, layers of molding, leather wingback chairs, dark mahogany paneling. At first glance, it was a beautiful room, but as he kept looking, it started to feel ridiculous, like some actress strutting down the red carpet in a silly designer dress.

He stopped in the middle of the room, hands still in his pockets, and faced the door. He'd been shown into this room ten minutes ago. He wouldn't be patient much longer.

He hadn't slept well the past two nights. He'd been unsuccessful in using his lowly contacts to find the man who'd attacked Liliana. Bando hadn't been happy with him for using those contacts for this, but Meric didn't care. His security had been watching his building closely, and no one who shouldn't be there had been seen. He'd just about convinced himself the attack on her had been simply a random act of violence.

But he still wasn't sleeping well.

Finally, the door opened. A man in his thirties with glasses and a bow tie walked in. "I'm so sorry for the wait. It simply could not be helped."

"I'm here to speak to the man in charge. Not a lackey."

The man's smile did not reach his blue eyes. "Unfortunately, he's quite busy."

"He agreed to this meeting."

The man kept his lips curved, like a crayon smiley-face drawing. "He unfortunately has to un-agree to it." He shifted backward toward the door.

"Then I'll be leaving."

"He wouldn't hear of you leaving without tea."

Tea? "No, thank you."

"Please let him make this up to you with a bit of civility. Tea is a lost art."

Meric started for the door.

The man turned, ran out of the room, and slammed the door. Before Meric could get there, he heard the lock click.

He gripped the item in his pocket more tightly but didn't remove it. There might be cameras watching him.

He glanced around the room. He'd already noted the high fixed windows and the lack of alternate exits, at least any obvious ones. Now, he looked more carefully, no longer concerned about making an impression during this meeting. He'd make an impression, all right.

One wall was floor-to-ceiling bookshelves. He saw nothing useful or out of place. The far wall held a massive fireplace with a fire burning. Also not helpful. Unless he decided to burn the house down. The two windows in the room were across from the bookshelves. They were unusually high on the wall—he'd thought it an odd architectural choice. Now he understood the reasoning. He paused to analyze what little he knew about the house. It sat on a high, steep hill, and this room was facing the front, which meant the drop from the windows would be too far to jump. He wouldn't waste time trying to access them.

Some thought niggled in the back of his mind—why this had happened. But he couldn't focus on that quite yet.

Meric was well known and powerful in his own right—it wouldn't make sense to trap him and then let him go later. No, the plan was surely to dispose of him one way or another. He had no phone on him; that'd been part of the stipulations for this meeting. He had no way to communicate. He was on his own.

He walked the perimeter of the room. He found no cameras, though it was impossible to be completely sure there were none.

As he was passing the fireplace, he paused at a new sound, an air handler turning on. He looked more closely at the shelving to the right of the fireplace—shelves with expensive knickknacks on top and cabinets on the bottom. The cabinet doors weren't solid, but an intricate wood design that was about 50 percent negative space. He knelt on the floor, opened the cabinet doors, and found what he was hoping to find. An air intake vent.

Quickly, he took the money clip out of his pocket, left the thick bundle of cash in his pocket, and flipped open the hidden knife from the clip. He used it to loosen the flat-head screws. An annoyingly slow process.

He kept listening intently for any sounds, footsteps, the sound of the doorknob. He hoped the plan was to let him sit in here imprisoned for a while, a sign of dominance, hoping he'd break down, show fear, maybe even beg. That sounded about right for the owner of this house.

Finally, the last screw came off in his hand. He carefully pulled the vent off. Luckily, there was enough room to lay it flat inside the bottom of the cabinet. He climbed inside the cabinet then through the hole in the wall. He reached back, barely able to move, and managed to get the doors closed.

Then he squeezed underneath the elevated air handler. He stood, just able to fit between the air handler and the door. He pressed his ear to the door and waited for the air handler to stop running so he could hear properly. It took forever but finally stopped.

He listened.

Nothing at first, but he waited a few extra seconds.

There was a door closing, somewhere far off.

He cracked the door and looked at where he was—a small

hallway with multiple doors and another hall branching off to his right. He eased out and closed the door behind him.

Footsteps, approaching.

He jetted to the room directly across the hall, went inside, and closed the door. It was a large laundry room. No windows. He listened carefully. A door opened and closed, and the sound of the footsteps faded.

Once the footsteps were gone, he slipped out and looked around. The door to his right would be the front of the house. Likely a small room, maybe a bathroom. He'd memorized the layout of the house as he'd approached, and he knew there were no more windows—they were all in the library. He turned, edged closer to the hallway that branched off, and looked around the corner. The hall wasn't dressed up like the main hall at the entrance had been, no molding or artwork. There was a wide doorway about halfway down, perhaps the kitchen. The hallway was long—risky. He moved toward the last door in this hall instead.

He heard nothing, so he opened the door. It led to another long hall, even narrower. A servants' hall, perhaps. Maybe there was an exit. He went in and closed the door. There were several doors. He tried each one, but they were all locked. Dead end.

He turned around. The only option was the long hall leading toward the kitchen.

He jogged silently and paused at the wide doorway to peer around the corner. He'd been right, a kitchen. No one was there. He rushed in and started opening drawers. A weapon—he needed a better weapon.

Finally, he found a drawer of knives. He grabbed one with a long but thin blade. Liliana would laugh at him for having no idea what kind of knife it was. That helped, thinking of her—it sharpened his mind. He imagined her face, how her eyes laughed when she teased him.

He flipped the knife into a reverse grip and clenched his jaw.

There was a butler's pantry in the back-right corner. He headed through and paused at the swinging door that surely led to a dining room.

Silence.

He slid silently through the door. Two sets of French doors opened onto a veranda, which overlooked a vast lawn. No one was outside that he could see, but he needed a better look. To the right was a wide doorway that appeared to lead to the huge main hall.

Could he be lucky enough to make it through the main hall to the front door?

An alarm blared, reverberating around the house.

Running footsteps, male voices.

They'd realized he was no longer imprisoned in the library.

He stepped back into the butler's pantry and just caught sight of men running inside through another set of French doors in the main hall. He waited, listening.

Nothing.

They must not have seen him.

He cracked the door and peeked out. He spotted a man locking all the outer doors with a key. He was locked inside. He could break the glass, but then they'd hear, and he had no idea what was behind the house. More security? A wall around the property? Dogs? He could see that the lawn was vast, no trees, no cover— too open, not a good idea.

The alarm continued to blare. It threatened to jumble his thoughts. He pulled up Liliana's image, held her there in his mind. She smiled at him, that smile that was barely there, but he saw it.

He slipped out into the dining room, only partially filled with a massive table seating ten. He stood to the side of the doorway and tried to get a look at the main hall. No one was in sight. He ran across the hall to a set of double doors. Unlocked.

He went inside and closed the doors. It was a large office, as big as the library. He locked the bolt and ran over to the window across the room. Before he even tried to open it, he saw it was no use. The land sloped away from this side of the house as well. It was too far up. And there was nothing in the room that could make a rope.

A desk, a couch, an armchair, one smaller chair on the other side of the desk, paneled walls, a few pieces of ugly artwork. Nothing useful.

Then he looked again at the paneling closest to the desk. Knowing what he did about the owner of this estate, he would expect at least one hidden room, and it would make sense for it to be off the private office. The shadow of the paneling was a little different on this section of trim, as if it sat a fraction of an inch farther from the wall. He walked over and looked closer. He pushed at it. There was a slight shift, barely discernible, as if the panel wasn't fully adhered to the wall. He ran his fingers around the edge of the trim.

At the top right, there it was. A latch. He pressed it, and there was a sound of a heavy bolt sliding. He pushed at the trim, and this time the whole panel slowly shifted to the side.

There was a room beyond. It was larger than he'd expect a secret room to be. He stepped in. Maybe there was a secret exit as well. There were no windows, and no light on. He found the switch on the wall.

He stopped and stared. Though he'd anticipated the purpose for the room, it still made him feel sick.

In his mind, he saw what happened in this room. This prison. To so many. Helpless innocents. Over and over. So many. They would scream. They would beg. But the owner of this room liked that part; it excited him.

So many innocents.

He heard them crying. Praying for help. Praying for it just to end.

Hoping for death.

Meric realized he was gripping the knife so tightly his hand was shaking.

He stepped out of the room and slid the panel back into place. He couldn't stand to see it. Rage threatened to take him over, like a ghost inhabiting his body, the ghost of all those innocents trying to find justice through him. He'd give them justice—he promised that. But right now it was time for strategic thought.

Liliana. Again he pulled her image close. He saw her standing at the windows in their apartment, looking out across the city. How the sun touched her skin, made it glow.

Their apartment, he'd thought. She probably didn't see it that way. She saw it as his. But it was hers. He was thankful he'd taken the time to change his will. Everything went to her. Everything he had—all the businesses, the properties all over the country, all his money, investments, everything.

He stood straighter and focused. He would have to try going back out into the main hall.

The door handle turned, someone on the outside. But he'd locked the door when he'd come in.

The alarm was still blaring.

Urgent voices on the other side of the door. "In here!"

A fist pounded on the door. "There's no way out of that room!"

But there was a way out. Through that door. Through the men on the other side. He was going to have to fight his way out.

Chapter EIGHTEEN

Liliana sat at her desk reading and rereading the letter, making sure the English was right, making sure it properly captured what she wanted to say.

> *You don't know me, and I'm sorry to intrude. I'm writing because I'm concerned about your safety. I recently escaped human trafficking with the help of a wonderful person. I was being transported to a buyer, and one of the men transporting me was the man you're currently living with—Carl Walsh. I pray he is not hurting you. He was not so kind to me. I will not tell you the details, mostly because I do not want to relive them myself, but I hope you believe me when I say he cannot be trusted and is not worthy of your kindness. I used to think everyone was worthy of kindness, but that was before I saw what real evil is and how it can eat away at your soul. There comes a time when you must protect yourself so you don't lose your goodness.*
>
> > *Sincerely,*
> > *a concerned friend*

She left it on Meric's desk with a request to please mail it. She didn't care to know the address—she just wanted that poor woman to be warned. It was possible, she supposed, that the woman was no better a person than Carl, but she didn't want to take that risk. Not when she had a shot at helping her.

But she had no idea when he was coming home. The last couple of days, he'd continued to avoid being at home. Sometimes, she heard him come in late at night or leave early in the morning, but she hadn't even seen him, not since the incident in the alley.

She went out every day to look for a job but hadn't been successful yet.

For some reason, she'd hoped Meric would come home tonight, maybe have a late dinner with her. She wasn't sure why. It wasn't as if he seemed to care what day of the week it was. He'd surely work all day tomorrow, whether it was Saturday or not. Though her gut told her he wasn't working all these hours. She had no idea what he was doing. Perhaps nothing other than avoiding her.

She forced her thoughts onto something else by picking up the tablet. He'd had some books downloaded onto it. She wasn't sure why she seemed to prefer reading the tablet rather than one of the books on the shelf. It was not because the tablet was a gift from Meric.

***

Four men. They were each holding a handgun and had a knife at their hip, and by the way they held themselves, Meric could tell they were very well trained.

Meric stayed back, closer to the desk, and watched them enter the room. It'd taken them a few minutes to get inside. He guessed the only key for this room was in possession of the owner, and there had probably been a discussion among these men on whether they should break down the door or simply leave him in there, trapped. He assumed they'd either called the owner and gotten permission or had decided he could not be left alone in this particular room, the owner's private office.

Meric had already removed his jacket. He'd looked around but had not found any weapons other than the knife he'd taken from the kitchen and the small knife hidden in his money clip.

Money clip . . .

He took the large wad of cash out of his pocket and held it up.

The men said nothing, but two of them looked at the cash.

"It's yours if you walk out of here." Meric watched each of them closely.

The one with dark hair and sun-worn skin, the oldest out of the group, didn't even glance at the cash, nor did the youngest, who was standing next to him. It was the other two who looked at the cash.

"Is the job worth it?" Meric asked.

"Drop the knife," the oldest one demanded.

Meric focused on the two standing to the left. He took a couple of steps and tossed the cash on the coffee table in front of the sofa. "Think of what you can do with that. Do you have kids?"

One of the men eyed the cash and then the older man.

"You can get another job easily," Meric said. "Think of what you can do for your kids." He was guessing they were just hired security and had no idea what went on here.

"Drop the knife," the oldest man said again. "The police have been called."

"No, they haven't," Meric said. Then he looked at the two wavering men. "Why do you think that is? Why do you think the standing order is to never call the police? Doesn't that seem a little off?"

"The owner of this property has his reasons," the older man said, surely more for his subordinates' benefit than Meric's. "We work for him."

"Thank you for confirming the police are not coming," Meric said.

The man scowled. "Drop the knife, and we won't hurt you."

"But you'll hold me prisoner." He looked to the other two men. "Does that set right with you? You know who I am, I assume. What does he have to gain by holding me prisoner? And why was this house built with that capability?" Meric watched the men closely. He hoped they would take the bribe, but he was also reading them, trying to confirm they didn't know anything about what went on here.

Finally, one of the men stepped forward and grabbed the cash off the table.

"Stop. Put that down," the leader commanded.

The man holstered his gun and headed toward the door.

The leader stepped back, looking over at the man. "I said stop. Now."

Meric rushed the leader, pushed his gun hand up, and raked the weapon out of his grasp. He released the clip and threw the gun to the other side of the room. He hoped he didn't regret that, but he didn't want to chance shooting and killing someone who knew nothing and was just trying to do his job.

The youngest man fired.

Meric leaned to the side, but the bullet grazed him, just barely. Pain burned across the skin of his shoulder.

The man with the cash ran out of the room, and the other one who'd wavered only stood there, watching, looking uncertain.

Meric attacked the younger man, while keeping him between himself and the leader. He disarmed him the same way he had the leader and again threw the gun. The man lunged with a fist toward Meric's jaw, but Meric blocked with both arms, more of a strike than a block, and threw the young man off-balance. Meric slammed the butt of the kitchen knife across his jaw, and he spun to the side. Before he fell, Meric grabbed him and tossed him toward the leader. They both fell.

Meric snatched the gun out of the wavering man's hand, tossed it, and roared at him, "Get out!"

He ran.

The other two were now on their feet, knives in hand. They held their fighting stances confidently.

Meric gripped his knife and took the small money clip blade out of his pocket. He remembered the first knife fight he'd been in. A very long time ago. They'd attacked Meric in his sleep, tried to steal his jacket and shoes. He'd had no training, no idea what he was doing. But he'd survived.

That made him think of Liliana.

He clenched his jaw and slowly circled, keeping just one in front of him.

The younger one lunged, aiming the blade at Meric's gut. He blocked, but of course, the knife still cut his arm. Meric slashed at the young man to try to get him to back up. Maybe he could get him to run away too. He didn't want to hurt either of them seriously, but he knew that probably wasn't realistic. Not if he wanted to survive.

The leader burst toward him. They traded several attacks. Block, counter, parry. Blood stained their sleeves. The younger man moved around them and attacked from the side. Meric slammed the small blade in his left hand down on his chest, hoping the blade was short enough not to hit anything major.

The young man stumbled back.

Meric blocked another attack from the leader, and then managed to smash the butt of the knife across his jaw. He spun, landed on the ground, and didn't get back up.

The young man attacked again. He got past Meric's block. Pain seared from the blade sinking into his flesh.

Meric lunged his shoulder into the man's stomach and took him down. He struggled to get up from underneath Meric and managed to stab at his back, but he didn't have much leverage.

Meric grabbed his shirt and slammed him against the floor, trying to get him to stop flailing. He slammed him over and over. Finally he stopped struggling.

Something flashed by the door. Meric looked up just in time

to see the man in the bow tie, the one who'd locked him in the library, running down the main hall toward the front door.

Meric forced himself to his feet and ran after him. He stumbled in the hall. By the time he got to the door, the man in the bow tie was in a car and tearing down the long drive. Meric turned back to the house only to catch a glimpse of a servant running down the main hall and disappearing down the hall toward the kitchen. There were surely several servants for an estate like this, but Meric had dealt only with the man in the bow tie and the security. None of the servants had seen him. He needed to keep it that way if he could.

He ran down the steps toward his car. The man in the bow tie had taken his key fob, but Meric had thankfully thought to bring his spare in a hidden pocket, and while he drove, he took the spare burner cell phone out of the console. He dialed.

"Hello?"

"It's me."

"What's going on? You were supposed to—"

"I need someone to meet me. I'm losing a lot of blood." His head was light, and his thoughts were starting to muddle.

Liliana, think of Liliana.

"What happened?"

"Just have someone meet me."

"Where are you?"

"I . . . I'm headed east away from the estate."

"Stay off the main roads." He took the phone from his ear and barked orders to someone in the room. Meric didn't understand most of it.

Liliana . . .

"Meric? Meric, stay with me."

He glanced over, and she was sitting in the passenger seat. She spoke, but her voice didn't sound right. "Stay with me. Meric?"

"I'm here," Meric said. He glanced at the road and then back over to her. She rested her hand on his leg. He reached for her hand but couldn't feel her. "Liliana?"

"Meric, what're you talking about? Liliana is at home."

Liliana spoke, but her voice was wispy. "Watch the road. Be careful."

Meric turned back to the road, surprised he was still driving. There was a truck coming at him. He swerved to miss it. Was the truck in the wrong lane or him?

She touched his arm. He focused on the road. He couldn't get in an accident and let her be hurt.

"All right, Meric. Are you still on the same road as the estate? I have a man parked behind the diner at the corner of Oak."

Meric saw the diner up ahead.

"Be careful," Liliana said again.

He nodded, still watching the road.

At the diner, he turned, jumped the curb, but managed to stop behind the car waiting for him. He opened the door. His vision turned spotty.

"I'm here," Liliana said.

He stumbled from the car and started to go around and get her door. But then there were arms around his shoulders. And then nothing.

Chapter

NINETEEN

Liliana lay in bed wide awake. She'd been lying there for hours, unable to sleep for some reason. The problem wasn't memories this time. Something felt . . . wrong. At midnight, she'd checked with the doorman to make sure everything was okay downstairs. He'd politely told her everything was fine but had seemed confused. Or maybe he'd thought she was crazy.

Finally, she got out of bed, went over to the windows, and looked out over the darkened city.

Her thoughts turned toward God, asking him to make sure everything worked out all right. What that "everything" was she had no idea.

The elevator dinged. *That has to be Meric coming home.* She walked out of her bedroom as he was walking off the elevator. The shadows were too thick to be able to see details, but she recognized the way he moved.

He glanced at her and hesitated, just for a second. Then he turned and headed toward his room.

Relieved to see him home, she shifted to step back into her room. Then she noticed something was off about the way he walked.

Meric closed his door with a quiet click.

She walked past the living and dining rooms to the entryway

and paused. His scent lingered in the air, but it wasn't right. Instead of his usual slight musky scent, almost unnoticeable, it was sweat mixed with . . . blood.

She went quickly to his door and knocked.

Nothing.

She tried the knob. Unlocked. She cracked the door. "Meric?"

Still no answer.

She opened the door wider. He wasn't in his bedroom. Then she heard water running in a sink. She walked in and crossed to the door on the left, following the sound. The door was open.

She stopped at the sight of Meric standing in front of the sink. His white dress shirt was tossed on the floor, covered in blood. His arms and back were covered in cuts.

"Meric! What happened?"

He stepped back, away from her.

She moved toward him, and he took another step back.

"What happened?" she asked again.

His expression was hard, and he kept his gaze over her shoulder, not actually on her.

There was a bandage on his side, and on his shoulder was a nasty gash. Blood slowly oozed from it and dried down his arm.

"Meric."

"Please go."

She paused at his cold tone. Then she said, "No."

He finally met her gaze.

She grabbed a washcloth from the counter and ran it under the hot water. Then she turned to Meric.

"I've already been to a doctor."

"Someone bandaged your side, but nothing else has been addressed. Nothing's even been cleaned."

"What do you think I'm doing?"

"There's no way you can reach everything. Now sit down." She didn't let herself keep asking what'd happened. Right now, she needed to focus on getting him cleaned up, making sure nothing got infected, reducing the discomfort. He had to be in horrible pain.

He stared at her with his cold gaze.

She moved closer, looking up at him. Then she rested her hand on his cheek. "Please."

He lifted his head away from her hand. But then he sat on the edge of the tub.

"Tell me if I hurt you."

He looked up at her, and she thought he was going to say something. But then he looked away, past her to the opposite wall.

As gently as she could, she cleaned the wound on his shoulder with soap and water, all while trying to figure out what could have possibly happened. She didn't want to push him for information for fear he would make her leave. All the other wounds looked cleaner, probably from blades, but this one was more of a gash, maybe a burn. And then she realized what it was, what made the most sense. A gunshot wound. The bullet had grazed his shoulder.

Her hands shook, but she didn't let him see.

What was Meric involved in? How in the world could he possibly be in a position to be shot at, let alone sustain all the knife wounds? And why wasn't he in the hospital? Why wasn't he talking to the police? Maybe he'd already been? But the police would've made sure his wounds were properly treated, wouldn't they?

What was going on?

After she got the wound on his shoulder as clean as she could, she started on his back. He angled himself on the edge of the tub so she could reach. She'd chosen his back next, not his arms, because these cuts had more dried blood around them and because she didn't want him to see her face and guess at how upset she was.

"Do you have any kind of antiseptic?" she asked. "Or bandages?"

"There might be some Neosporin in the drawer." His tone sounded so distant.

She opened the drawer. Behind his razor and can of shave cream, she found a tube of Neosporin and some medical tape. But no bandages. She looked around the room.

"What are you looking for?"

"Bandages."

"I'll be fine."

"You'll get blood all over everything. Do you really want Teresa wondering why your bed sheets are covered in blood?"

He stood, walked into his bedroom, opened a dresser drawer, and removed a white undershirt. Then he took a small pair of scissors from a different bathroom drawer and handed them both to Liliana. He resumed his seat. His movement was stiff. Though he would probably never admit to it, she could see how much pain he was in.

She started cutting up the shirt.

She carefully applied Neosporin to the now-clean cuts and used the medical tape and cut-up shirt to cover the wounds.

"I think some of these need stitches," she said.

"It'll be fine."

She didn't push any more, thankful he was allowing even this much.

Once she'd done as much as she could with his back, she started on his left arm. Most of the cuts were on his forearm. She guessed they were defensive wounds. He'd obviously been in a knife fight.

Meric continued to stare past her. He never flinched or made a sound, but she noticed his muscles seemed especially tight, his posture rigid.

When she started on his right arm, she asked, "What happened to your side?" If that one was bandaged, it must have been a lot worse than any of the other wounds.

"It's fine."

She continued treating the cuts.

"Does it feel any better?" she asked. "Do you have any aspirin?"

"I'm fine."

Finally, the words that'd been crawling up her throat burst out. "Have I done something wrong?"

He looked up at her, brows drawn.

"You don't talk to me anymore," she said. "You're never home. You don't even look at me."

He hesitated, and his voice was finally thawed. "I'm sorry. It's nothing to do with you."

"Then what is it to do with? What's wrong, Meric?"

"Nothing's wrong."

"You were in a knife fight, and someone shot at you."

He said nothing, didn't deny it.

"I know I'm not really your wife. But you are important to me. I care about you."

He nodded, and his gaze shifted away from her. "You're not really my wife."

"Why won't you talk to me? What have I done to make you pull away from me so much?"

He looked up at her. "You haven't done anything."

"Something happened. Something's changed."

"Nothing changed."

She shifted closer and rested her hand on his cheek. "Please, Meric. I'm scared for you."

He pulled away. "There's no reason for you to worry about me."

"How can you say that? You were in a knife fight."

"Like you said, you're not really my wife."

Her voice was soft. "But you are my friend. You saved my life." She rested her hand on his cheek again. "You're important to me."

He didn't pull away but also didn't look at her. Finally, he said, "I can't."

"Why?"

"I'm sorry I put you in this position. I shouldn't have married you."

She felt like he'd stabbed her in the chest.

But she pushed that overwhelming pain away, shoved it all to the side, so she could focus on him, on whatever was wrong. The pain she saw in his eyes looked like how she felt. She had no idea what he was involved in, but whatever it was, it was killing him. Not just the physical pain, but something else, something worse.

She moved even closer, and carefully she pulled his head to her chest. He tensed at first. She thought he would pull away, shove her back. But then he wrapped his arms around her, hands splayed across her back, and let her cradle his head against her. He closed his eyes and took deep, slow breaths.

She held him tightly, a little surprised she didn't mind having him against her chest, even in her nightgown, or having his arms around her. Maybe because she knew he wouldn't take advantage.

Because she trusted him. He was involved in something dangerous, something he wouldn't talk about. But he'd earned her trust anyway—it was in all the little things, his kind gestures, the respect he'd always shown her, how he always protected her.

And she knew, right now, he was protecting her. She had no idea from what, or if it was even needed, but he was protecting her by not telling her what was going on. It was frustrating to be kept in the dark, but she would not push him right now, nor was she sure she had the right to. He was letting her take care of him; that was all she'd ask. For now.

They stayed there for a long time. She ran her fingers slowly through his hair.

Then he nuzzled into her more and tightened his grip. She leaned over him and kissed his hair.

The feeling between them changed, and she wasn't sure what it meant, what to think. She stepped back. He didn't try to hold on to her.

He looked at her like a dog that'd been beaten and was resigned to being beaten again. Not upset, just resigned. "I'm sorry."

She was so confused.

She walked out of his room. Part of her hoped he would follow, and another part hoped he didn't. And why was he sorry? Had she hurt him?

She ran the rest of the way to her room and closed the door.

Chapter TWENTY

Liliana didn't sleep. All the confusion tumbling through her mind, like blocks knocked over by a toddler, wouldn't let her rest.

Sometime before dawn she put on jeans and a shirt and went out to the kitchen. She'd make him breakfast, and they'd talk. That would help. She could make sure he was okay, that she hadn't ruined what they'd built.

As she passed the island, something caught her eye. There was a note on the counter, handwriting hurried but legible.

I'm sorry I made you uncomfortable. I promise to do a better job of giving you space. But if you need anything, I'm here.

He'd already left. She couldn't talk to him. But she needed to. What was he talking about? He hadn't done anything wrong, and why did he think she wanted space?

She jogged back to her room and grabbed the phone he'd given her. She texted: "Are you busy? Can I talk to you?"

No response. She gave him several minutes, and still no response.

She called. It rang several times, and then went to voice mail and his cold recorded voice. "This is Meric Toledan. Leave a message."

"Will you call me back when you have a chance?" She ended the call.

She set the phone down and tried to make herself find something to eat. She opened the refrigerator and stared at it for a few seconds. Then she closed it.

She walked back over to the island and stared at the phone.

Something felt wrong. Just like it had before he'd come home last night. Was this just residual from last night? Or was she fretting over his note?

Over the next couple of hours, she called several more times. She stopped leaving voice mails.

She texted a few more times.

No responses.

She looked up the number for his office, but of course there was no answer. It was Saturday, and the receptionist who would answer the phone wouldn't be there.

She couldn't get herself to sit down, so she made laps around the apartment. The sun peeked over the horizon, and sunlight bounced off the glass buildings like a laser show.

Finally, she decided she would go to his office. Although none of his employees should be there, maybe he was. She was pretty sure she could remember how to get there. She grabbed her shoes from the closet and put them on, then pressed the button for the elevator.

The phone rang.

She looked at the screen, expecting to see Meric's name, but it was Alfred. She hadn't realized any other numbers were programmed in the phone.

"Hello?" she answered.

"Good morning, Mrs. Toledan. I'm so sorry to bother you on a Saturday. I can't find Mr. Toledan. Is he home?"

"No. He left early. I've been calling."

Silence.

"Do you know where he was going today?" she asked.

"He was supposed to meet me at the office. He said he'd review some loan documents for me. I'm trying to buy a condo."

"Maybe he stopped somewhere along the way, and he doesn't have a good signal?" The elevator doors opened, and she held it.

"He's already late. He's never late. I wouldn't have called you otherwise." Meaning Alfred was worried. And if he was worried, there was probably good reason to be.

Her hands shook.

"Is there any other way to get ahold of him?" she asked.

"He always responds to his phone. If he can't take a call, he'll text." Then he added, "And I don't think he'd ignore your call. Even if he was in a meeting."

"I'm going to walk from here to the office. Maybe I'll find him along the way." She got on the elevator.

"I'll stay here in case he shows up."

"See you in a little while." She ended the call and slipped the phone in her pocket.

In the lobby, she paused to ask the doorman if he'd seen Meric, but he hadn't seen him since early in the morning. She walked out to the mall area, which wasn't bustling yet.

"Liliana, there you are." Wilmer grabbed her arm.

"I'm sorry. I can't talk." She tried to walk away, but he held on.

"I'm getting you out of here." He started to drag her.

"What are you doing? Let me go." She pulled her hand and slipped it out of his grip.

"You need to leave, Liliana. While you have the chance."

"What're you talking about? I have to find Meric. He's missing."

He looked at her like she was crazy. "He's not missing. Don't you know?"

"Know what?"

"He was arrested this morning. Right out there." He pointed to the sidewalk outside.

"Why would he be arrested? What are you talking about?"

"The news is saying it was for human trafficking."

"What?"

"That's what he's doing to you. That explains everything. He trapped you, and once he's bored, he'll sell you to someone else."

Rage burned from her gut up through her chest. "Meric would never do that."

"You barely know him. You've admitted as much."

She wanted to tell him he'd saved her. He'd risked himself for her. And he'd never once tried to get her into bed. He didn't even touch her if he could help it. But she couldn't let anyone know the marriage wasn't real. What if that stopped her from being able to help him somehow? She didn't know how the legal system worked.

Wilmer took her arm again. "I'll make sure you're safe."

"No," she demanded and pulled her arm away.

The glass door leading to the lobby opened. "Is there a problem, Mrs. Toledan?" the doorman asked.

"I'm fine. Thank you."

He hesitated but then let the door close and returned to his desk.

She turned back to Wilmer. "I appreciate your concern. But stop it."

He opened his mouth, obviously about to argue again, but she walked away quickly, exiting the doors to the outside. This early on a Saturday, there weren't many people around. She took her phone out and dialed Alfred.

"Did you find him?" Alfred asked.

"Will you check the news? Someone told me he was arrested." Alfred would be faster than her at finding a news article to confirm it.

"What? Hang on." There was a pause, and then he cursed. "I need to make some calls. Can I call you back?"

"Do whatever you have to. Take care of him."

"Someone's going to answer for this." He cursed again. "I'll keep you updated."

"Tell me if there's anything I can do."

"You got it." The call ended.

She stood there on the sidewalk, feeling helpless. Now what? Go back upstairs? And do what? She needed to do something to help him. But what? She didn't understand the legal system. Alfred—he would take care of it, right?

But why was Meric arrested in the first place? And was Wilmer right that it was for human trafficking?

He was involved in something dangerous, something he wouldn't tell her about, something that got him shot at. But she knew—she knew—he was not a human trafficker. He'd *saved* her. He'd protected her. She'd thought the police investigation would end up with nothing, and the officers would be laughed at for thinking something so ludicrous. They had to have something pretty solid to be able to arrest him, right? But what?

"Mrs. Toledan?"

She whipped around. A white man in a suit was approaching her from a black SUV parked at the curb.

"You're Mrs. Toledan, right?" he asked. "Meric's wife."

"Who are you?"

"We should talk privately."

"Not until you tell me who you are." She shifted closer to the mall doors.

He took a business card out of his wallet and handed it to her—Agent Bando of something called the FBI. "We need to talk privately."

Chapter TWENTY-ONE

Meric sat leaned back in his chair with his cuffed hands in his lap. The pain, especially from the knife wound in his side, screamed, but he showed no emotion. It wasn't a choice so much as how he lived life. He'd learned on the streets not so show emotion in any form, and it'd stuck.

"Let's hear it," the detective with a gray mustache said. He was standing on the other side of the metal table from Meric.

"I would like my phone call, please."

"I would like information. Let's start there. We both know what's going on, what kind of scum you are."

"I would like my phone call, please."

"I would like to know why you buy and sell innocent women." Meric stared him down.

The detective blinked. "Where you really messed up was marrying one of them. What is that all about anyway? Wanted a slave at home? Do you really think she won't jump at the chance for protection?"

"You've sent someone to talk to her," Meric surmised. "Again."

The detective crossed his arms.

"That didn't work out so well for you the first time." He ground his teeth together to stop himself from threatening him not to touch her. Liliana was strong and could handle herself. But she would very likely leave him after this.

He couldn't let himself think about that right now.

"She didn't feel safe yet," the detective said. "With you in here, she'll be able to talk to us."

"Is that all you have? The hope you can get her to give you what you want?"

The detective smirked. "We have photographs."

"Of what?"

"You at a location we've been watching."

"The warehouse," Meric surmised.

"Are you admitting to being there and participating in what goes on there?"

If they had solid evidence of what went on there, they'd have raided the place, caught him there rather than outside his building. "Phone call."

"We also have pictures of you associating with known criminals."

Meric didn't doubt he had pictures like that. They could be of him with any number of people, though he was always careful no transactions happened in an environment not perfectly controlled. Any pictures they had couldn't be anything more than circumstantial.

"It's only a matter of time," the detective said. "My partner is on his way to your penthouse. If you talk now, I might be able to put in a good word with the DA."

"Phone call."

The detective picked up the metal chair and slammed it down on the floor.

Meric gave no reaction and just kept looking at him.

"Talk!" the detective demanded.

The door opened. "Hughes."

Hughes glared at Meric.

"Now," the man at the door said.

Hughes shoved the chair against the table and stalked out. He slammed the door shut, and the glass quivered.

Meric sat perfectly still, silent, and listened. Between catching every few words and reading lips, he could understand the conversation fairly well.

"Is that Meric Toledan?" Meric assumed this man was the detective's lieutenant.

"We got this under control."

"We? Where is Johnson?"

"He's picking up more evidence."

"What evidence?"

"We got it covered."

"We're talking about Meric Toledan. You better have your ducks not just in a row but stacked and mortared like a brick wall."

"It's solid."

"What's solid? What do you have?"

"An eyewitness."

"Willing to testify? Have they signed a written statement? What do they know?"

"No written statement yet. She needed to feel safe. Johnson went to pick her up. With Toledan here, she'll tell us everything."

"Are you talking about Toledan's wife? As in a spouse who cannot testify against her husband?"

"It can hardly be called a legal marriage when she was forced into it. She's more possession than wife."

Meric's whole body tightened as he controlled himself.

"Plus," Hughes added, "we have him at a site—photos and video."

"What site?"

The detective glanced over, through the window at Meric. Meric diverted his gaze for a moment so it wouldn't look like he was paying such close attention. Hughes turned back to the lieutenant. "Give us just a little leeway on this. We all know he's dirty, and he's here already. Let's make the most of this opportunity."

The lieutenant's voice was a rumble. "Make. It. Stick."

Hughes walked back into the interrogation room.

"Phone call," Meric said.

◼ ◼ ◼

"How can I verify you are who you say you are?" Liliana held up the business card the man had handed her.

He glanced around and spoke quietly. "He came home last night with a bandaged stab wound and a lot of defensive wounds."

"That proves you know him, but it doesn't prove you're not the one who caused those wounds."

He raised an eyebrow. "Touché, Mrs. Toledan." He paused in thought, still looking at her as if assessing. "Has he ever mentioned me?"

She crossed her arms.

He pursed his lips. "You've heard my name, but you can't verify I am actually Agent Bando."

That was part of it, but she also couldn't be sure he wasn't part of Meric's problems. She'd only heard the name that once, while overhearing a conversation when she'd first come to live with Meric. She had no idea of the context of that conversation.

He took something from his pocket, looked like a wallet of some kind, and opened it. There was some kind of ID badge inside. "I don't suppose this helps."

"I don't know what that is."

He closed it and put it back. "Understandable. You're new to the country. Your English is impressive, by the way."

She continued to stand there with her arms crossed. "How do you know Meric?"

"I can't really tell you much. Honestly, I've told you more than I'm supposed to."

"You haven't told me anything."

"You're not supposed to know anything is even going on."

"Then why are you here?"

"I need to secure his office." Then he added, "And I need to verify how much you know and make sure you don't talk to the press."

"You mean reporters?" And why was he worried about Meric's home office and not work? Or maybe someone else was there too? Or maybe this had nothing to do with his business.

He nodded.

"I wouldn't talk to reporters."

"Good. Best to keep things quiet."

"I'm not letting someone I don't know into Meric's office. Not unless he tells me to, but he can't right now."

"This is for his protection."

"Prove you're his friend."

He took a heavy breath as he thought. "All right. He doesn't share about his past, but I assume he's shared quite a bit with you. Not even the gossip rags have been able to dig up much about his youth. I know he lived on the streets for some time. I know about his mother, where she came from, that she was brought here by human traffickers."

Several things clicked together in her head, but she was careful not to show surprise.

She started toward the mall doors. "Come on."

The doorman nodded a greeting as she passed and got on the elevator with Bando, but the doorman couldn't quite hide his curiosity at her leading another man upstairs. Surely he'd never seen Agent Bando, not if she was right about Meric's relationship with him.

The elevator doors opened, and she walked off and turned toward Meric's office. While Agent Bando flipped through file folders, she stood by the door, watching him. She still didn't fully trust him.

But she did trust Meric.

"Do you see anything?" she asked.

"No. I think it's clean. If he has any hard copies, they're not in here."

"What about his phone? He has that on him."

"Our emails are encrypted. Not impossible to break, but certainly above the paygrade of local police cyber specialists."

"Wait, I think I saw him reading something to do with his undercover work." She started down the hall toward his room.

"He told you what he's working on?" Bando sounded concerned.

"No, you did." She continued walking.

He followed. "I didn't tell you anything about my relationship with him. We could simply be old friends, and I wanted to secure his office as a favor before the police riffle through it. I didn't give you details."

She stopped and looked back. "Not in so many words, but he's obviously working undercover. That's why the police think he's involved in human trafficking—he is, but not in the way they think."

He raised his brows.

Once in Meric's room, she paused to look around. She tried not to let Bando see that she'd been in there only a few times. She hadn't paid much attention and didn't know where Meric would put papers. This was where she'd seen him reading documents about a shipment from South America.

She tried the nightstand drawers and noticed the gun holstered on the side closest to the bed. Nothing else other than a flashlight and a few books. Then she thought more—he wouldn't leave anything easy to find, not when he let people into the apartment regularly when he wasn't home. Anything important would be locked up.

Maybe a safe in a wall? Maybe behind that painting on the wall opposite the windows? She'd seen that in a movie once when she'd gone with her mom to work. No, the bathroom was on the other side of that wall, specifically the shower. There wasn't space for a safe to be hidden in that wall. Then she glanced at the made bed and noticed drawers underneath. They were wood, looked like normal underbed storage, but one of them had a combination lock. She knelt and rattled the drawer to see if it felt and sounded like a normal drawer. It felt heavier and the sound was deeper, like thick metal. The wood must be just cladding.

"Do you have the combination?" Bando asked.

She shook her head and stared at the lock, wishing she had some way of guessing what the combination might be.

"Mrs. Toledan." It was the doorman's voice coming over the speaker in the kitchen. He sounded urgent and stressed.

She stood and jogged out to the kitchen. She pressed the button to respond. "Yes?"

"They had a warrant. I had to let them up."

Chapter TWENTY-TWO

"I understand. Thank you for telling me." Liliana let go of the button that allowed her to talk to the doorman.

"Local police." Bando had followed her out from the bedroom.

"What's a warrant?" she asked. "Does that mean they can search?"

"Yes. You can't tell them who I am."

"Why?" Then she added, "They can't search you?"

"They could search my person only if they had a warrant for that specifically. We can't let them know who I am. Meric's identity as an undercover informant has to be protected. He's too famous; we have to control who knows about him very carefully."

"I'll say you're a friend."

"They'll probably assume you're stepping out on him."

She guessed that meant she was cheating. She'd figured the same thing. Bando was slightly older than Meric, but was clean-cut and attractive, though in a different way than Meric. Bando was more like the boy next door who'd played high school sports and went to a good college. Meric wasn't like that at all.

"Meric will understand," she said. "And I don't care what they say about me. As long as he's safe."

She thought she caught a smile in his eyes, but then the elevator dinged and the doors opened.

She turned to face the officers stepping off the elevator. The detective in front was one of the men she'd met before, the younger one with reddish-blond hair. If he was here, she was willing to bet the aggressive Detective Hughes was with Meric.

She reminded herself Meric could handle himself better than anyone she'd ever known.

Four uniformed officers followed Detective Johnson off the elevator. They scattered in different directions. She hadn't had time to clear out her room and make it less obvious she lived separate from Meric, but she couldn't worry about that at the moment.

Detective Johnson walked up to her and handed her a folded piece of paper, presumably the warrant. "Liliana, I'm sorry to put you through this, but it's over now."

"What's over?" And where did he get off using her first name?

"Toledan is in custody. You're free."

"I'm in America. Of course I'm free." She stopped herself from saying more.

Bando stayed back several feet and kept quiet. She wondered if he'd be able to keep quiet for long.

Detective Johnson's voice was soft. "You're free from Toledan. We'll keep him locked up for a very long time. You just need to tell us how it all happened."

"How what all happened?"

"Your abduction."

"Meric didn't abduct me. Meric saved my life."

Something dark flashed across Johnson's expression, but then he pulled it back. "He's controlling you, Liliana. Step back and look at it rationally, without fear. I'm here to protect you from him."

She took a breath to control herself. "I realize you don't know me very well, but I'm not an idiot. I understand very well what's going on. I made my choices myself, with my eyes open. Or don't you believe in a woman's right to make her own decisions?"

His tone turned condescending. "Liliana—"

"That's *Mrs. Toledan*, Detective Johnson," she said. "You think you need to come in here and *rescue me*? I hate to break it to you, but I'm perfectly capable of thinking for myself."

Johnson crossed his arms.

"If you're depending on me to give you something you can use to hurt Meric, you're going to be disappointed. Meric has done nothing wrong."

Johnson walked away, down the hall, and called out, "What've you got for me?"

Liliana made herself stand there in silence while the officers tore apart Meric's home. They ripped off couch cushions, tipped over the armchairs, tossed food from the refrigerator across the counter. She didn't let herself look over at his office—that room was surely even worse.

Johnson came back down the hall. "What's the code?"

"If you think he's holding me against my will, why would you think he would give me codes to anything?"

A uniformed officer came up behind Johnson. "I've never seen anything like it before. We can't get it open."

"Take it out."

"It's anchored into the building's structure. I'm sorry, it's not coming out, and it's not opening without the combination."

Johnson pushed the officer back down the hall and growled, "Find *something*."

With all the officers out of the room, she glanced back at Bando. He smirked.

Another fifteen minutes passed before the officers gathered at the elevator. Johnson joined them a minute later. He had some files in his hand.

"What is that?" Liliana asked.

"Call me when you're ready to talk. Just hope I'm still willing to listen."

When the doors opened, he stepped on the elevator, followed by the four officers. None of them looked at her, but she swore one of them scowled when Johnson talked. The elevator doors closed.

Liliana ran back to Meric's bedroom. The safe was still closed. She knelt to inspect it. It didn't look like it'd been pried open. The files Johnson had taken must've been something from Meric's office.

Bando followed her. "There wasn't anything in that office. Whatever he took isn't anything, just him pulling at straws."

She looked up at him with drawn brows.

"Sorry. It's an expression. It means he's desperate and trying anything."

She stood. "You need to get Meric out of there."

"It's going to be tricky, but I'll get it done." He took a step toward the door but paused. "Are you all right? Would you like someone to stay with you?"

"Just focus on Meric." Her voice came out terser than she'd intended.

He nodded and then headed down the hall. He pushed the button for the elevator.

Maybe there was something else he could help her with. "Wait." She caught up to him. "Do you have the address where Carl is staying?"

"The guy who was transporting you?"

She nodded.

"Why?"

"He obviously doesn't have the protection of anyone, right? Whoever hired him isn't communicating with him anymore."

"We're fairly certain of that, yes."

"That woman he's staying with—she deserves to know who he really is."

"You want to write her a letter?"

"I've already written it. I just need the address."

"You can't trust her."

"I realize that. I didn't let her know my name or where I am."

Then she added again, "She deserves to know. What if he tries to do the same thing to her? Isn't that what you're fighting? Maybe we can help her before it's too late."

"How about this—I'll send the letter for you."

"Thank you." She quickly grabbed the letter, thankful it hadn't gotten completely lost in the mess, and gave it to Bando.

As he got on the elevator, Bando asked, "Are you sure you're all right alone?"

"Just help Meric. I'm fine."

He nodded. The elevator doors started to close, but he put out a hand to stop them. "When he first told me he'd gotten married—to someone he'd just met—I didn't react with congratulations. I worried it was dangerous, reckless. But I suppose I should've trusted him." He let go of the doors, and they closed.

She understood why he would've felt that way. She wasn't sure why Meric had married her either.

She took her phone out of her pocket and called Alfred. He didn't answer, but he texted a few seconds later. "Sorry—can't answer. On the phone with someone. Working on it. Will let you know when I have something."

Between Agent Bando and Alfred, they'll get Meric out. He'll be all right. She set to cleaning up the mess the police had made of the apartment. She was thankful to have something to keep her busy. She didn't touch his office or bedroom though. Those were his private spaces.

At one point, the doorman called and asked if he could let Wilmer up to see her. She ignored him.

The revelations she'd learned from Bando kept turning over in her mind. The knife fight he'd been in had to be related to his work for Agent Bando, but how? What did he do exactly? How much danger did he put himself in on a regular basis? And then she wondered if some part of him wanted to be sacrificed to the cause, an atonement.

She finished up the last of the cleaning and realized night had fallen.

She looked at her phone. She'd texted with Alfred here and there, but the last thing he'd sent was over an hour ago. She texted, "Anything?"

No reply.

She set her phone down on the kitchen island and moved to gaze out the window. *Please, Lord, please help him.* She leaned her head against the glass and took a deep breath.

Her phone beeped, and she snatched it off the counter.

Alfred had responded. "He's being released." Another text: "I'm still on the phone, but I just got confirmation. He'll be out within the hour."

She bowed her head. *Thank you, God.*

Then she texted Alfred, "How did you do it?"

There was a pause before he responded. She was impressed he could be on a phone call and still hold a conversation with her in text. "I'm not sure actually. I tried a bunch of different routes, but I didn't think any of them were working."

She wondered if Agent Bando had nudged along some plan Alfred had started. He would possibly know about some of the connections Meric and Alfred had and could maybe push things along in the background.

She paced in front of the elevator, while staring at her phone, hoping Meric would call as soon as he walked out of the station. She wanted to go wait for him downstairs, but she didn't want to risk having to deal with Wilmer or reporters.

And so she continued pacing.

Finally, the elevator doors opened, and Meric walked off. "I'm sorry you had to deal with that." He turned toward his office and then closed the door behind himself.

Chapter

TWENTY-THREE

Liliana watched Meric disappear into his office. She hadn't anticipated much from him but at least a greeting, mentioning being grateful to be home, something.

She followed and walked into his office.

He was picking up papers off the floor. He didn't look up. She'd half expected him to appear disheveled, but he looked the same as always. Just as cold as usual.

"It wasn't your fault, Meric."

He stopped and looked at her. Through the coldness, she could see something, the same thing she'd seen from the beginning.

"Whoever hurt your mother," she continued, "that's their doing. You may be the product, but you were not the cause."

He stared at her, completely still.

She met his gaze.

Quiet surrounded them. She wasn't sure if he was shocked she knew, angry that she'd talked about it, or perhaps sorting a hundred different thoughts.

He turned and picked up more papers off the floor.

She stayed there. She wasn't going to let him freeze her out, not this time.

Several minutes passed while he continued to pick up papers and right furniture.

He set several folders on the desk. "You didn't need to clean up the rest of the apartment."

"I didn't touch this room or your bedroom. I didn't want your privacy to be disturbed any more than it already has been."

"Then why would you talk about my mother?" He didn't look or sound angry—more detached than anything.

"Because you need to hear it."

"How in the—" He stopped before the curse exploded out of his mouth.

"Agent Bando came to make sure anything important was secure. They couldn't get the safe under your bed open, by the way. I made him tell me something only you would know before letting him in the apartment. He said he knew your mother was brought here by traffickers."

"How did you know I'm—"

She kept her voice gentle. "You said she should've aborted you."

He turned away, toward the window. Several seconds passed.

"I knew they wouldn't get in the safe," he said. Then he added, "I'm just sorry you went through that."

"I'm fine. Agent Bando was here while they searched, so there will most likely be rumors. But they didn't question Bando or even ask his name. It'll be more bad gossip about you, but I doubt it's any worse than you've endured in the past."

Still turned toward the window, he said, "You shouldn't have to endure that. When I married you, it didn't occur to me that they would target you too."

"You married me to protect me. Just like I'm sure you always did for your mother."

A long pause.

"She shouldn't have had to—" He ran his hand through his hair.

"No, she shouldn't have had to go through that. My heart breaks for her. I can understand the pain she went through. I'm betting she barely survived it."

He lowered his head.

"But God blessed her with a child. He knew she needed help to survive, and he sent her a beautiful soul to give her purpose and love." Liliana moved closer, just behind him. "She needed to feel purpose, a reason to make it through another day. She needed you."

He didn't respond, didn't move.

"Think back through your childhood," she said. "She was happy when you were happy, right? She worked hard to support you because you were everything to her." She didn't know anything about his childhood, but she felt in her gut she was right about this.

She rested her hand on his back. He was tense, hard.

She felt him take a breath.

"You are the man you are because of her," she said. "Because she showed you strength and kindness. You are her legacy."

A long pause.

"I'm not—" He stopped. "I'm not like her—gentle, kind." He growled the words, "I'm like *him*."

"Did you know him?"

"No. Her captor was never caught, and she didn't tell me anything about him. She may not have even known who exactly my father was, probably some random man who paid for *time* with her. But I know the kind of man he was—cold, violent, domineering."

She moved around in front of him and looked him in the eye. "You *stop* men like him."

"You don't really know me, Liliana."

She shifted even closer, rested her hands on either side of his face, and whispered, "I know who you are."

He met her gaze.

Then he blinked and stepped back. "What do you mean I stop men like him? What did Bando tell you?"

Her hands felt cold without his stubbled skin to warm them. "He didn't actually tell me much of anything."

"Then what—"

"The police think you're involved in trafficking because that's the part you're playing—you work undercover for Bando, pretending to be a wealthy buyer. That's why you have reports about shipments from South America. That's how you realized so quickly what Josh and Carl were doing at that truck stop."

He returned to straightening the papers on his desk.

"Bando is lucky to have you," she continued. "You're the perfect image. You're wealthy enough to afford to be a buyer, and no one really knows much about you, other than rumors. How long have you been working for him?"

He took two papers out of the mound on the desk and started a new pile.

She stood there and waited for a response.

He sighed and looked up. "I don't want you involved in this."

"I get that you're trying to protect me, but I handle things better if I have some idea of what's going on." She also thought it might help him to have someone to talk to.

He continued sorting papers.

She remained standing there.

Finally, he said, "A few years."

"What happened yesterday? How were you hurt?"

He looked up. "I went someplace, dealt with a security issue, and came home."

She crossed her arms.

"I'm not allowed to talk about this," he said.

"I already know you're working undercover, and Agent Bando knows that I know. I'm not asking for names and addresses, just some basics."

"Why would you want to know? I'm trying to give you time to heal. This won't help with that."

Her voice hardened. "What would help me heal is knowing garbage like that are being taken down by someone like you."

He took a slow breath, and she felt an understanding develop between them.

Finally, he said, "Come here. Sit down."

She sat on the corner of his desk, the one spot not covered in papers and file folders. He took his chair, only a foot or so between them.

"We're working on a few things, some small-time and some bigger," he said. "That rural highway where we met is a route frequented by traffickers. We think a particular major player we've been tracking has been using it. I took that on my way back from a business meeting to scope it out, see if I could find anything that might possibly help."

"What about Detectives Johnson and Hughes? Do you think they could be working with a trafficker?"

"I think Johnson and Hughes are acting in good faith. While I believe their main goal is to make a big arrest, I do think they're honestly concerned about you. That tempers my anger. That and the fact that I heard them getting ripped by their lieutenant when I was leaving."

"Are you sure? Why are they coming after you so hard?"

"We think Johnson and Hughes received an anonymous tip. Hughes knew I've been to a particular transaction point—a warehouse. It's a place used by multiple traffickers. The ownership runs through a shell corporation, probably leading to a midsize trafficking operation, and legitimate business is run out of it as well to throw off anyone who might watch it. I suspect that major player I mentioned is the tipster. He doesn't use that warehouse, and we think he's been working on taking out competition."

"What about yesterday? What were you working on?"

"Nothing I couldn't handle, and nothing you need to worry about."

"Were you at that warehouse?"

"No. An estate."

"It was that major player, wasn't it?"

He didn't answer.

"Why would he tell you to meet him there and then attack

you?" she pushed. "He has to know you're working undercover. You're not safe."

"Bando and I have found enough information to be confident he doesn't know I'm working with the FBI. He sees me as competition. I'm working to convince him I can be an ally. Then I can get a meeting, and then we can take him down."

"But the fact that you got married—won't that look odd with the role you're playing?"

"It's not uncommon for these guys to be married. Especially someone like me. I have the money for multiple homes, and I travel extensively for my business. The wives of these men are in the dark. Usually a trophy to hang on their arm at social functions, a way to make them look more legitimate. You're probably exactly the kind of woman people in those circles would expect me to marry."

Someone they assumed he could control. So, she wasn't hurting his ability to do the work. But that didn't make her any less nervous. "Have you ever gotten hurt like that before?"

"Not since I was a teenager. It's not a common occurrence. There's nothing for you to worry about."

"But it could happen again. You don't know."

He gave no response.

"Will you tell me your plans from here?" she asked.

"It's not a good idea. You already know too much."

"I'm worried about you."

He held her gaze for several seconds.

Then he stood. "I've told you enough to show you everything is fine. You don't need to know anything else." He walked out of the room and down the hall.

His tone had been cold, maybe even condescending. But her gut told her that was just a cover, a way of protecting himself. But from what?

Chapter TWENTY-FOUR

"They haven't gotten a good picture of you yet." Meric was standing in the middle of the living room, remote control in hand, watching the news—a segment on his arrest.

Liliana continued out of her room, surprised to see him. She'd grown used to his seldom being around. "I don't know why." She'd come out to find something for dinner.

"I think when you leave the apartment, you leave too early for them to catch you outside." He kept watching the TV.

"They probably wouldn't guess at who I was even if they did see me."

"I doubt that." The segment ended, and he clicked off the TV and turned to walk away.

She wasn't surprised news of his arrest had leaked. The police had come through the public mall downstairs when they'd come to search the apartment, and they'd arrested him on a public sidewalk. It'd been early, but obviously people had still been around to witness it.

"Stay for dinner," she said. "I'll make you something."

He paused at the kitchen island. "Thank you, but I'm not hungry." He faced her properly. "I just wanted to make sure you're all right. I left you abruptly earlier."

Did he do anything *not* abruptly? "Were you waiting for me? How long were you standing there?"

"Are you all right? Did Johnson upset you?"

"I was really worried about you, is all."

He gave no reply, but started to head down the hallway.

"Are there rumors about my cheating yet?" she asked.

He hesitated before looking back at her. "It's not on the news, but it's hit gossip sites and social media."

"Is it bad?"

"It's reality. It wouldn't have mattered—that rumor would've started no matter what."

"Why?"

"Why would anyone be faithful to coldhearted Meric Toledan?"

"I am."

He looked at her with those cold, dark eyes that weren't really cold, not if you looked deeply, not if you knew him. She didn't know the details of his life very well, but she had a feeling she knew him a lot better than most people ever had. Or ever would. That made sadness rush through her.

"I know we're not in love," she said, "and we won't be together forever. But I am faithful to you."

"I know you're not about to sleep with anyone, not after what you've been through."

"Obviously. But that's not really what I meant. I mean I'm loyal."

He didn't respond.

"When I get the chance, I stand up for you. I would do what I could to protect you. I know I can't do much, but sometimes what really matters is that someone tries, that someone sees something in you to make them want to protect you."

He stepped closer. "What do you mean you stand up for me? Has someone been bothering you?"

"No. It's just an older man who lives in the building. He's really kind to me, but he listens to the media too much."

"Does he bother you?"

"What would you do? Kick him out of the building?" She laughed.

"Yes. If he bothers you, he'll be gone by tomorrow."

"You wouldn't do that."

"Does he bother you?" His expression was calm, but his eyes were hard.

She wasn't sure how to react, wasn't sure what to make of him. "No, he's fine. He's nice to me."

"He doesn't think I'm good enough for you."

"He listens to the media too much." She didn't tell him about Wilmer's behavior earlier today, being almost forceful. She had a feeling if she did, Meric would follow through on his threat to kick him out of the building by tomorrow. She was angry at Wilmer and didn't want to see him anytime soon, but she didn't want him kicked out.

"Tell me if anyone in this building upsets you."

She nodded.

He held eye contact for an extra second, perhaps making sure there was no action to be taken, and then he turned and headed for the hallway.

"Meric."

He stopped and looked back.

Her voice barely made sound. "Thank you." For so much she couldn't put it into words.

"Anything." He walked away and she heard his bedroom door close quietly.

What had he meant by that?

She went to the kitchen, but she wasn't very inspired to prepare dinner. In the end, she decided to keep it simple—just a sandwich. She still felt frazzled from today and didn't have it in her to do anything more interesting.

After putting her plate in the dishwasher, she made another sandwich and brought it to Meric's bedroom. She knocked on the door. There was no answer.

She knocked again. Maybe he'd fallen asleep? But he hadn't eaten all day. He needed to eat.

Cautiously she opened the door and peeked inside. He was sitting on his bed, wide awake and looking as sharp as always.

"You need to eat." She shoved the plate into his hands before he could protest. "And no throwing it in the trash. You'll hurt my feelings." She tried to sound harsh, but it came out a bit playful.

There was a grin somewhere in his eyes. She loved seeing that, knowing no one else did. There was something so genuine. It was like watching someone when they thought they were alone.

She left and closed the door behind her.

■ ▦ ▪

Meric set the plate on his dresser near the door and turned back to the open safe under his bed, intent on continuing to work. It upset him that Liliana had been brought into this.

But then he tossed the paper he'd been reading back inside and closed the safe. He grabbed the plate off the dresser, sat in the chair by the window, and took a bite of the sandwich. He hadn't felt hungry, but now he was famished. Maybe it was the smell that'd made him hungry.

Or maybe it was the fact that she'd taken the time to make something for him.

He leaned back in the chair and let himself enjoy the simple meal. The taste was good but different. He lifted the bread to see what was on it. Orange-colored sauce was slathered on the meat. Chipotle sauce. He wondered if she'd somehow figured out that was his favorite.

No, it'd been just luck.

He took another bite and looked out over the darkened city. Maybe he should step back from his work with Bando for now, at least for a while. At least until Liliana left. He knew she'd leave eventually. She'd find an employer willing to sponsor her green card and then have their marriage annulled.

He set the plate with the half-eaten sandwich on the floor.

Liliana kept listening for any sign of Meric, but he didn't come out the rest of the evening. She supposed she should be getting used to it. This was probably how he'd been when he lived alone. She couldn't expect him to change his life just because he was now saddled with her. But she wasn't getting used to it.

It seemed harder every day.

She needed to find a way to free him, but now she was also concerned about what he was involved in. It sounded stupid, even inside her own head, but she didn't want to leave him alone. What would've happened last night if she hadn't been there to help him clean and bandage all his cuts?

She sighed. He would've been fine. He'd been about to take care of it himself when she'd walked in on him.

But she still worried about him.

She tried yet again to read the book in her hand but couldn't manage to concentrate. Instead, she continued to stare at all the lights dotting the city below. She'd never seen anything like it. It was mesmerizing to be able to see so much from this high perch, yet see no details, nothing of the humanity down there. It reminded her of those stupid reporters who attacked Meric. Sitting high above, thinking they had a far-reaching view, but not actually understanding anything.

Meric could have been like that. He could be sitting in his penthouse, unconcerned about what happened below. But he wasn't. He was out there in the dirt, fighting for people he didn't know. He got no credit for anything he did, and it didn't even occur to him to care.

She was so lost in thought that she jumped when her phone rang.

She walked over to the desk and picked up the phone. It wasn't Meric or Alfred—those were the only numbers programmed. She hesitated to answer—who else could possibly be calling her?

"Hello?"

"Liliana?"

"Agent Bando? Is something wrong?" It couldn't be Meric. She was sure he was still at home. She'd gotten to be very good at listening for the elevator.

"No, no. Everything is fine. I just wanted to check on you after the day you had." Then he added, "Meric gave me your number just in case there was any trouble in the future."

Like if he got arrested again, or hurt, or worse. "Meric is home, and he seems fine."

"But are you okay? You handled everything beautifully, but I worried it would catch up with you later."

"I'm all right, but thank you for asking." Then she added, "Was that really the reason for your call, Agent Bando?"

"Meric was right about you." There was a smile in his voice.

What had Meric told Bando about her?

"Tough as nails, I think was the phrase he used. And a little scary if you really want to be."

"Meric said that?"

"He's an excellent judge of character. I'm learning to trust that about him."

"Are you worried that I know what he does? What he works on with you?"

"Surprisingly, no. In fact, this whole thing might have worked out for the best."

"What do you mean?"

"To be honest, Meric won't be happy with me, but I think he'll understand in the end. Maybe. I think you might be the perfect person to help."

"Help with what?"

"Catching a predator."

TWENTY-FIVE

Liliana sat at the dining table. Light was beginning to peek over the horizon. By the time she'd finished talking to Bando last night, it'd been late, so she'd decided to catch Meric in the morning. She had no idea how he was going to react. She'd considered for just a moment not telling him, but she wanted to be honest with him. How else could she expect him to be honest with her?

She heard his door open and stood from her chair.

"Good morning." He didn't pause on his way toward the elevator.

"I need to talk to you."

"I have somewhere to be."

"It's Sunday morning."

He continued walking.

"Please, Meric. It's really important."

He turned back to her, and his icy façade melted around the edges. "Is everything all right?"

"I talked to Agent Bando last night."

"Why would you talk to Bando?"

"Do you trust him?"

His brows pulled together.

"Do you trust him?" she repeated.

"Yes."

"Why?"

"What's going on?"

"Please answer."

"When I first met him, I dug into his past. He has a few disciplinary notes in his file, but it was all for actions he'd taken to protect people. He follows the rules unless he has no other way to save an innocent. He thinks for himself and has honest motivations."

"Have you tested those motivations?"

"Nothing he knows about."

"Good. If you trust him, then I feel comfortable trusting him."

He shifted closer. "Why would you need to trust him?"

The doorman's voice came over the intercom. "Mr. and Mrs. Toledan, I have a gentleman requesting to come up."

She walked over to the screen on the kitchen counter.

The doorman added, "He says he's an old friend. I believe he was here yesterday." He turned the camera and showed Agent Bando standing at the counter downstairs. Then he turned the camera back around to himself. "Shall I allow him up?"

Liliana pressed the intercom button. "Yes, please."

"Yes, ma'am." The screen went blank.

"Why is Bando here?" There was a cautious edge to Meric's voice.

"You said no one has pictures of me yet. No one knows who I am."

He didn't respond.

"I can fit in perfectly. Because I am one of them. And I want to help."

Meric stared at her. She started to wonder if this was the only reaction she'd get.

The elevator doors opened, and Bando stepped off.

Meric lunged and grabbed Bando's jacket in both fists.

"Meric!" Liliana rushed over.

Meric growled, "She's been through enough."

Agent Bando's eyes were wide.

"What are you thinking, asking her to do this?" He was only about an inch taller than Agent Bando, but he seemed so much bigger in this moment.

"Meric," Liliana said. "Please."

Meric glanced at her. Then he let go of Agent Bando's jacket and stepped back.

Agent Bando blinked once slowly.

Liliana stood between Meric and Agent Bando, facing Meric. "Please hear me out."

Meric continued to glare at Agent Bando over her head.

"You said he has honest motivations," she said.

He pulled his gaze from Bando to her. "He can find someone else to go undercover. You've been through enough. You deserve time to heal."

"Meric—" came Agent Bando's voice from behind her. He stopped short when Meric skewered him with another look.

Meric turned back to Liliana, and his anger evaporated like mist.

He took her hand in his firm but gentle grip and led her through the living room to her bedroom. She wondered why this room and not his office, which had been closer, and then she figured he wanted to make sure Agent Bando didn't hear this conversation. He let go of her hand as soon as they entered the room. He closed the door behind them.

"I'm sorry to hit you with it like that," she said. "I wanted to talk to you more before Agent Bando showed up." She was still covering her shock at his reaction. She'd figured he probably wouldn't be excited about it, but she hadn't anticipated his being that angry.

He moved closer and rested his hands gently on her cheeks. He murmured, "Please."

She looked up into his dark eyes.

"Please," he murmured again. "I'll beg if you want me to."

She had no idea how to respond to that.

Several seconds passed.

A cloud shifted, and the rising sun filled the room with light.

Finally, she said, "I have to help if I can."

"You've been through enough."

"I need to do this, Meric."

He turned away, toward the window. The sun made his skin glow.

"I need to help," she said. "And I can. I can blend in with these women better than anyone. I am uniquely qualified to help. God put me here, right now, so I could help these women. For my family, for their memory."

He faced her. "You don't owe anyone anything."

"It's for me too," she admitted. "I need this."

"You need to heal."

Her voice strengthened like a gladiator about to go into battle. "They didn't break me. They will not break me. They hurt me, but I'm still here, still fighting. They cannot stop me." Her voice rose, and tears pricked her eyes. "I will fight until my dying breath. I'm stronger than them. I have to be."

Silence.

"I can't . . ." His voice trailed into nothing.

"I want your support."

He lifted his chin, and she saw that same focus and determination usually in his eyes. He opened the door and walked out of the room. She quickly followed. She was pretty sure he wouldn't hurt Agent Bando, but she wasn't positive.

Agent Bando straightened when he saw Meric coming.

"I'm going with her," Meric demanded.

Agent Bando glanced to her and back to Meric. "I don't think—"

Meric growled, "Make it work." Then he walked down the hall.

Agent Bando watched him go and then turned to Liliana. "How'd you do that?"

"Do what?"

"Meric Toledan doesn't just change his mind like that."

She wasn't sure how to respond, so instead, she said, "Do you have the information you said you'd bring?"

He took some folded papers out of his overcoat pocket and handed them to her. "Make sure these are put into Meric's safe."

She nodded. Then she said, "I think you should probably go for now. Call me when you have a date and time?"

"Yeah. I won't come back here unless I need to. Don't want people to wonder who I am and how I'm connected to you or Meric." He pressed the button for the elevator.

"Okay."

"But we'll set up a meeting to go over details and make sure you're ready."

She nodded.

The elevator doors opened, and he stepped on. "Your letter was delivered, by the way."

"Thank you." He must've had it messengered or something. Maybe he was worried about the woman too.

The doors closed.

Liliana sat at the dining table for a little while and went over the papers. They were targeting a small group buying women, currently looking to acquire a young Latina. Her English was good enough that she felt mostly comfortable with the information, with the aid of the Spanish/English dictionary, but she wanted to go over it with Meric to be totally sure. And she wanted to talk to him.

She folded the papers back up and headed down the hall toward his room.

Chapter TWENTY-SIX

Liliana was halfway down the hall when Meric came out of his room. He held his hand out. "The papers."

She paused.

"The combination for the safe is 225121. I'm not trying to take this away from you. I'm going to help make sure it's done right."

"Promise me."

He met her eyes. "I give you my word."

She handed him the folded papers. "I want to look at them later."

He nodded then walked back in his room, set the papers in the safe, closed the door, and came back to her. "But if you decide you want out of this, the slightest doubt, I'll make it happen. No matter what."

She nodded once.

"Come with me."

She went with him down the hall. "I've never been this way."

"You don't explore when I leave you alone all the time?"

She shrugged. "Why would I?" It wasn't her house.

"To check out the strange guy you live with. You can go anywhere in the apartment you want."

"Why do you leave me alone all the time?"

Silence.

He went into a doorway on the right. It was a big almost-empty room. There was a weight bench in the corner closest to the door and a hanging bag in the opposite corner, chained to both the ceiling and floor. The rest of the room was empty, just a wooden floor and windows covering two walls looking out across the flat white roof gleaming in the morning sun.

Halfway across the wooden floor, he paused. "It's not you." He turned and looked at her. "The reason I leave."

She kept her tone muted, careful. "We don't lie to each other, right? We may not tell each other everything, but we don't lie." She didn't understand why he always left, why he felt the need to "give her space." Maybe her situation reminded him of his mother and that was too difficult to be reminded of all the time?

The muscles in his jaw tightened. "I don't regret what I did. I need you to know that. I will never regret it. No matter how all this works out in the end."

"It was reckless. I know you well enough now to know that's not like you."

"You don't know me that well."

"I think I do. I may not know all of your history, but I think I know how you work."

He didn't respond.

"I want to do something like that," she said. "I want to—what's the English phrase?—pay it forward."

"You don't owe anyone anything. You don't need to pay anything forward."

"I owe you."

He stepped toward her. "Don't do this job with Bando. That's how to pay me back."

"How many times have you gone undercover? How many people have you saved?"

He sighed, almost a growl.

"I want to do this for them too, all those people you've saved. For all of those who are too broken to pay it forward." Then she said, "Teach me how to defend myself. That's why you brought me here, right?"

He met her gaze for several seconds.

Finally, he said, "The self-defense you said you learned from reading—show me what you know."

"Not much. With that vagrant in the alley, I focused on causing pain and disorientation. I'd read about the best places to hit and how to do basic strikes."

"Like what?"

"Preferably nose and groin, but also instep, knee, solar plexus."

"Not the eyes?"

"I'd rather not, but I would if I had to."

"Why would you rather not?"

"I don't want to blind someone."

"You're going to need to set that kindness aside, at least this once. If you're not willing to do whatever it takes, you could hesitate to take action, and that could get you hurt."

"If I have to take action to help an innocent, I won't hesitate."

"Remember you're an innocent as well."

She wasn't. Not anymore. She was no longer clean, and she hadn't saved her family, hadn't even fought. "Will you teach me how to do strikes properly?"

He led her over to the hanging bag. "Let's do palm strikes first. It's one of the easiest strikes. Aim for the nose with the heel of your palm. Curl your fingers just enough so that your fingernails get the eyes." He struck the bag with his right hand, opposite from where the most major of his knife wounds was.

She jumped at the slamming sound and then the chains rattling.

He reached out and steadied the bag. "I'm sorry. I should've warned you."

"No. I need to get stronger. I'm fine."

"But also remember those reactions. Use them when you're

there—that'll help you blend in and appear to be just another of their victims."

She nodded.

"Show me your palm strike."

She positioned her hand with the palm jutting out and then set it on the bag to get a feel. Then she pulled back and struck. The sound was more of a whack than a slam like his had been. "How can I get stronger?"

"It's not so much about strength as it is about hitting the right target with the right tool."

Frustration wiggled up her spine. It would take time she didn't have to get a lot stronger. Plus, she was so much smaller than Meric—she would probably never be able to exert the kind of power he could.

"And you probably won't need to fight anyway," he added. "This is just a precaution."

She nodded once, her movement stiff.

He hesitated, perhaps considering suggesting again that she didn't need to do this. What she appreciated was that he'd never said she *couldn't*. Never suggested she wasn't capable.

Then he grabbed a large handheld target from a hook on the wall. "I'll show you something you'll like better." He showed her how to do a front kick, something easily used on the groin. After a few minutes of practice—once he assured her that holding the target wouldn't hurt his wounded side—she was able to hit the target and make a pounding sound fill the room.

Then he moved on to fisted strikes. He held her hand and curled her fingers to show her how to make a proper fist. There was more to it than she'd thought. He showed her several ways to use a fist to strike, and then they moved on to a few common scenarios.

"Are you okay putting your hands on my neck?" he asked.

She reached out and set her hands lightly on his neck. "I'm a lot better than when I first came here. You don't have to be quite so careful." Then she added, "But thank you for caring how I feel."

"I will always care how you feel."

She was suddenly very aware of how close they were. How his skin felt against her hands, stubbled closer to his jaw and smooth closer to his shoulders. How warmth seemed to radiate from him. Or was that from her? His scent was comfortable, already familiar, and yet it seemed to do odd things to her.

They met each other's gaze. His eyes were so dark, like a cavernous room with no light. At first, there appears to be nothing, just endless blackness, but if you're patient, let yourself adjust, you can see through the darkness.

His lips parted just slightly.

Then he stepped back.

"We'll finish this tomorrow," he said and headed for the door.

She followed him to his room. "Meric? Is something wrong?"

He turned back briefly, gave her a half smile. "I worked you too long. You should get some rest. Mentally prepare."

She reached out and grabbed his hand. "Do you really think I can rest when I have no idea what's going on with you? This is not the first time you've walked away from me. What is it?"

He faced her but took his hand out of her grip. "There's nothing you need to worry about, nothing related to me, anyway."

"Of course I need to worry about you. You're the only person I have in the world."

"I'm the guy who happened to be there at the right time. I'm nothing to you."

"How can you say that?" She reached out to take his hand again, but he pulled away. "Sometimes it doesn't matter how short a time you've known someone. You're important to me—and I trust you."

"You shouldn't trust me."

"Why?"

He just stood there with that cold expression of his.

"Meric."

Several more seconds passed.

Finally, he spoke, but his tone threw her off. She'd expected cold or maybe even harsh, not a soft murmur. "Please—just leave me alone for a little while."

"I'm concerned for you, Meric. I don't want to see you hurting." She shifted closer. "You're the only person I have."

"You and I are just a twist of fate. You'll leave eventually, and then I'll be nothing to you, which is what I should be."

Her throat tightened. She didn't understand why his words felt like a punch to the face. A part of her wanted to go away and hide alone in her room, yet she wanted to help him if she could—she owed him that. "You said I need to mentally prepare—to have my head straight—but there is no way I can do that if I don't know what's troubling you."

He closed his eyes and sighed, as if defeated.

She waited.

He met her gaze. "I'm attracted to you."

Chapter TWENTY-SEVEN

"I'm sorry, Liliana." He made himself stand there and wait. If she attacked him, he'd let her hurt him however she wanted, whatever she needed.

He made himself look at her out of respect, but he struggled not to think about how beautiful she was. After all she'd been through, how she could hold herself in such a strong way, be so persistent, and still be kind too? She'd lost everything, had been molested—just shy of being raped, he was pretty sure—and tortured, had seen death right in front of her, and yet she hadn't let any of that take away who she was.

She was quiet for so long, he considered walking away. If they'd been anywhere else in the apartment, he would have. He feared she didn't feel safe in this room, a man's bedroom, though he wasn't sure how to get her out without making everything worse. A part of him hoped she'd attack him. Maybe that would make her feel better. So, he stood there.

Finally, she asked, "Is that why you're always gone?"

"I don't want you to feel unsafe." Then he added again, "I'm sorry."

"You've never done anything—"

"I won't. I promise. I've tried . . ." He closed his eyes. How had he let this happen?

"You've tried what?"

He opened his eyes. He realized what she might think he'd been trying to say. "I won't try anything with you. You have my word."

"What were you saying?"

"I've tried to convince myself you're not as beautiful as you are. I've tried to pretend." He paused. "But I can't believe a lie that big."

"I don't understand."

"I knew you were beautiful when we met, but I didn't realize how much I—Not until you were here, fully clean, no longer running and terrified. I looked at you, and I knew it'd been a mistake."

Her voice was so small. "Mistake?"

"I should've found a different way to help."

"You regret what you did?"

"I don't regret helping you." He felt like he could barely string sentences together. "I regret making you feel like this. I should've found a better way." He ran a hand through his hair. "I don't know."

A tear slowly slid down her cheek.

He shifted closer but stopped. "I'm so sorry."

She wiped the tear off her cheek with an aggressive swipe. "You haven't done anything."

"Except make you feel like this."

Quiet.

"This is why I tried to keep it from you," he said. "I didn't want you to feel disgusted and . . . unsafe."

"I don't feel unsafe."

But she must feel disgusted. All the times they'd touched ran through his mind. He knew she would replay those moments, now knowing how he truly felt, and she'd feel dirty all over again.

He made her feel dirty.

"I'm sorry." He walked into his bathroom and closed the door. With his back to the wall, he slid down to sit on the floor. He stared at the tile and tried not to feel anything.

Liliana stood there in Meric's room.

She didn't really understand what any of it meant, how it changed things. She'd had such little experience with men other than her father until they'd taken her. There hadn't been any boys her age in their village growing up. She really didn't know much about how interactions between men and women worked. Was the American culture any different in that respect?

How could he be attracted knowing everything that'd happened, that she was used?

It was all confusing.

Then she started thinking back through her time with Meric. All the times he could've taken advantage of her, starting with that first night when he'd had to carry her to bed. The nights he'd come to soothe her when she had nightmares. Just now in the gym, working so closely together. Not only had he never done anything vaguely flirtatious, he'd done everything he possibly could to hide from her. To protect her. From everyone, including himself.

And now he was torturing himself.

She knocked on his bathroom door.

No answer.

Of course he wasn't going to answer.

She cracked the door, hoping he wasn't undressing for a shower or something. He was sitting on the floor, back against the wall and knees bent to the sides, staring at the floor with his hands in his hair.

She walked in and knelt on the floor with a couple of feet between them.

He didn't look up. "I'll get you an apartment. Something with good security so the media can't bother you too much—once they figure out who you are."

"I'd like to stay here. For now, anyway," she said. "As long as you're okay with that."

He looked up at her.

Her voice came out as a whisper. "I trust you."

He hesitated. "Are you sure?"

"I'm really confused," she admitted. "About a lot of things. But there are two things I'm sure about. I want to help other people if I can. And you're my best friend." She reached over and gripped his fingers. "Those two things I'm really sure about."

He turned his gaze back down to the tile floor. And then he gently squeezed her fingers.

◼ ▦ ◼

Liliana left Meric alone for a while. She sat at the dining table reading. She'd been making herself read books in English, not the ones that were in Spanish, so she would continue getting comfortable with the language. She had to focus a lot more, and she read more slowly, but it helped.

She heard when Meric walked down the hall but didn't let herself look up. She felt how upset he'd been, how much he'd beaten himself up, and she didn't want him to feel like she was watching him. Though she was still hopelessly confused about so much, she wanted to show him she trusted him.

He set papers on the table and took the chair across from her. "Do you want to go over the information Bando gave you?"

She set her book down. "Do you mind helping? My English is getting to be pretty good, but I want to be sure I don't misunderstand anything."

His tone and expression were back to normal, but she thought she saw something more in his eyes. Maybe they'd built a stronger friendship? "I'll make sure you're as prepared as you possibly can be."

Meric meticulously went over every detail Bando had provided about the group looking to purchase a young Latina. He also added information and thoughts from his own experience, which was more extensive than she'd thought.

"What I said about going in with your head straight is important," he said.

"How do you make sure your head is straight?"

He sat back in his chair. He met her gaze for a few seconds but then looked out the large windows. "Most of the time, I have to keep anything personal out of my head. Focus completely on the task."

"Most of the time?"

He continued looking out the windows. "Sometimes, when things go bad, it helps to think of certain things. The things most important to me."

"Like what?"

He turned back to her. "It's different for everyone, I suppose."

"How do I know when I should do that?"

"When everything is sideways and the plan has gone out the window, when you need something to help you keep going, keep fighting."

"Do you ever think of God?"

He paused. "Maybe. But not directly. If that makes any sense."

"Maybe it's more like you let yourself feel his presence."

"I don't know."

She wasn't sure how he'd react to this next question. "Do you believe in God?"

He looked out the window again and was quiet.

Maybe that was too big a question with everything that was happening right now. All the stress he was under. But she wanted to ask it, hoped he accepted God's comfort, especially when she felt like she was the one person who really couldn't offer him comfort.

After a full minute passed, she realized he wasn't going to answer. Maybe she should resume reading her book and leave him to his silence?

His voice finally broke the silence. "I haven't thought about it in a long time."

She waited for him talk as much or as little as he wanted.

"When my mother died, when I was close to starving or when

someone tried stabbing me for my shoes, when I remembered everything my mother had been through, I just couldn't see it. Where was this benevolent Being my mother had loved so much?"

"I get that. I had moments when I doubted," she said. "But there are good things too."

He looked at Liliana.

"If there was no God," she said, "if there wasn't a divine spark in humanity, how could there be any good in the world? Being self-serving is easier and in a lot of ways more expedient. So why do people sacrifice for others?" Why had Meric saved her?

He looked at her for several seconds. Then he stood. "You haven't eaten all day, have you?"

She stood to follow him. She liked to make his meals if she could—it was a tiny way of trying to thank him. She also wanted to keep this conversation going, though she wasn't sure if that was because she so wanted him to feel God's love or because she just didn't want to be alone. She opened her mouth to suggest a meal she could make, but then his phone rang.

He took it from his pocket and answered. "Yes?" He paused to listen. "You're sure it's him? . . . Any evidence? . . . Thank you for letting me know." He ended the call and turned to Liliana.

"What happened?" she asked.

"Carl Walsh. He's dead."

Chapter

TWENTY-EIGHT

"His ex-girlfriend kicked him out," Meric continued. "He was found dead at a bus station. The police are working on it, but right now, they don't have any leads."

Liliana covered her mouth with her shaking hand.

Meric shifted closer but didn't touch her. "Are you all right?"

"I didn't mean for . . . I just wanted to make sure she was safe. It's my fault."

"Whatever happened to that excuse for a man is not your fault."

"I didn't mean for him to die. I just wanted to make sure he didn't hurt her."

His voice was gentle. "Liliana, what do you mean?"

She dropped her hand and took a deep shaking breath. "I wrote a letter. To the woman he was staying with. I told her what he'd done. I just wanted to make sure she was safe."

"How did you send her a letter? How did you get the address?"

"Agent Bando agreed to send it for me."

Meric was quiet. She wondered if he was disappointed in her.

"I should've known what would happen," she said.

His voice was still gentle. "How could you have possibly known that? All you were thinking about was keeping that woman safe. There is *nothing* wrong with that. The reason he's dead is because of what he did and who he chose to be involved with."

She felt herself start to calm.

Then he headed for the kitchen. "You need to relax for a bit. Sit and eat something."

She followed him into the kitchen. "Will you sit with me?"

He closed a cabinet door. "Are you sure?"

"Yes." She opened the refrigerator and started taking out ingredients for something simple.

A little while later, they sat to eat but didn't talk much.

"How are your dressings?" she eventually asked. He was wearing a long-sleeved shirt, so she couldn't see if he'd changed them or if there was any sign of infection. She'd worried about his holding the target for her, but she'd watched him carefully for any sign of pain and had seen none.

"Fine." He stood to take his plate to the dishwasher.

She followed. "Remember—if I'm worried about you, my head won't be straight."

He faced her and crossed his arms over his chest—the movement was more careful than usual. "Are you trying to manipulate me?"

"Is it working?"

There was a flash of humor in his eyes, and then he was serious again. "I'm fine. You have my word."

"One of Bando's people stitched the wound in your side, I assume?"

"Yes. The blade didn't hit anything major. I've had to be careful not to twist too much, but otherwise, it's not hindering me."

She figured he must have a high threshold for pain, which made her a little worried he would push himself too hard.

"Would you help me practice on the hanging bag some more?" she asked. But she wouldn't let him hold the handheld target again.

He hesitated but agreed.

The rest of the day, they worked on strikes on the bag. He didn't attempt any physical contact at all, didn't even stand close. When they were done, they agreed to start again at six a.m.

Then he went to his room, and she didn't see him the rest of the evening.

Over the next few days, they went running in a nearby park each morning before sunrise, and when Meric returned each day from the office, they worked on the heavy bag. On Friday, the day before her assignment, they went for their final run in the park.

As they jogged the several blocks toward Sam Houston Park, her mind wandered. What would it be like if this was every day? He didn't talk much to her if he could help it, and sometimes he barely looked at her, but she still found herself looking forward to this time together, to not being alone.

She noticed him glance at her peripherally.

With his black hoodie up, she couldn't see his face unless he looked directly at her. He'd said the hoodie and going out so early were to make sure no one recognized him and then realized who she was. She needed to stay anonymous for a few more days.

Once they crossed the street into the park, he paused. "Do you want to rest for a few minutes?"

She grinned, and then she sprinted forward.

His quick steps followed.

A man came running from the garden outside one of the historic houses along the trail. "Miss! Miss! Do you need help?"

She paused her running, and Meric caught up. He murmured, "He thinks I'm chasing you."

She grinned. "You were. You are dangerous, you know."

"You have no idea." The corner of his mouth quirked, a partial grin. An actual grin.

Her stomach did an odd little flip. "You go ahead. I'll deal with him." They couldn't risk anyone recognizing him.

"I won't be far." He continued down the path.

The man ran up to her, dressed in work pants and jacket. "Are you okay?"

"He's my husband. I'm fine."

He glanced over at Meric. "Are you sure? Looked like he was chasing you."

"He was. I was trying to show him I'm faster."

The man hesitated and glanced at Meric again, who'd stopped running and was watching from a distance, far enough that shadows covered his face. She had to admit Meric did look menacing, not just because of the hoodie hiding his face in shadow but also his height, lean build, and the strong way he held himself.

She smiled at the man. "I promise I'm fine but thank you so much for keeping an eye out for people in trouble." She continued forward at a light jog.

When she got to Meric, she wrapped an arm around his back under his arm and rested her head on his shoulder.

Meric stiffened.

"Put your arm around me," she murmured. "We don't want him calling the police."

He wrapped his right arm around her shoulder and gently rubbed his hand over her upper arm. They walked forward at a meandering pace. She enjoyed looking at the historic sites in this park when they went on their runs. They passed the Yates House on the right, a late-1800s house with a two-story porch and gray siding, and approached the little pond on the left.

"He can't see anymore." Meric took his arm away and put some distance between them. "Are you ready to keep running?"

"Race you around the big field." She took off past the bandstand and toward the larger of the two walking path loops. "Better keep up," she called over her shoulder.

He caught up before they made it to the larger loop, but he seemed to have to work hard at it. He kept up a fast pace, and she stayed with him. She'd grown up doing plenty of manual labor, and they'd never had a car, so running was something she was used to and pretty good at. He'd been pushing her on these runs, and she'd pushed herself even harder. She'd decided her goal with the training was just as much about putting his mind at ease, showing him she was in good shape and strong.

Once they made their second lap of the bigger loop, they slowed to a light jog and started toward the smaller loop. They passed the bandstand and took the path that cut through the middle of the smaller loop, through some trees. They were both able to catch their breaths quickly.

He kept his focus forward as he spoke. "Your endurance is good. You're fast."

"Thank you." Maybe that would help him relax.

He stopped and faced her. "If anything seems off, anything at all, don't hesitate. Just run. Run as far and as fast as you can. I'll be there."

She could feel tension rolling off him in waves. "I will."

"Promise me."

"I promise."

The ring of Meric's phone broke the silence of the park. A bird nearby rustled the trees as it took flight.

He took his phone out of his pocket and glanced at the screen. She could just see Alfred's name. He always answered Alfred's calls.

She gestured to the left, a split in the path. "I want to look at the pond."

He nodded and answered his phone.

This small pond was made from concrete and had bronze statues of foxes. The foxes looked as if they'd wandered out of the trees, one on a boulder and another sniffing the edge of the little pond. At this time of year, the plant life wasn't as green, but she liked the foxes and the boulders and the view of the historic houses dotted throughout the park.

She meandered through and draped her hand over one of the foxes before pausing to look at the Staiti House, probably the newest of the restored houses, surrounded by a decorative black metal fence. To her right, skyscrapers towered over the park.

A man came around the left side of the house. She figured he was probably a worker. She turned to the right down the path and tried to keep track of the sound of his footsteps, just in case, but he was extremely quiet.

Another man came around the other side of the house, jumped the fence, and stood in her path.

She shifted to run, but someone grabbed her from behind, one arm around her waist pinning her arms and another pressing her head firmly back against his chest with a hand over her mouth.

Her words to Meric from just a few minutes ago came back to her—*I promise.*

She scraped her foot down his shin and stomped his foot.

He lifted her up off the ground and started carrying her away, the opposite direction from Meric.

The other man followed and sneered at her. "Quiet."

She struggled and tried to make any kind of sound, but the man was strong—she couldn't get a hand free. She kicked at his legs, missed the first couple of times, but then landed a hard strike on his shin.

He cursed in her ear. "Get her legs."

The other man bent down. She threw her weight forward the best she could and kicked him in the face, the kick Meric had helped her with. He stumbled and fell.

"Get up," the man who was holding her said to the other man. "Toledan can't be far away."

They know Meric, that I'm connected to him. Who are these men?

Rage coursed through her.

She rammed her foot back and up. She hoped the fact that he was holding her up off the ground would make it possible for her to reach his groin. After a few tries, she felt her foot connect.

His breath expelled in her ear, and he cursed. "Get her legs," he growled again.

The other man was still holding his face. Blood seeped out from between his fingers.

"Now," the man holding her said.

She tried kicking his groin again, but he shifted her to his hip. She took advantage of the change in grip and struggled even harder. She found a little room for her left arm and shot an elbow back at his ribs. Then she reached down for his groin and gripped as hard as she could.

He whimpered and then called her what she assumed were some very nasty names for females.

She squeezed and twisted.

He fell to his knees. His grip relaxed enough that she was able to push away from him. She landed in the grass and quickly rolled over, ready to use her legs to kick them off her.

And then Meric was there. She couldn't see his face, but she knew how he moved. She'd never seen him run so fast. He punched the man who'd been holding her in the face so hard he went limp and smacked to the ground.

Then he faced the other man.

The man turned and ran. Meric grabbed him by the back of his collar and slammed him to the ground.

Liliana struggled to her feet. "They said your name. They knew I was with you."

He looked over at her. Then he ripped the hood back off his face and knelt over the man he'd just dropped. He grabbed his shirt in shaking fists and growled, "Who sent you?"

The man shook his head. Blood trailed down his face.

Meric pounded him against the ground. "Who?!"

"I don't know," the man blubbered. "We just took an assignment."

"What assignment?"

"Get the Latina woman who lives with you. That's all I know."

"What were you supposed to do with her?"

"Deliver her."

"To who?"

"I don't know."

"What were the directions?"

"We're supposed to drug her and then put her in a locker at a truck stop up off 45. That's all I know. I swear." He whimpered. "Please don't kill me."

Chapter

TWENTY-NINE

Liliana touched her hand to Meric's cheek. "I think he told you everything he knows. Let's go home," she said. "Please."

Meric let go and shoved the man back against the ground. Then he stood.

Liliana lifted his hood back up and took his hand. They cut through the trees.

"We'll look less out of place if we're jogging," he said.

She figured he was right, especially given the clothes they were wearing. She let go of his hand and started jogging. He stayed with her, closer than usual, and kept glancing around them.

Once they were in the building and on the elevator, Meric dropped his hood and looked at her. "Are you all right? Did they hurt you?"

"I'm fine." She was pretty sure, anyway.

He took out his phone and dialed. She assumed the person on the other end of the line was Bando. He explained what had just happened.

The elevator doors opened, and they walked into Meric's apartment.

"She's right here." Meric pressed the speakerphone button.

"Liliana," Bando said. "Are you all right?"

"I'm fine." She was starting to feel like she actually was. She'd fought back successfully, and thanks to working with Meric, she felt more confident in her ability to fight.

"Do you want to cancel tomorrow?" Bando asked.

"No. I'm ready."

Meric's hand squeezed the phone more tightly, but he didn't say anything.

"It's okay if you need some time," Bando said.

"I'm ready," she said again. Then added, "You said these men we're going after are actively trying to buy women. What if they buy someone else while I take time? I can't let that happen."

"We'll call you later this evening," Meric said.

"All right," Bando said.

Meric ended the call and set the phone down on the kitchen island. He shifted as if to move closer to her but stopped. "You need to go into hiding. I can make you disappear, keep you safe."

"I know you can."

"But you're not going to let me."

"Not until after."

"The buyer—the man who paid to have you kidnapped and your family killed—he's after you. I'd been hoping he was just cleaning up loose ends with Josh and Carl, but now we know he wants you and he knows where you are."

"I know."

"Then let me hide you," he said. "Please."

"You and Agent Bando both agree that the man who kidnapped me and the people we're targeting tomorrow are different people and run in different circles, right?" She knew Meric had already made very certain of that. They didn't know much about who had kidnapped her, but they knew a lot about the organization they were going after tomorrow. They were dangerous, but they weren't nearly as well buried underground.

"We're certain."

"Then I'm in no more danger than I was before."

"Please," he said. "Be reasonable."

"I'm going to disappear. Whoever it is who's coming after me won't know where I am." She paused. "And there are women sitting in bondage right now who I might be able to help. I will *not* leave them there." She took a breath. "After that, I'll go wherever you want."

"Do you give me your word on that?"

"Yes." She didn't want Meric involved in this, but she figured if he was hiding her, he would also be hiding himself. Those men had known who Meric was, had obviously watched him to know that they could find them in the park. She wanted him to disappear as well.

Meric turned and ran his hands through his hair.

"I'm prepared," Liliana said. "I fought off those men, and I would have been able to get away."

His voice was quiet, but she couldn't tell if it was from calm or defeat. "You would have."

"You'll be there for the sale," she said. "And Agent Bando will follow when they transport me."

"I will follow."

"Did Agent Bando approve that?"

He faced her. "I don't care what Bando approves or not. I will be there."

The slightest smile curved her lips. "Good."

They stood in silence for a minute or two.

Finally, she asked, "Are you going to work soon?"

"I'm not leaving you."

Relief washed through her. She didn't want to be alone right now, and she really didn't want Meric out there alone either.

Her voice sounded small. "I'm sorry I got you into this."

"You didn't get me into anything. I decided to get involved at that truck stop. I asked you to get married. You have never once asked me for help."

She turned her head to look out the window.

"Liliana?" he asked.

"Why is this happening?" She turned back to him. "Who is this, and why won't he leave me alone? Why me?"

Meric walked over to the dining table, pulled out a chair, and motioned for her to sit. She took the seat.

He pulled out another chair, set it down in front of hers, and sat. "I won't pretend or lie, okay?"

She nodded.

"It's pretty obvious now that you were specifically targeted. This person, whoever he is, wants you in particular, not just a beautiful Latina woman, but you."

"I don't understand why. I'm just a poor girl from a little rural village. I thought they'd picked me because I was an easy target."

"We shouldn't get too deep into this right now. You need to focus on tomorrow. But I think the reason you were targeted is fairly obvious."

She lowered her brows in confusion.

"You're a beautiful woman, Liliana. You have to know that."

She studied her hands in her lap. This wasn't something she liked to think about. "There are a lot of women."

"I've never seen a more beautiful woman." He took a slow breath. "I can usually block physical attraction out of my mind. But with you . . . You're the exception." He sighed.

She looked up. "I don't understand."

"I know you don't. And you probably never will." Then he added, "And I promise you I will never ask anything of you. I will always treat you honorably."

"I trust you."

"I will do everything possible never to break that trust."

She had so many more questions and thoughts to ponder, but she shoved them to the back of her mind.

"Let's focus on tomorrow," he said.

She straightened her posture. "Will you help me review the plan again?"

Meric called Alfred and told him he wasn't coming in to work.

Then he went and got the papers out of his safe and laid everything out on the dining table.

They went over every intricate detail. He answered every question she could think of, even if it was a little silly or probably irrelevant. He treated her every thought seriously.

Eventually they ordered food, and then continued working on the couch, with the contents of the file spread out on the glass coffee table. The conversation veered a few times, but Meric always brought it back.

At some point in the evening, she fell asleep on the fluffy white couch.

She woke before sunrise. It took her a few seconds to remember how she'd fallen asleep on the couch and what was happening today. There was a soft blanket on her—she assumed Meric had done that.

She noticed Meric on the chair next to the couch. He was staring at the papers on the table, or more like staring through them.

Her voice was muted and a bit raspy. "Did you sleep?"

He blinked and looked over at her. Then he stood and walked to the kitchen.

The morning passed quietly.

At noon, she changed into the outfit Meric had helped pick out. The person they'd communicated with had requested she be cleaned up and presentable. The outfit was very fitted but also covered her well—jeans that were basically spandex and a long-sleeved top that showed peeps of skin in an artful, if not tactful, way. Meric had said the outfit would work and wouldn't look out of place, but she had the feeling he'd pushed the limits as much as he could for the sake of her comfort.

Meric grabbed a bag from his safe, as well as the papers, and they headed down to the car Bando had left for them in the garage.

Meric pulled to a stop and turned off the engine.

"This is where the meeting is?" Liliana asked. It was a run-down house in a dilapidated area of town. The gray paint was peeling and chipped, the roof shingles were falling off, and the wood porch post was so crooked she wasn't sure how it was still holding up the roof. He'd parked in what had once been a gravel driveway on the side of the house.

"Not a lot of cameras or nosy neighbors in a neighborhood like this." Meric reached into the back seat and grabbed the bag he'd brought.

"A bag to put the money in?" she asked.

"That too." He took a mask out of the bag, one that would cover his entire head and neck, as well as gloves.

"To keep you anonymous," she surmised. She was glad he'd be completely protected.

"Are you ready?"

"You said Bando checked the camera already?" She still wasn't sure she could believe there was a camera in the one button at the neck of her shirt.

He glanced at his phone screen. "He's parked a block over." A text came through, and Meric smirked and held the phone up for Liliana to see. It was a text from Agent Bando: "Tell her I see and hear, so please no touchy feely stuff."

She nodded. Then she reached back to check her hair again, making sure it was in a secure braid so it wouldn't get in the camera's way.

"He might require you to pull your hair down." Meric's voice was cautious, like he was waiting for her to start freaking out as what she was about to do became more real.

She strengthened her posture and buried her fear deep in her gut. This was too important. There were women out there who needed her to be strong today. Tomorrow, she might break down, but not today.

"It's time." Meric pulled on the hooded mask. There weren't

eyeholes—instead there was very thin fabric over his eyes, thin enough for him to see, apparently, but she could no longer see his skin tone or eye color. He slid on the sleek black leather gloves and then stood from the car.

She followed.

In his perfectly tailored black suit, the mask, and gloves, he looked oddly polished, but even more menacing than he had in his hoodie in the park. He walked around the car to her and spoke in a low voice. "I have to treat you differently now."

She nodded. "I know. I'm ready."

"I just want you to remember this isn't me."

She gave his hand a quick squeeze.

He held her arm just above the elbow and guided her to the back door of the house. She tried to pretend he was dragging her, though his grip was gentle.

"Does he speak Spanish?" she whispered.

He responded in Spanish, but his tone was hard, like he was rebuking her. "We don't believe so, based on our research."

She nodded. It was so odd his talking to her with that tone. It made her realize more clearly what he normally sounded like when he spoke to her, how different from when he talked to other people. When they'd met, she'd thought his tone was cool with everyone, including her, but now she heard the distinction. Maybe because the difference was becoming more pronounced. Because they were friends now.

They walked up crumbling concrete steps and into the back door. An old screen door creaked shut behind them. The kitchen they walked into was so grimy it made her think of what her mother's reaction would be. *Would have been.*

Emotion threatened to clog her throat, but instead of fighting it back, she let it show on her face. At least some of it.

They stood there in the kitchen not talking, Meric holding her arm. The arrangement was for them to arrive first, and then the buyer would come about ten minutes later. Meric had said he didn't trust them not to show up early, and so they stayed in their respective roles, ready.

She didn't let herself look at Meric. She was suddenly aware that it would be almost impossible to stay in character if she did. She needed to look afraid and confused, but his presence helped her feel protected and calm.

Finally, the screen door squeaked open. Meric had guided them to the other side of the kitchen, by the archway leading to the living room and the front door. He continued holding her arm but squeezed a bit more, pulling her closer to him, as a man walked in the back door.

Chapter
THIRTY

The man was wearing a mask as well, but just a standard ski mask. She could see his eyes and the light skin around them. He looked her up and down.

Disgust convulsed through her.

Meric squeezed her arm, and she perfectly understood what he was communicating—*you can change your mind. I'll get you out of here.*

"She speak English?" the man asked.

Meric's voice was low, more gravelly than his normal tone, well-disguised. "A few words here and there. Better if she doesn't know too much."

The man nodded. "I can make sure she obeys without words."

Meric's hand on her arm flexed. She swore she could feel his rage transmitting through his hand. Her rage flared as well. How many women did he have already? What did he do to them to make them "obey"? She ground her teeth. She was going to stop this pig.

"Do you speak Spanish?" Meric asked. "Or anyone in your group?"

The man shook his head. "Not necessary." Then he added, "How long have you had her?"

"Not long. She hasn't figured out she's now property. She thinks she's going to work as a maid."

The man's laugh was muffled by his ski mask. "She can do that too."

"Where's the payment?" Meric asked.

From the inside pocket of his blue jacket, the man took a bundle of cash. "Spin her around first."

In Spanish, to keep up the pretense that she didn't understand English, Meric told her, "Spin."

She did as told, and then Meric held her arm again and tugged her a little closer to his side.

"You weren't lying about the quality. I'll take her."

Meric held his hand out. "Money."

The man slapped the bundle of cash into Meric's palm.

Meric turned to Liliana. His voice remained gravelly and harsh, but he switched to Spanish. "We can get him arrested now for human trafficking. You don't have to go with him."

She made her voice sound weak, confused. "We won't get the other women out if we don't." They didn't know where he kept them.

"I can tell him I changed my mind, and then we can still follow him like we planned."

"What if he doesn't go straight there? If he doesn't have me to drop off, he might not have a reason to. And what if there are other houses with other women? I am getting them out of there."

"Let's go. Let's go," the man said.

Meric gripped her arm tighter. She couldn't see his eyes, but she could feel his gaze boring into her.

She murmured in Spanish, "I'll be fine."

"I'll be right behind you," he said. "I promise."

"I know."

The other man stepped forward, grabbed her other arm, and yanked her toward the door.

She looked back at Meric and lifted her hand slightly, telling him to stay there, to let her go. He stayed, but she could see how tight his posture was.

The man dragged her out the door, and she stumbled on the steps.

"Don't slow me down, do you hear me?"

She kept her eyes widened in confusion, pretending she had no idea what he was saying.

He led her to the other side of the house from where Meric had parked, equally as hidden from the road. The car was nothing noteworthy, just a boring beige sedan. It would be easy to lose track of.

But she trusted Meric wouldn't lose her. Bando was the one watching, the one with the badge, but it was Meric she trusted.

The man tossed her in the passenger seat and sat in the driver's seat a few seconds later. He threw the ski mask in the back seat before starting the engine and backing onto the road.

She made sure to not let him see that she took in every detail—the fact that he was right-handed, that he had a little scar on his right ear, that he had a unique way of holding the steering wheel with just his thumb, that he watched the map on his phone in this immediate area but put it away as soon as they crossed a certain intersection. She memorized every street, everything she could see, but also continued to pay attention to the man.

At a stoplight, he looked over at her in the way someone might look at a thoroughbred horse, assessing build, tone, value as a possession.

She made a decision. This guy was getting punched in the face before she was done. She had to focus not to sneer at him.

About half an hour later, he pulled into the attached garage of a large gray house on a generous plot of land. She'd imagined closer neighbors. *Not to worry*, she told herself. *Just play your part.*

She started to get out of the car, but he grabbed her upper arm and yanked her against the armrest between them. Pain throbbed in her ribs. "Stay," he growled.

I don't speak English, remember?

She remained seated while he got out of the car, tapped a button on the wall to close the garage door, and came around to her side of the car. Instead of opening the car door to help her understand, he demanded, "Get out."

She looked at him through the window with her round eyes.

"Now," he demanded.

She pretended to fumble with the door handle and got out of the car.

Now that they were alone and secluded, she kept her guard up even more, careful of the distance between them.

His phone rang. He took it out of his pocket and answered, "You'll like what I picked up this time, man. Just like you asked." He took her arm and dragged her toward the door to the house. It led to a rather nice kitchen—wood floors, shiny tile backsplash, and stone countertop—although it was filthy with trash and open food containers.

He kicked the door closed with his foot, and two other men came into the kitchen.

"Go all right?" one of them asked.

The first man was still on the phone. He nodded toward her. Both men smiled. "Nice merchandise."

She'd underestimated how difficult it would be to keep a blank expression and not kick them. Meric had helped her with technique, and now she felt quite comfortable with her front kick. She was comfortable with several techniques, but the front kick was her favorite.

The man on the phone caught her attention. "Sure you don't want me to dress her up, or rather down, first? . . . All right, no problem. Sending you a text in a sec." He held his phone out as if to take a picture. He said to his friends, "Get her positioned. I need a pic."

The man closest to her, who had skin darker than hers and a black goatee, pushed her to the side so the island wasn't blocking a clear view of the phone. She'd looked over at the darker man, and he grabbed her chin and forced her to look at the phone. Yeah, the urge to kick them was really hard to control.

The first man snapped a picture and then held the phone to his ear. "Tell me when it comes through." There was a pause. Then his expression changed as he listened. "That's an awful unusual request. We'll block off her time whenever you get here. You can have as much as you want. But until then, she's a commodity. I laid a lot of money down for this one." As he listened, his lip curled. "I'm in the services business, not in the procurement business." He listened more, and when he finally answered, his voice was raised. "All right. All right. You better make it worth it." His eyes widened. "Yeah, yeah. Just get here quick. I'm not waiting too long to reap the rewards." He ended the call and cursed, though she couldn't tell if it was out of anger or something else, perhaps a combination of emotions. Then he looked over at the dark man, who was now standing a lot closer than she liked. "Step back, man. We can't touch her."

Both men looked at him.

"What?"

"I got a buyer."

"That's not how we work," the third man, whose hair looked reddish in the light, said.

"It's a big payday, man. No way I could turn it down."

"How big?"

The first man said what sounded like a very large number, though her grasp of American currency wasn't perfect yet. Both men cursed in shock.

"We can have some fun while we wait." The dark man turned back to her and lifted her chin.

"No." The first man pushed him away from her. "He said untouched."

"Are you serious?"

"You wanna risk a payday like that? We got plenty of others upstairs."

Liliana started jabbering in Spanish about being a good maid, and she'd get this place clean so it shined. She walked over to the sink, next to which was a roll of paper towels. She tore off a handful, wet them, and started wiping the counters.

"What's she doing?"

"The guy I bought her from said she thinks she's interviewing to be a maid. She doesn't speak English."

There was a pause. She didn't turn to look at them but listened carefully, fully aware of the distance each of them was from her.

"I say let the dumb chick clean," the first man said. "We might as well get some benefit while she's here."

There was a click sound, and she could just see peripherally as the first man locked the door with a key. He shoved the key back into his pocket. She assumed the rest of the house was secured in much the same way.

The men walked out of the kitchen into the adjoining living room.

Liliana sent up a silent prayer of thanks. She'd known this wouldn't be pleasant, and she knew Bando was watching and wouldn't sit by while something happened to her, but it'd still terrified her. Her hands shook while she opened cabinets looking for trash bags.

※ ※ ※

Once he heard the car back onto the road, Meric ran out of the house while ripping off the hood and gloves. He paused at the corner to watch the beige sedan, which direction it went. Then he ran to the gray car he had waiting at the curb in front of the neighboring house. If the buyer was watching for him, he'd be watching for the car he'd driven there in, which was parked at the side of the house where they'd met. This car looked like an old worn coupe, unmemorable, but it still had a good engine. He got in, started it, and punched the gas. He knew Bando had agents following her, but he didn't want Liliana out of his sight for any longer than absolutely necessary.

The beige sedan didn't take a meandering route and didn't change up speeds, which confirmed the guy didn't know he was being followed.

Meric got closer than he probably should have a couple of times. He wanted to see through the windows that she was all right.

Out in the suburbs, the beige sedan pulled into a garage attached to a house.

Meric pulled around a corner that was blocked from view by the house next door, parked along the side street, and took a good look around. The homes in this area were older, a good amount of land connected to each one. Behind the houses was a small but dense patch of woods. He peeled off his black suit jacket and white dress shirt, leaving just a white T-shirt. Then he reached in the back seat for a worn brown bomber jacket and a tattered ball cap.

He got out of the car and headed leisurely down the sidewalk. Neither the house where Liliana was nor the house next door had a fenced backyard. As he passed the neighboring house, he could see the back of the target house—and was visible to anyone who happened to look out the window. He strolled into the woods.

He took out his phone and speed-dialed Bando.

Bando answered before the first ring stopped. "She's fine. Hang tight while we listen." Meric could vaguely hear the audio in the background.

The background noise faded, and Bando said, "There's another buyer. Offered high dollar."

"But this guy isn't a broker."

"Offer was too good to refuse, apparently. But the good news is the buyer wants her untouched."

Meric wanted to feel relief, but he couldn't quite manage it. That just meant Bando would leave her in the house longer, and he knew she wouldn't ask to be extracted any sooner than necessary. She would gather as much information as she could.

Bando filled him in on the rest of the conversation and what Liliana was doing. She'd managed to get them to let her walk around unhindered.

She is amazing.

"Where are you?" Bando asked.

"Woods in the back. I have eyes on the house."

"I'm parked a few houses down. I've got it covered."

Normally, Meric would feel comfortable with that, if he was the one undercover. But not this time. He didn't answer Bando. Instead, he found a log to sit down on and watched the house, ready to jolt into action. The constant urge to rush in there and get her out threatened to overwhelm him, but he reminded himself this was her choice. She was in control. And he trusted her.

Chapter THIRTY-ONE

They didn't talk a lot, at least not about their "business," and Liliana had no way to instigate such a conversation. So she patiently and slowly continued cleaning, all while listening intently and watching them as much as she could without raising suspicion.

"I think we should use some of the money to buy more stock."

Liliana's ears perked at the conversation in the front room. It was the first man's voice. She'd determined his name was Rick.

"We got enough. They're trouble enough as it is." That was Johnny, the dark-skinned man, she was pretty sure.

"They're gettin' worn," Horace, the one with reddish hair, said. He explained what he meant in graphic terms. "They're not gonna be worth much pretty soon."

"Think big picture," Rick said, surely directed at Johnny. "Do we want to be major players? Bring in *real* money? We need to diversify. Have a selection. That's why I've been trying to get a Latina. When you go to the ice cream shop, do you want to choose from just vanilla and chocolate? No, you want thirty-one flavors, man."

The urge to punch that man in the face continued to grow.

"All right," Johnny said. "But why would we pay for stock? Not when we can get it for free."

Meaning kidnapping women from the street and out of their homes. Just like what had happened to her. Not that buying "stock" was any better.

"I found this new pipeline. If we get stock originally pulled from far away," Rick said, "less chance someone traces them. Even better if we get it from outside the US, especially underdeveloped countries—no one's looking for them. No missing persons reports, no investigations."

"Too much risk to pull locally," Horace agreed.

Johnny acquiesced. "Yeah, I guess. It's just so much cost up front."

"Price of doing business. At least until we can set up our own pipeline." Then Rick added, "We in agreement?"

How much did Rick know about pipelines? If they could shut down the transport over the border, that could save so many. The cartels might still kidnap women for their own interests, but if they had no way to transport, that would effectively shut down their trafficking industry. At least in this country.

She wanted as much information on these pipelines, as well as the local clientele, as possible, and she wanted it before Bando came in and shut them down. She didn't want one of these pigs using that information to get themselves a lesser sentence. She wanted them to rot.

She murmured in Spanish, loud enough for Bando's Spanish-speaking agent to pick up, but not loud enough for them to hear in the next room. "Leave me here for the night. I can get more on them."

"There you are." Horace walked into the kitchen, took her arm, and dragged her toward the stairs.

She didn't fight him, but she was ready to if needed.

He led her up to the second floor, down the hall, and then up another flight of stairs. The attic stairs were unfinished and creaked under their weight. At the top was an open room with bare sloping rafters. Lining two sides of the large room were chain-link cages. He opened the door to the middle cage on the left side of the room, tossed her inside, and closed the door. Then he secured a padlock on the door.

She glanced around. There were four other women, all huddled in corners and watching him with terror in their eyes. She wavered in her resolve to stay the night. These women deserved to be freed. Now.

But if she waited, she might be able to help more.

She decided if anyone tried to touch any of the women, she'd call in Bando. If not, she'd wait and see what more information she could gather.

Horace went over to a table under the one window, tucked in the peak directly across from the stairs. He opened one door at a time and dumped bread and some kind of slop on the floor in each inhabited cage. Directly on the floor.

Once he relocked the last door, he demanded, "Eat."

The other four women slowly crawled out from their corners, picked up their bread, wiped the slop off the rough wooden floor, and ate it.

Horace stepped up to Liliana's cage and glared. "Eat."

She managed to keep her confused expression.

He pointed at the floor.

She picked up the bread—stale and moldy—ripped off a piece that was still white and put it in her mouth.

Horace went back down the creaky stairs, and she heard a lock click a few seconds later.

She spit the bread out on the floor.

"You better eat," said a weak voice on her left. "They get mad if you don't eat." That woman had jet-black skin, darker than Liliana had ever seen. Her fine features, barely visible in the fading light from the window, contrasted with her wild black hair.

"They got a highfalutin' one this time," a voice from across the room muttered. "Won't be long 'til she just like us." All Liliana could see of that woman was that she had light skin and very light hair. Even though she was tucked in the shadows in the corner by the stairs, her hair still looked almost white.

The woman directly across from the dark woman didn't look

up, just mopped up her dinner with her head down. All Liliana could see was that she had brown hair and a very small build.

Liliana turned to look at the woman in the cage to her right. Her bright red curly hair managed to catch some of the sun. It was dirty, but Liliana guessed that if her hair was clean, it would shine like a jewel in the sun. The woman glanced at her, showing her perfectly freckled skin, but said nothing.

Their own personal ice cream parlor—with as many varieties as they could get.

In each of the cages, there was nothing, no furniture, not even a blanket. Once they were done eating, the women huddled back into the dark corners.

Liliana shifted closer to the cage wall separating her from the dark-skinned woman and sat down. "I'm Liliana. They don't think I can speak English, but I can."

The woman just looked at her. Even in the dying light, Liliana could see a glimmer of fire in her eyes, buried under fear, but there.

"What's your name?" Liliana asked.

"Who you think you are?" the blonde in the opposite corner demanded.

"I'm just trying to make friends," Liliana said.

"Friends? This here, girlie, ain't no place for *friends*. Or maybe you don't quite realize where you are yet."

Liliana paused, not sure how to proceed. Or if she should. Maybe it'd been a mistake to tell them she could speak English. Would the blonde tell the men?

She looked around the room, trying to assess.

And then the small woman across from the dark-skinned woman finally looked up. Only she wasn't a woman. She couldn't be more than fifteen at the most, probably younger.

Emotion immediately clogged Liliana's throat. She looked away, toward the wall.

She thought for a long time, debated. She wasn't completely

sure of her next steps. All she knew was this was going to end with that girl's freedom. And freedom for the rest of them too.

■ ■ ■

Meric didn't sleep. He sat there in the dark, keeping watch. He wasn't even sure if he blinked. Bando had confirmed Liliana was safe for the night. A cage in an attic was not Meric's idea of *safe*. But she'd told Bando she wanted to stay, so Meric would honor that.

But he also planned. He'd observed the house closely, had brought binoculars to be able to see details. He knew the best entry point, and he'd made Bando give him the layout of the house based on what they'd been able to see. If anything seemed out of place, if he got any indication something was wrong, he was ready.

He ran through his planned assault of the house over and over again in his mind.

All night long he sat in the pitch black, as if caged by the darkness of the woods, staring at the house.

■ ■ ■

The door flew open and banged against the wall, and all the women jumped. Light had finally begun to filter into the room through the one window. Horace, the man with reddish hair, walked in with mini bottles of water in his hands. He threw one toward each cage.

Each of the women reached for their bottle, just barely fit it through the chain link, and guzzled it down.

Except the youngest girl couldn't reach hers. It'd landed too far outside her cage for her to reach. The man just watched her, amusement in his eyes.

Then he turned to leave.

Liliana started jabbering in Spanish. She stood and made motions as if sweeping the floor. She let her accent muddle her words. "I make clean. Yes?"

The other women looked at her but said nothing of her much clearer English from last night. Thankfully.

The man crossed his arms and watched her jabber. She'd seen this before in Carl—he liked to be in control, liked to watch others flailing around helpless, while knowing he had the power to help and then choosing *not* to.

"Clean. Yes?" She wanted to suggest something specific that would be more tempting—like a clean bathroom—but she wanted to be careful not to let on she knew more than those few words. "Yes?" She continued making brooming motions. Then she switched to making motions of wiping off a surface about toilet height. She looked up at him again. "Clean?"

He took keys from his pocket and walked over to her cage door.

A clean bathroom—yes, she had a feeling that would do it.

He opened the cage door, and she headed for the stairs.

He grabbed her arm and jerked her back so forcefully her arm felt like it was millimeters from being dislocated. His hand around her arm was like a vice. Holding her inches away from him, he snarled in her face. "Behave, little girl."

She widened her eyes, creating a mixture of confusion, shock, and fear.

He dragged her toward the stairs. She didn't have to pretend to stumble. Down the stairs and then down the hall, he shoved her into a bathroom.

She immediately started picking up towels from the floor.

He walked away.

She paused for a few seconds and listened. Once she was sure he was downstairs, she silently ran back toward the attic stairs. She was careful on the creaky attic stairs. Then she grabbed the water bottle still sitting in the middle of the floor and slipped it through the chain link toward the young girl.

"Take it," Liliana whispered.

The girl slowly reached out and took it.

"Don't worry." Liliana smiled at her.

"What do you mean *don't worry*?" the blonde said. "What're you playing at? Who are you?"

Liliana shifted over to her cage and spoke quietly. "Please don't tell them I'm not who I'm pretending to be."

The blonde crossed her arms.

"I know trust is a crazy idea for you right now. I get it—I've been where you are. But I found someone to risk trusting, and it was worth it. I can be that person for you. Just give me a few more hours."

She didn't answer.

"All I ask is that you keep quiet. That's all."

The blonde looked around at the other women, and for the first time, Liliana saw why she was so aggressive—she was protecting them. She looked back at Liliana and gave one curt nod.

"Thank you." Liliana turned toward the stairs. But then she looked back at each of the women. "If any of them come for you, if they try to hurt you in any way, you scream as loud as you can."

"If we scream, they make it worse," the dark-haired woman said.

"Trust me."

The woman hesitated but then nodded.

Liliana glanced one last time at the youngest girl, who was huddled in the corner. Then she ran back downstairs. On her way down the hall, she peeked in each room—she didn't see anything of interest, nothing that seemed to indicate she'd find any information by searching.

She returned to the bathroom, cleaned what she could without proper cleaning supplies, and then picked up all the dirty towels and headed downstairs. She'd seen the laundry closet by the kitchen yesterday and figured they wouldn't object to her doing laundry—and this way, she might be able to overhear something. They were in the kitchen talking about some kind of sports team.

They went on and on.

Finally, she couldn't pretend to do laundry any longer. She was pretty sure they hadn't noticed her, so she didn't start the washing machine and alert them to her presence. Instead, she slunk down the short hall. She passed a half bath and then found an office. She glanced behind her and then slid into the room and closed the door silently.

There were papers and mail strewn across the desk. She quickly shuffled through them—a bunch of junk mail addressed to "Resident." And then she found an envelope addressed to Rick Spenker. At least she had a last name. She checked the address on each piece of mail, hoping to find something other than this house's address, maybe another house where other women were being kept. But there was nothing.

She took the folded paper out of the envelope addressed to Rick. It was from a hotel in Del Rio, Texas, something about his having left something in the hotel and they were returning it to him. It must have been small to fit in the envelope, and he'd apparently already taken it out.

Isn't Del Rio on the border with Mexico? In his conversation on the phone yesterday, he'd said something about "this time," as if she wasn't the first Latina he'd procured. Had he picked up a different girl in Del Rio?

She folded the letter and stuffed it into the pocket of her jeans.

The door opened. "What're you doing in here?" It was Johnny.

Liliana produced a scared expression. "I clean. I clean."

He moved toward her. "You don't look like you're cleaning."

She shifted around the desk to keep him at a distance.

"Hey!" Johnny called toward the door. "Get in here."

Before she could get out the door, both Rick and Horace appeared.

She focused on Horace. "I clean. Yes."

"Did you let her out?" Johnny asked.

"I left her in the bathroom to clean. What's the harm? It's not like she can get out of the house. We might as well get something from her."

"What's she doing in here?" Rick asked.

All three of them looked at her.

"I clean." She tried to squeeze past them out the door.

Johnny came around the desk and grabbed her by both upper arms. "What are you doing in here?"

She looked at him with wide eyes.

He shook her so hard she felt dizzy. "What are you doing in here!" he demanded.

She looked at Horace. "I clean, yes?"

Johnny slammed her against the wall, and all the air in her lungs expelled in a gust. She coughed. *This is it. I have to get something from them. Now.*

She blinked hard, forced her eyes to refocus. She addressed Johnny in perfect English. "It's too late. We know about the other house."

She had no idea if they did have another house or if they had multiple houses, but one other house was her best guess. They weren't sophisticated, so the operation wasn't likely large, but they probably had at least one more Latina somewhere.

The men looked at one another.

Johnny slammed her against the wall again, and the sound reverberated through the house. Her vision blurred, but she kept an arrogant little smirk on her face.

Johnny picked her up and threw her across the room. She fell and banged her head on the windowsill.

The men walked out of the room and closed the door. Liliana scrambled to get up and run over to the door. The room spun around and around. She ran into the desk and almost fell again.

But she made it to the door and pressed her ear to it.

"Who is she?"

"Who'd you buy her from?"

"It was anonymous. I don't know—"

"How much does she know?"

"How could she know anything?"

"She knew about the house on Paddington."

Liliana smiled.

The door shoved open and knocked her back against the wall. Before she could get her vision to focus, there were hands on her throat.

Chapter THIRTY-TWO

Meric's eyes burned from staring at the house. His body ached from sitting perfectly still for hours, not wanting to make any sound on the chance he might miss hearing something from the house. He'd been texting Bando, but he'd abruptly stopped answering. He could've simply received a call he had to take or was giving direction to one of the agents. But Meric focused even more on the house.

If he ran in there at the wrong time and ruined Liliana's careful strategizing, she wouldn't forgive him. That was the only thing keeping him sitting here.

A thud came from somewhere inside the house. Like the sound of someone being slammed against a wall.

Meric exploded from his hiding place in the woods and sprinted across the lawn.

The framing around the back door looked old and not maintained properly, possibly rotted. He ran up the couple of steps and back-kicked the door. It flung open. He drew his gun from his waistband and walked into a mudroom.

At the door from the mudroom to the hall, he looked around and listened.

There were voices coming from down the hall, all male. He moved quickly but quietly in that direction.

"FBI!" It was Bando's voice coming from the front of the house.

If he was breaching, either Liliana had asked to be removed or she was in trouble.

The door closest to him opened, and a man appeared. Meric pressed the barrel of his gun to the man's head.

There was a crash as Bando's team broke down the front door.

"Where is she?" Meric demanded.

The man in front of him only stared with wide eyes. Another man appeared behind him.

With his left fist, Meric punched the first man square in the face. Blood splattered from his nose, and he stumbled to the side.

Meric rushed forward, grabbed the neck of the other man and pressed his gun to his head. "Where is she?"

Before the man could answer, Meric caught movement from the corner of his eye, saw Liliana—being choked. He smashed the heel of his gun across the jaw of the man in front of him, threw him to the side.

He rushed toward the man hurting Liliana, but before he could attack him, Liliana slammed her leg up toward the man's groin.

The man dropped.

Liliana gasped for air.

FBI agents swarmed the room.

Meric tucked his gun into his waistband. "Are you all right?"

She coughed and couldn't seem to catch her breath.

"Get paramedics!" Meric roared at the FBI agents.

■ ▓ ■

"I'm okay," Liliana rasped.

"Are you sure?"

She nodded. Her head pounded, and the room still spun a bit. She tried to step away from the wall, but her leg strength gave out. She stumbled.

He caught her, wrapped his arms around her, and held her against him.

She relaxed in his arms and rested her head on his shoulder,

224

let him hold her until the room stopped spinning. He smelled different, more earthy than usual, but that didn't diminish how familiar he felt. He stroked his hand over her hair.

She'd never felt so safe in her life.

She closed her eyes and let herself calm down.

She heard Bando talking, heard the cursing voices from the men they were arresting, but that was all background. What she really listened to was Meric's regular breaths.

"Is she all right?" It was Bando's voice.

She didn't bother opening her eyes, not yet.

Meric lightly rested his hand on her head. "I think so." Then he added, "What did they do to her?"

Liliana stood straight as she remembered. "I have to get them out. They must be terrified." One of the agents was walking Horace out of the office. "Wait." She took the keys out of his pocket and ran down the hall and around the corner toward the stairs.

On the way, she saw Rick being escorted out, noticed his bloody nose. Meric had taken care of her promise to herself to punch him in the face before all this was over. She'd have to thank him later.

As she swung around the newel post, dizziness made her pause. She held on to the post to keep from falling.

And then Meric was there, an arm around her waist. "Are they upstairs?"

She nodded.

"Tell me where." He helped her up the stairs.

She told him where to go, and he kept an arm around her. She was thankful he didn't insist she slow down and wait for the agents.

They made it up to the attic, and the dizziness had mostly passed.

The women were standing at the cage doors looking out curiously, but when they saw Meric, they all shrunk back into their corners.

Meric stopped. "I'll stay here. You should let them out, explain what's going on."

She went to the blonde first. She guessed the others might come out more easily if she got the blonde out. She unlocked the door and opened it. "It's safe, I promise."

"Who is *he*?" she demanded from her corner.

"He's . . ." She glanced over at Meric and then turned back to the blonde. "He's my husband. He helped get you free. He won't hurt anyone, I promise."

"I ain't never met a man who don't *hurt*."

She walked into the little cage and squatted in front of her. "He saved me. He didn't even know me, and he saved me. He's why I did this—to pay forward the kindness he showed me."

She looked past Liliana to Meric. "He don't look kind."

Liliana reached for her hand. "Just like you. Yet you've been protecting these women the best you could."

Tears filled the woman's eyes.

"You don't have to anymore."

The tears rolled down her face.

Liliana stood and helped her to her feet. They started toward the open cage door.

Bando appeared at the top of the stairs, and the blonde stopped.

"He's an FBI agent." Then Liliana addressed Bando, "Could we get some water for them? They've barely been eating or drinking."

"Of course." Bando went back down the stairs.

The blonde stayed with Liliana as she unlocked the redhead's door. The blonde helped her to her feet. Liliana went to the dark-haired woman's cage, and the other two followed. When the cage door opened, a sob bubbled from the woman's chest. The other two knelt on the floor and comforted her.

Liliana went over to the youngest girl's cage. The girl stared at her as she opened the door. Then her gaze darted from Liliana to Meric, to the other three women, and back to Liliana. She opened her mouth, and unintelligible sound came out, more of a cry.

As it struck her again how young the girl was, tears filled Liliana's eyes. She knelt in front of the girl and held her tightly.

The girl sobbed uncontrollably but didn't hug her back. "I couldn't . . . They . . ."

"It's over," Liliana said.

The girl cried.

"You need to remember one thing," Liliana whispered. "This." She squeezed her fiercely. "This right here. This is what life is about. Don't be afraid of it. Don't ever for a moment think you're not worthy."

"I couldn't . . ."

"You need something good to hold on to. Remember this, how this feels. The relief. Remember someone loved you enough to come for you. Remember you are worthy. Remember this. When things are hard later, when the past comes back in your thoughts, remember this. This right now. This moment. Remember."

The girl finally hugged her back, hugged so hard, Liliana's breaths were a little tight. But she held her back, cradled her head. The girl's voice was muffled against Liliana's shoulder, strained. "Remember this."

"When you wake from bad dreams," Liliana whispered.

"Remember this."

"When memories try to overwhelm you."

"Remember this."

"You're in control of your mind. It'll be hard, really hard. But when it gets hard, flood your mind with this. Remember how this feels, every detail." Liliana rubbed a hand gently over her upper back. "Remember that someone loved you enough to come for you."

Another sob.

"Remember this."

The girl rasped out in a whisper, "Remember. Remember."

They held each other for a long time.

Liliana whispered against the girl's hair, "Dear God, watch over her."

Peripherally, Liliana saw Meric set a bottle of water on the floor next to them. Liliana had noticed Bando slip the waters to him and then disappear back down the stairs. Then Meric stepped back away from the cage.

The girl's hold finally started to relax, and her breathing evened out.

"Do you think you can drink some water?" Liliana asked.

The girl nodded.

Liliana took the bottle of water, cap already off, and gave it to her. "Slowly."

The girl drank.

Liliana squeezed the girl's hand. "What's your name?"

"Jessa."

"Are you ready to leave this place?"

"Where will I go?"

Meric's voice was quieter than usual, surely his attempt to be gentle: "The FBI is taking you someplace safe."

Liliana looked up. He was standing near the doorway to the cage with the other women, a few feet separating them. The women huddled together, holding one another's hands.

"Can we stay together?" the blonde asked.

"Can't they go home?" Liliana asked.

The blonde said, "We ain't got . . ."

"None of you?"

"That was probably part of why they were targeted," Meric said. "They focused on targets they thought no one would come searching for."

Based on the conversations Liliana had heard between the men, that made sense. But she'd assumed they'd have families to go back to, who would help them heal.

The blonde said, "Jessa ran away from the foster system. Awiti was brought over from Africa years ago as a child and sold several times. Imogen was taken from a homeless shelter."

"What about you?" Meric asked.

The blonde's gaze snapped to him.

He returned her gaze. Liliana could see he was trying to be gentle and comforting. But he wasn't as successful as she'd seen from him in the past, when he'd comforted her.

With an arm around Jessa, Liliana helped her stand.

Meric took a step back from the cage doorway, leaving plenty of space. He was obviously being extra cautious, knew his presence there was difficult. But she was glad he was here. She wanted them to see there were good men.

"What's your name?" Liliana asked the blonde.

"She's Victoria," Awiti said.

Liliana smiled at Victoria. "That suits you. Where are you from?"

"My mama died when I was sixteen. I been working the clubs since."

Strip clubs?

"Until one of those pieces of garbage learned your story, realized you had no one, and took you," Meric said.

She looked at him. Her expression changed a bit this time. Instead of pure distrust, there was a little hope mixed in. She finally answered, "Yeah. Exactly." She turned back to Liliana. "You said he's your husband? He saved you?"

"I was trafficked too. He saw what was going on. He had no idea who I was, no connection, no reason to care. But he saved me. I was lucky. God must have put him in that place at that moment." Then she added, "There are good people in the world."

Bando reappeared at the top of the stairs. "Ready to go?"

"Do your people need to talk to the women?" Liliana asked.

"We'll do that at the safe house. I'm sure they want to get out of here."

"But they can stay together, right?"

Bando smiled. "Definitely." He addressed the group of women. "And I have female agents assigned to you. I figured that might be easier."

Victoria hesitated. "Thank you."

Liliana looked down at Jessa. "Are you okay going with them?" Then she looked over at Bando. "She's underage. Does that change anything?"

"I'll work it out with Child Services."

Victoria held a hand out to Jessa. Jessa took her hand and let herself be guided toward the stairs. Before following Bando down, they stopped.

Jessa looked back, and in a small voice she said, "I'll remember."

Liliana smiled at her.

Then the four of them went down the stairs together.

Liliana took a shaky breath.

Meric shifted in front of her. "Are you all right?"

"Can we leave? I don't want to be here anymore." Now that it was over, now that the others were safe, she felt her strength slipping.

"I think I should take you to a doctor."

"I'm fine now."

"I think—"

"I'll tell you if I get dizzy again or feel any pain. I promise." She was confident she was fine, and she really didn't want to deal with anything more right now.

He led her down the stairs. He didn't put an arm around her like he had when they'd come up, didn't hold her hand.

Several agents were still in the house searching it for anything else useful. Liliana took the button camera off her shirt and the letter out of her pocket and gave it to one of them. Then Meric led her outside to a car parked at the curb around the corner.

He drove, and she watched houses flash by out the window.

They pulled up to a stoplight.

Then she noticed Meric's hand—it shook slightly.

Chapter THIRTY-THREE

Liliana looked at Meric. He glanced at her but then focused out the windshield on the stoplight.

"You made it into the house so fast," she said. "Even before Bando. How?" He hadn't had the benefit of the camera to know what was going on inside the house.

"I heard it. Someone slammed you against a wall."

"How did you—"

"I was in the woods behind the house."

"You stayed there all night?" She'd figured he'd stay in the car. He didn't answer.

She knew he'd had to have been close, plotted the best way to get in, perfectly focused on the house. She'd known he hadn't wanted her to do it, obviously, but she'd figured it was mostly out of a sense of responsibility for her.

"I'm sorry," she murmured.

He looked over at her.

"I'm sorry I put you through that."

"It was the right thing to do." His voice was normal, strong, a little cool like usual.

She took his hand from the wheel, and she could feel the slight tremor. She held his hand in both of hers.

He closed his eyes and leaned his head back on the headrest.

"I'll go with you," she said. "Wherever you want. I'll go into hiding."

He squeezed her hand in response.

Finally, he opened his eyes and looked around at traffic before driving forward.

They were quiet all the way back to his building. She kept hold of his hand, a little surprised he didn't try to pull away.

He parked in the parking garage, and they walked into the building. Inside his apartment, she went to her room and he to his.

She paused just inside. Would she come back here, or was this her last time in this room? She'd become attached without realizing it. As she opened a drawer, she realized she didn't have any kind of bag to put anything in.

A sound behind her made her turn. Meric set a suitcase just inside the door. Then he walked away.

Is that his suitcase? What will he use?

But she didn't argue.

She filled the bag with all the clothes, toiletries, the tablet, everything he'd given her. The bag was packed full.

She walked out of the room. The suitcase rolled behind her, clacking on the tile grout lines. Meric was already standing in the kitchen with a duffel bag on the floor next to his feet.

He was on the phone. "Communication primarily via email. If you need to call, use the number I just emailed you."

She figured he was talking to Alfred. Why was he telling him to use a different number?

"I will. Thank you." He ended the call. "Is there anything you need before we leave?"

"I don't think so."

"Where's your phone?"

She took it out of her pocket and handed it to him.

He set it on the counter. "We need to leave it. Do you mind?"

"You think someone could be tracing it?"

"I'm not entirely sure what to think. I'm just not taking any chances."

She nodded. He was the only one she ever called anyway. "Do you need the tablet?"

"No. I have VPN set up as well as a chain of proxy servers."

She had no idea what that meant but trusted he knew what he was talking about.

He led her back down the elevator and to the garage, this time to his personal car, not the ugly one he'd driven this morning. He loaded their bags in the trunk, and they both got in.

He started driving.

It wasn't until they left downtown that she asked, "Where are we going?"

"A cabin in North Carolina." Then he added, "It's a long drive."

She didn't know where North Carolina was, but she was a little surprised it didn't really matter to her where they went. "How'd you get it set up so fast?"

He glanced over at her. "I set it up about a week ago."

"Why?"

"Just in case." He turned onto an on-ramp.

Had he set it up after the incident in the alley, when Barrett had come to help her?

"When can we come back?" she asked.

"As soon as Bando figures out what's going on and makes the needed arrests."

"Should Bando be focusing on this? Doesn't he have bigger things to worry about?" She'd looked up the FBI, what kinds of cases they took. This—someone targeting her—didn't seem like a big enough problem to warrant Agent Bando's attention. It was just her being targeted, and they didn't even know for sure why.

Meric didn't respond.

"Meric?"

"Whoever is behind this might be a big player."

"But we don't know that. We don't really know much of anything, not even if that guy in the park was telling the truth."

"It's getting handled."

"Did you . . . ask Bando to do this as a favor?"

"It's getting handled," he said. "I brought you some water and a snack. I doubt you ate or drank properly over the last twenty-four hours." He gestured to a bottle of water and a couple of granola bars in the console.

As the freeway flashed by, she thought about how she should be scared, how she'd known Meric for such a short time and shouldn't trust him like this, shouldn't allow him to take her away to some secluded place. But she did trust him.

But she also needed to think about contingencies. She would stay with Meric for a little while, but when it came to it, she would find a way to free him. She would not put him in danger.

She watched trees and towns pass by. So many things were different from home.

Meric stopped for gas and to grab food from a convenience store, and then they drove for several more hours. She wished she could help him drive, but she didn't know how. Her family hadn't owned a car.

It'd been dark out for a while when Liliana suggested, "We should stop at the next town."

"You can sleep. I'll keep driving."

"Did you sleep last night?"

No response.

"You need to sleep," she said. When he still didn't respond, she added, "Please."

His gaze flickered to her. Then he moved into the right lane, toward the approaching exit. At the end of the ramp, they came to a stop. There wasn't much around.

"There." She pointed out the window. "A hotel."

"A motel."

"Is there a difference?" She'd never stayed at either.

"Yes." He took a phone out of his pocket, different from his usual phone, and pulled up a map application.

She leaned over so she could look at the screen. "Doesn't look like there's much civilization for a while."

"Motels aren't as safe, generally. I want you to feel safe."

"I'm with you."

He looked over at her. She was still leaning on the armrest, closer to him than usual. Something intensified in the air between them. Maybe just because of the darkness.

He focused on the road, pressed the gas, and turned toward the motel. She sat back into her seat.

Down the road, he parked in one of the few spaces available, and they both walked into the little motel office. The place was definitely old but seemed clean.

The elderly man behind the counter looked up. His withered face brightened into a smile. "You folks needin' a place to lay your head tonight?"

"Yes, sir," Meric said. "What do you have available?"

"You're in luck. I have one queen bed available."

Meric glanced at Liliana, and she understood what he was thinking—they'd have to share a room. She nodded.

He hesitated but then turned back to the old man. "Thank you, sir." He took his wallet out of his pocket and extracted a couple of bills, as well as an ID, which had a different name on it. She wondered if that was something Bando had given him or something he'd procured for himself.

The old man handed him a key, and Meric and Liliana walked out of the office. The room number on the key was only a few doors down, so they left the car parked where it was, and Meric took their bags out of the trunk.

In the room, Liliana flipped on a lamp and glanced around at the paneling that'd been painted a cream color and the pretty paintings on the walls. The bedding was all white and looked newer, and the place smelled like fabric softener.

Meric set her bag on top of the low dresser and his duffel on the floor. "I see why the place is booked out." He took off his jacket. "We should get to sleep. I'd like to get going early tomorrow."

Liliana opened her bag and brushed out her hair. She debated between sleep and a shower. After spending last night in a cage, sleep in a comfortable bed won.

Meric opened the closet door across from the bathroom and looked inside. Then he glanced at the bed. He walked over, took one of the pillows and dropped it on the floor.

"You're not sleeping on the floor, are you?"

"Yes." He sat in the one chair, a wooden rocking chair, and slipped off his shoes and socks.

"There aren't any extra blankets." She could see the empty shelf inside the open closet from here.

"Not a big deal."

"The whole point of stopping was so you could get some sleep. You're not going to be properly rested after sleeping on the hard floor with no blanket."

"I'm certainly not letting you sleep on the floor."

A memory popped into her head of sleeping on the floor of the shack where Carl and Josh had kept her. They'd zip-tied her hands to an exposed pipe under the bathroom sink. She hadn't been able to sit or lay properly, and her body had screamed with pain. Sometimes, she still caught herself rubbing at her wrists where they'd been rubbed raw from her struggling against the plastic ties.

"We can share the bed," she said.

He looked over at her. "No."

"We're adults and friends. We're married. It's okay to sleep in the same bed."

"You know why I can't do that." He lay down on the floor and stared up at the ceiling.

She took a slow breath, and then walked over and knelt next to him. He didn't look at her. He'd said he was attracted to her, but he didn't act like it. It couldn't be that strong a feeling.

"I trust you." She held his fingers in her hand. "I'm not letting you sleep on the cold, hard floor."

"I don't see that you have much of a choice."

He had a point. She couldn't exactly force him to do anything. Instead, she lay down on the narrow strip of floor next to him.

He popped up to his feet. "What're you doing?"

She sat up. "You're right—I can't force you to do anything."

He closed his eyes and sighed. "Liliana, please."

"I'm not letting you sleep on the floor. You might as well give up now and get some rest."

He opened his eyes, and his voice was quiet. "You know why I can't."

"You've hugged me before. Even in your bed that one time."

"That was when you were upset and I could focus on just that, on trying to comfort you."

"You did it once, you can do it again."

"Liliana, I don't think you understand." His voice quieted even more. "I don't trust myself to be that close to you, lying next to you in bed."

She moved closer. "I trust you." She took his hand gently in hers and pulled him closer to the side of the bed. She pulled back the covers and moved him closer to sit. She was surprised he let her maneuver him. Finally, he lay down, and she brought the covers up.

She took off her jacket and shoes and then walked around to the other side of the bed, flipped off the lamp, plunging the room into darkness, and slid under the blankets.

■ ■ ■

Meric lay there in the darkness and tried to forget Liliana was lying next to him. Not so easily done. He kept thinking about her long hair brushed out and laying over her shoulder. It looked like a black river, perfectly calm, soothing.

He glanced over at her, at her beautiful profile and how the small amount of moonlight filtering through a gap in the curtains touched her hair, made it shine. She looked peaceful, apparently not having nightmares for once. Thankfully.

His thoughts raged, thoughts of what it would be like to really share a bed with her.

He closed his eyes. *No, she's not for you.*

He was honored he could be her protector—he needed to learn to be content with just that. That was all she needed from him. And soon enough, she wouldn't even need that.

Sleep. He knew he needed to sleep, but he wasn't sure if that was going to be possible.

She rolled over, and in her unconsciousness, she lay her hand on his chest.

He took her hand gently off his chest and placed it on the blanket between them. He tried to let go of her hand, but she held on.

He gave up and let himself hold her hand. This would have to do for him. With this little amount of contact with her, he was able to find sleep.

▪ ▦ ▪

Liliana woke to dull sunshine feebly pushing its way through the gap in the curtains. She was lying on her side facing Meric. Holding his hand. He looked peacefully asleep. She didn't want to move, didn't want to disturb him, so she lay there and watched him sleep.

She'd never had the chance to look at him this closely before. Dark shadow covered his jaw. He usually shaved every day. Unlike her father, Meric would have a full beard if he chose to grow one. His lips weren't terribly full, but there was a softness to them, perhaps only while he was relaxed like this. She'd thought his nose was straight, but now she could see a little imperfection in the angle, as if it'd been broken before. Given his background, that was probably the case. His lashes were dark, thick, and long, a pretty feature that didn't seem to fit him. But then, she suspected the Meric he showed the world wasn't who he really was.

He opened his eyes and looked over at her, as if he'd felt her gaze on him. There was a softness in his eyes, the usual cold gone.

Chapter THIRTY-FOUR

Meric abruptly stood.

He paused and glanced around the room, as if getting his bearings. Then he walked over and squatted by his bag on the floor.

"Are you ready to get up?" He continued looking through his bag.

She sat up and flipped the covers off her. "Did you sleep all right?"

"You can shower first. I'm sure you're anxious to after the experience you had."

She thought about letting him go first, but he was right, she really wanted to shower and get into her normal clothes. "Thank you." She grabbed what she needed from the suitcase and went into the bathroom.

She was as quick as possible and came back out to find Meric sitting in the rocking chair, reading a book. He stood, exchanged his book for some clothes he had sitting on top of his bag, and entered the bathroom.

Curious, she glanced down at the book he'd been reading. It was worn with frayed corners. O. Henry short stories. She didn't know who that was.

He was quick in the bathroom and came back out with his dirty clothes neatly folded. He was wearing just a white T-shirt and jeans. The sleeves pulled tight against his arms and across his shoulders. He ran his fingers through his still-wet hair to pull it back off his forehead.

Liliana looked away, focused on making sure her things were packed.

Before they walked outside, Meric slipped on his black hoodie.

"Trying to make sure no one recognizes you?" she asked.

"I should've been more careful last night when we checked in. The last thing we need is gossip of a Meric Toledan sighting."

"You were too tired last night." Though he *had* used that fake ID.

"You're probably correct."

They checked out of the motel, he loaded the bags in the trunk, and they drove down the road. He stopped at a fast-food restaurant, hood still up partially obscuring his face, and ordered breakfast. They ate as they drove.

A few hours later, he stopped to put gas in the car and to grab something to eat and drink.

And they kept driving.

It was dark again when they reached the hills of North Carolina. Following a hand-drawn map, Meric drove up a steep road crowded by trees.

After what felt like forever, he turned off on an even tighter road. They bumped along, and around a bend a cabin came into view. An actual log cabin. Meric parked in a patch of dirt and gravel.

"It's colder here than you're used to," he said.

She stood from the car and was immediately shivering. She'd never been this cold before.

He came up behind her and wrapped her in his hoodie.

She was about to argue that he was now going to be cold in just that thin T-shirt, but he was already walking up the steps to the front porch of the cabin. She followed. He took a key from the top of the doorframe, unlocked the door, and walked inside. She'd hoped it would be warm in here. It was not.

He knelt in front of a massive brick fireplace and stacked wood into it. "No heating other than the fireplaces."

"Give me the car key."

He pulled the fob from his pocket and handed it to her.

She walked back out, while pushing her arms through the sleeves of his hoodie and stopped on the porch. It overlooked hills. The moon was bright, so she could see the muted colors of the trees—reds and yellows and some bare branches here and there. The trees and hills went on forever, miles and miles. She looked forward to seeing it in the daylight.

The breeze smacked her with more cold. She wrapped her arms around herself, continued toward the car, and popped the trunk. When she walked back into the cabin with both of their bags a minute later, Meric had the beginnings of a fire going.

He looked up. "I thought you were going to sit in the car."

She smirked. He'd thought she would sit in the car with the heater running while he got the fire going. *Right.* She closed the door, handed him the key fob, and then looked around the place. It was tiny—just a couch in front of the fireplace, a row of cabinets along the side wall with a round table in front, and two doorways on the wall opposite the front door, presumably to a bedroom and bathroom.

He followed her gaze. "Couldn't find a remote cabin with two bedrooms. I plan to take the couch—it looks comfortable."

It annoyed her a little, but she decided not to argue, not with how the night at the motel had gone. Though once she'd gotten him in the bed, it'd been rather nice. She'd slept a lot better than usual.

Fire now growing, he stood. "It's a little rough. The electricity is only solar, so it's limited to how much the sun decides to give us. Sewer is septic, and water is well. Completely off the grid."

She walked over to the kitchen and ran a hand along the butcher-block counters.

"I'm sorry it's not nicer," he said.

She faced him. "I keep forgetting you have no idea how I grew up."

"I only don't know because you haven't told me."

She turned and opened a kitchen cabinet to find small stacks of plates and bowls. "We didn't have electricity. The first time I went with my mom to her job—cleaning a fancy house—seeing all the lights flip on was like magic."

She turned to face him again. He had an expression she couldn't quite read. It wasn't disgust at how she'd grown up, but maybe . . . respect? He headed toward the door on the left.

She followed and stood in the doorway while he got the fire in the bedroom going. The room was small but with a large bed in the middle covered in a quilt and several pillows. It took him only a few minutes to get the fire started.

"Are you tired?" he asked.

"I was when we were in the car. I'm awake now."

"There's some food in the kitchen. Should be some fresh food but not much."

"I'm sure we've both made do on worse." While their backgrounds were so different, there were some distinct similarities. She'd pretended not to be hungry more than once growing up, and she was sure he'd gone hungry many times.

They found some food to pick at and then sat on the couch and watched the crackling fire.

"Warm enough?" he asked.

She nodded. She hadn't taken off his hoodie. She didn't need it anymore, but she didn't want to give it back yet either.

He took his phone out of his pocket and looked at emails. She should have been surprised he had a signal all the way up here, but she knew him too well to think he hadn't planned for everything.

"Bando says they found the other house," he said.

She'd been leaned back in the corner of the faded brown leather couch, and now she sat up. "Did they find more women?"

"Several more." He looked up from his phone. "Some of them were pretty banged up, but they're okay." He looked back down at his phone and added, "Most of them have agreed to testify and also to try to identify the clients."

She took a relieved breath. *Please, God, watch over them.*

Abruptly, he stood and took her hand. "Come here?"

"What?"

He led her over to the big window to the left of the fireplace. She gasped. "Snow."

"I assume you've never seen it."

She shook her head. All she could do was stare at the big white flakes drifting down from heaven. She'd never seen anything like it. Closer to the cabin, she could see the individual flakes, but as she looked farther out over the distant trees, it was a veil of sheer white. Slow. Calm.

She leaned closer and rested her fingertips on the cold glass.

It was so quiet. Other than the flow of white drifting from the clouds, the world stopped. There was nothing ugly or sad. There was just this calm white. That and Meric's hand still holding hers.

God was in this moment.

"I'm not broken."

She didn't fully realize the whispered words had come from her lips until Meric squeezed her hand.

She looked at him, and her voice was stronger. "I'm not broken."

"I know."

She smiled a little. "I didn't know. I was determined not to let them win, not to stop fighting, but I didn't know if I was still whole anymore."

"What made you realize? All of a sudden."

She turned back to the snow. "It wasn't all of a sudden. It was a little bit every day. Every moment."

He squeezed her hand again.

Every moment. Little by little.

"No one can break you, Liliana." The quiet certainty of his voice seeped into her like the heat from the fire.

They stood there in silence, watching the quiet snow, holding hands.

"Now that you're healing"—Meric's voice brought her back to the present—"what's next?"

"I don't know."

"When you were little, what did you want to do with your life?"

"I guess I really just wanted to help my family. I was looking for a job to help support us, take some of the burden off my parents."

"Anything in particular?"

She shrugged. "I was trying to find a cleaning position, hopefully one like my mom. She kept a vacation house for a wealthy family. My dad worked whatever odd jobs he could find."

"What about in your dreams?" he asked. "If anything were possible. If you don't have to think about work visas, money, anything other than what you want."

"I don't know. I've never thought about it."

"You should think about it. Take your time." He added, "You can go to school if you want, find an industry you like and start working, start a nonprofit, volunteer, write a book, explore the arts—you're so smart you could do anything."

"You think I'm smart?" Her parents had always said so, and she'd done well in the little schooling she'd had, but it felt like more coming from him, someone who'd built so much from nothing.

"I think you're brilliant. Objectively brilliant. And you're brave. And have a kind soul." He seemed more open than perhaps she'd ever seen him, no walls up, no coldness, just Meric.

Her heart felt tight in her chest. She didn't know how to respond, so she turned back to the snow.

"I want you to know," he said, "you can stay with me as long as you want."

She liked being with him. He already knew her story, had already accepted everything about her. She could be herself with him. But she also saw how uncomfortable he was so much of the time. Distant. Was that distance simply because of his past, because he didn't know how to be close to people, or was it specifically related to her? Did her presence hurt him somehow?

"Thank you for letting me bring you here." He let go of her hand and walked back toward the couch.

The main reason she'd agreed to leave with him was to get him out of danger. Whatever was going on, someone knew she was connected to him, and that could put him in harm's way.

He opened a chest behind the couch and pulled out a blanket and pillow. She took that as her cue and headed for the bedroom.

She pushed the extra pillows over to the far side of the bed and lay down. It was a waste for only one person to sleep in this huge bed, but she wasn't going to try to force the issue again. She didn't want to make him any more uncomfortable than she already had.

* * *

Meric lay on the couch and watched the crackling fire.

He'd gone too far, been too open.

He needed to keep his distance. Which wasn't going to be easy in this tiny cabin. But he had to do it.

For her.

* * *

Liliana woke early, straightened the bedding, and walked quietly out to make some tea. She'd noticed Meric liked tea. She wanted him to wake to that pleasant scent.

But he was already up and working on his laptop at the round table.

She put a mug of tea on the table for him and then some breakfast. Then she went outside to the porch.

As the sun rose, some warmth came with it, but only to maybe fifty degrees. She sat on a rocking chair on the porch for a while looking out over the view. The snow melted, revealing the brightness of the colors on the trees—the deepest reds and the brightest yellows mixed with oranges and browns.

She sat on the porch for a long time, thinking.

Around lunchtime, she went back in, made something simple, and set a plate on the table for Meric.

"Thank you." He continued typing.

She grabbed a book from one of the narrow bookshelves flanking the fireplace in the bedroom. The books were more evidence of the amount of preparation Meric had put into this place. The books ranged in subject, but were all things she was interested in, and some of them were in Spanish. Apparently, he'd noticed that even though being fluent in English was important to her, sometimes she just wanted to relax into a pretty story in her native language. She sat on the couch in the main room and read for a while.

This was so different. He still ignored her like usual, but now he did it while they were in the same room.

Maybe *ignored* wasn't the right word. She was sure that she caught him watching her several times, but he didn't speak to her.

Finally, as the sun began fading, she asked, "Everything okay at work?"

"I'm sorry I'm so absorbed. I have a deal I'm working on out in California. It's proving to be tricky." He resumed typing.

She got up to find something to make for dinner. He said something about her not needing to feed him, but he did eat what she put on the table for him. He mentioned the time difference between North Carolina and California, that the other coast was still in the middle of the workday, and kept working.

She'd hoped maybe they could talk a little more tonight, like they had last night, but when he finally closed his laptop, he grabbed the blanket and pillow out of the trunk and lay down on the couch. She went into the bedroom.

Hesitant to go to sleep, she sat on the rug in front of the fire. She'd dreamt last night. That wasn't anything new, but the content of the dreams was. She couldn't remember most of the details, but she knew Meric had been there, not Carl or Josh or even Rick, Johnny, or Horace. Something about the dream made her feel on edge.

It was late by the time she finally gave in and lay down in bed.

What felt like only a short while later, she woke with a start. She jumped from bed and silently crept out to the main room. She needed to see Meric. Needed to make sure he was alive.

Chapter THIRTY-FIVE

Meric was there on the couch sleeping. Liliana tried to take slow breaths to calm herself down. The dream had felt so real.

She couldn't get herself to go back to bed, so she sat in one of the chairs at the table. She turned it to face the couch so she could see his chest slowly rising and falling.

He's alive. He's fine.

It was just a dream.

Finally, her heart rate calmed back to normal. She stayed in the chair, watching him, no matter how irrational she knew it was. The firelight danced over his features, and his breathing was even.

When he shifted in his sleep, she stood and moved quickly back to the bedroom.

Only a little while later, she heard him get up.

She took her time getting a shower and dressing. Then she went to the kitchen to make something for breakfast. There was tea and a plate with eggs and toast sitting on the counter. She thanked him and sat at the table to eat. He was already working at his computer.

The day passed the same as the previous day.

When it was time to go to bed, she fought against it. She sat on the rug in front of the fire and read. She struggled to stay awake and made it several hours until sleep crept in and abducted her.

Meric woke. He wasn't sure exactly why. He lay there for a few minutes and tried to go back to sleep. Unsuccessfully. An unsettled feeling gnawed at him.

Though he didn't particularly feel the need to use the restroom, he got up and started across the room. Anything to try to get rid of this unsettled feeling.

He noticed she again hadn't closed the bedroom door. A part of him wished she would, just to add another barrier, a little healthy distance between them. When he saw her lying on the floor, he stopped. His instinct was to pick her up, lay her in bed, and cover her in warm blankets, but that went against his personal directive not to touch her unless absolutely necessary.

He took another step toward the bathroom.

He couldn't leave her on the floor.

At the doorway, he looked around the bedroom. The bed was still made. He crept by her and pulled back the covers. Then he knelt on the floor in front of the warm fire. She was curled up on her side, facing the fireplace. The flames threw light and shadow across her face. He leaned closer to see her better. Her expression was strained, and a tear fell from the corner of her eye and crept down her cheek. She hadn't been having nightmares, at least not nearly as often and not as powerful. He would've heard. And he definitely would've noticed if she'd had one at the motel when they'd shared a bed—she'd slept peacefully that night.

He forced the memory of sharing a bed with her out of his head.

"Liliana," he murmured.

Her expression strained more.

He leaned closer, just a few inches from her but careful not to touch her, and murmured again, "Liliana. Wake up."

Her eyes opened. She looked toward the door and then stared up at him.

He shifted to get up, step back, but she caught his hand and held him there.

"I'm sorry to wake you," he said. "I think you were having a bad dream."

"You're alive." She gripped his hand in both of hers tightly.

He wasn't sure how to respond and said simply, "You're all right. It was just a dream."

"You're alive." Her voice was barely a whisper. She closed her eyes and rested her head against the floor. Her lips moved, but he couldn't hear all of what she said over the crackle of the fire. Was that a prayer? He felt like he should leave, but she didn't let go of his hand. If anything, she gripped more tightly.

Finally, he said, "You should get in bed. You'll be warmer."

She opened her eyes and stared up at him again. Tears clumped her long lashes together, and her hair was a mess all over the rug. Maybe it was the juxtaposition of the wild unkemptness and her delicate features, but to him she'd never been more beautiful.

He shifted again to get up, to escape.

"Please stay," she whispered. "I need to see you're all right."

"What do you mean? Of course I'm all right." Then he added, "Did something happen in your dream?"

She nodded, barely a movement.

She'd dreamt about him.

Before he let any ridiculous thoughts form in his head, he reminded himself he was the one steady thing in her life at the moment. It made sense he would pop into her dreams once in a while. It didn't mean anything.

"Everything's all right," he said. "It was just a dream, I promise."

"He killed you, and I couldn't stop him." Another tear fell. "I tried. I swear, I tried."

"Who killed me?"

"The buyer. He came for me, and he killed you."

He leaned closer. "A lot of people have tried to kill me, including several traffickers. I don't die so easily." He rubbed his thumb over the back of her hand. "He won't find you. I've made sure of that." His voice hardened. "And even if he did, I would not lose that fight."

"I don't want you to be hurt. Not for me."

Fear that she might run away to protect him gripped his throat. He lay down on his hip and elbow, facing her. "No one is going to hurt either of us. If we stay here, no one can find us. There is no way to trace us here. The trail of ownership goes through ten shell corporations. There are no utility accounts. Nothing to tie us to this place."

She didn't respond.

"Do you trust me?"

She hesitated.

He gripped her hand. "Do you trust me?"

"Yes."

"We're safe here."

She took a deep slow breath, and it shook on the exhale. Then another. Finally, her breath didn't shake.

He glanced at the door.

"Don't leave," she said. "Please."

His desire to be close to her warred with his determination to protect her.

She finally let go of his hand only to reach around him. Before he could figure out what to do, how to escape, they were holding each other. He pressed his cheek to hers and held her against him.

I need to let go. Right now.

But he couldn't get his body to move. He could feel her now-calm breaths against his neck, feel her hands on his back.

Please, God, give me strength. It was the first prayer he'd muttered in almost twenty years.

He managed to get himself to pull back a few inches, and he tried to think of what to say, how to come up with a way to leave.

Looking up at him, she rested her hand on his cheek and lightly brushed her thumb over his cheekbone. He'd never been looked at like this before. He'd seen attraction in women's faces, but this wasn't that. This was trust, honesty. A bond.

Everything about him melted. His body, his brain, his logic. His resolve liquified, evaporated in the fire.

He leaned slowly closer. They held eye contact. He wanted to be nearer to her, strengthen their bond.

He touched his lips to hers.

He wanted to groan with pleasure, with relief, but he managed to stay silent. The kiss was soft. She curled her fingers into his hair and held him close to her. He tilted his head, and she sighed softly against his lips.

That one small sound made blood rush through him like water from a fire hydrant.

But he remembered to be gentle, slow. She'd been hurt. She deserved someone who would be careful with her, move at whatever pace was comfortable for her. He was surprised she seemed to be enjoying the kiss . . .

He ripped away from her and stood.

She sat up. "Meric?"

He walked out of the room, over to the bathroom, and locked the door. *Please, God, forgive me.* He prayed for forgiveness over and over again. And when his mind returned to Liliana, how her hands, her lips, had felt, he prayed harder. He pulled his shaking hands through his hair and begged forgiveness.

■ ▓ ■

Liliana stared at the doorway. What had she done? Had he not wanted to kiss her? Had she done it wrong? Confusion overwhelmed her. Confusion about what had just happened, Meric's reaction, how she felt about it. Should she go find him? Would that just make it worse? She didn't want him to regret kissing her. Her first real kiss, the first one she'd given freely, which in her book counted as her first kiss.

And she'd liked it. She was shocked at how much she'd liked

it. She touched her fingers to her lips. She could still taste him. She tried to memorize it, all of it—how he'd made her feel on fire and also protected and cared for.

Even though the kiss had been soft and simple, her mind had rushed forward. Could something more grow between them?

She shook away that thought. Obviously, he didn't want that. He'd admitted to attraction, and with her pulling him close, he'd given in to it for a moment. But he clearly did not want more. That had to be why he'd pulled away. He didn't want to lead her on and hurt her, knowing he didn't want anything real and lasting with her. There was no other explanation.

She stood and silently closed the door.

Chapter THIRTY-SIX

Liliana stayed in bed longer than usual, thinking. The most logical explanation for his behavior was that he didn't want a real marriage with her, which was surely why he'd always kept her at arm's length. She accepted that. But why did he often seem to reject even her friendship? All while showing her unending kindness at every turn. She had a theory, but she knew it would be difficult to get him to talk about it.

She was finally starting to feel like she was healing, and she felt mentally clearer than she had in a long time, her mind less muddled with fear and grief. He'd helped her so much with that progress. He'd pushed her when she'd needed to be pushed and comforted her when she'd needed comfort. She was determined to do the same for him.

She walked out to the main room to find him sitting at the table, typing on his computer. There was a plate with a bagel and fruit sitting on the counter—a blueberry bagel, cantaloupe, and honeydew—all her favorites, though she'd never told him. He didn't look up, didn't acknowledge her in any way.

Not sure how to start the conversation she wanted to have, she took the plate and sat at the table. She picked at the food.

"I've read some articles about you," she said.

He glanced at her but then refocused on his computer.

"There are some accounts from women who've said they dated

you, but what they say about you makes it very clear to me they've probably never even met you."

His typing slowed, but he didn't look up.

"I figure you probably don't set anyone straight for a few reasons. One, you don't particularly care about gossip. Two, if anything, the reputation the gossip gives you probably improves your ability to help Agent Bando undercover. Three, setting them straight would mean you'd have to give interviews and create a public persona, and I know you well enough to know that's never going to happen."

He continued typing. "Is there a point to this?"

"I've read enough of those silly stories to read between the lines."

He stopped typing.

"Why don't you date?" she asked.

He finally looked up.

"I don't think you've ever dated anyone, at least not seriously," she said. "Why?"

He leaned back in his chair and crossed his arms.

She met his cold gaze and tried to emanate determination but also kindness.

"That's an unusual question," he said, "coming from my *wife*."

"We both know I'm your wife in name only." Which he'd made perfectly clear last night.

No response.

"Answer the question, Meric."

"Why would you care about any of this?"

"Just answer the question."

He stood and looked out the window, his back to her. Several seconds passed. "I'm sorry for what I did," he said. "Last night. It won't happen again."

An ache crept up her chest and throat. She swallowed to try to get it to go away.

"That's why I've tried to keep my distance," he said. "To stop something like that from happening. I should've sent you here with Alfred or one of Bando's agents—anyone but me."

She swallowed again. "But why don't you date?"

He turned to face her, and the kindness in his voice had frozen over. "Have I made you talk about anything you didn't want to?"

"You made me talk when I needed to. The fact that you're pushing back so hard on this simple question tells me it's something you need to talk about."

"Our circumstances are entirely different."

"You might be right. I've genuinely needed you. It's hard for me to admit needing help, but it's the truth. And I'm grateful."

His voice softened a bit. "You don't need anything, Liliana. Least of all me."

"That's not true. God blessed me by letting you find me at just the right moment. You specifically. I will do everything I can to repay you."

His jaw clenched. "You, of all people, know why I don't date. You know where I came from."

"You come from your mother. She raised you."

"I'm not like her!" he snapped. "I'm like him! But I will not become him."

"Of course you won't."

"You know better than anyone how easily it could happen." He pointed at the bedroom. "I took advantage of you last night."

"I kissed you back."

He ran his hands through his hair again. His arms were so strained she could see each tendon.

She wanted to comfort him, maybe lay a hand on his arm to soothe him, but she had a feeling this was not the time to touch him. Not because he would ever do anything to her but because it would make him intensely uncomfortable. She didn't understand it, but she swore she could feel what he was feeling.

Finally, he dropped his hands and looked at her. His voice was hard but quiet. "I control everything around me. That's my job.

I'm good at it. I've made millions, built companies into household names. All because I control every aspect." He sneered. "But I will not do that to a woman who simply wants companionship. I'm not capable of caring for a woman the way she deserves. A relationship should never be *controlled*."

"So, you've turned the control inward."

"That's the only way it can be. I have to control the part of me that is my father, or else I'll become him."

He turned and walked out the door. The door closed loudly behind him.

She took a slow breath. That had been difficult, but she was thankful. She had a better understanding of him, how deeply the pain of his origins went. She was determined to help him, to give back a little of what he'd given her. Now, she had to figure out how.

Please, God, guide me.

She looked out the window to see where he'd gone, to make sure he hadn't driven away or disappeared into the woods. She felt certain he wouldn't do that—he was too determined to make sure she was safe.

He was sitting on the porch steps, staring into the trees to the side of the cabin. He sat with his knees to the sides and his elbows resting on them, apparently not bothered by the cold, surely more evidence of his time on the streets where he'd adjusted to being cold.

She grabbed his black hoodie and stepped out onto the porch.

He didn't move, even as she draped the hoodie over his shoulders.

She wanted to say so many things, force him to see, but God whispered to her that Meric wasn't ready to hear any of it. The best thing she could do for him now was be there, listen if he needed to rage, answer every action with kindness—and hopefully, eventually, be there to comfort him when he was ready to accept it. She prayed that day would come, but she wasn't entirely sure it would.

She went back inside and stood at the window, watching him. A few minutes later, he pushed his arms through the sleeves but remained sitting there.

If she had to guess, he'd probably learned shortly before his mother died about how he'd been conceived. That would mean she hadn't had time to help him deal with it in a healthy way. And it would help explain why he'd refused to stay in the foster system and had opted for the streets instead. Isolating himself seemed to be his way of dealing.

And now she feared he would isolate himself from her even more.

Chapter THIRTY-SEVEN

It was over an hour later when Meric finally came back inside. She stayed on the couch, plenty of room beside her, trying to be approachable. But he went into the bathroom and showered.

When he came back out and resumed working, she had to keep reminding herself not to push him, but it was difficult.

She stayed inside all day to be near him. She didn't sit on the porch and enjoy the view. She tried reading but ended up staring at the fire.

In the evening, when he finally stood and brought his computer over to the couch, she watched him curiously.

He handed the laptop to her. "You received a letter."

She pulled her brows together but then looked at the screen. On it, there was a picture of a handwritten letter. She looked up at Meric.

"Bando sent it." He didn't sit next to her but didn't walk away either.

"Why is Agent Bando sending me a handwritten letter in an email?"

"Read it. It's worth it, I promise."

At the return of the kind tone of voice he seemed to use only with her, the knot in her chest started to loosen a bit. She turned back to the screen and read.

Dear Liliana,

Agent Bando was kind enough to tell me your name. He said he could get this letter to you. I really wanted to tell you thank you. I don't think I would've survived much longer. Some days, I still don't think I will, but then I remember. There are good people in this world. I'd stopped believing that, but you showed me. That's what keeps me going.

I also wanted to tell you we're all doing fine. Agent Bando is letting us stay in one of the FBI safe houses as long as he can manage it. It's really weird finding myself trusting a man. I hope that gets easier. Victoria, Awiti, and Imogen are getting jobs and planning on finding a place to live together. They decided it'll be easier if they pool resources, and sometimes it's easier to be with people who understand what you've been through, you know? Victoria is trying to become a foster mom so I can stay with them. Agent Bando said he'll do whatever he can to help make that happen.

Words aren't enough to express how thankful I am.

I will always remember.

Love,
Jessa

A tear fell down Liliana's cheek, and she wiped it away.

Meric took the laptop and set it on the coffee table. She wanted him to sit next to her. She wanted to hug him. But she didn't.

He squatted in front of her. "Worth it?"

She nodded, and another tear fell.

"What you did for them was amazing."

She wiped her eyes. "It's no different from what you've done. I'm sure you've saved a lot of people."

"You didn't just free them physically, you helped start the healing process." He stood and took his laptop back over to the table.

She prayed he was right, that Jessa and the others would find a way to heal. If she'd helped them heal, maybe she could help Meric heal too.

"Can I ask you," she said, "how did you start working with Agent Bando?"

He paused, as if considering whether or not he would answer. "I was too much of a pain."

"Huh?"

"I kept calling and pushing them to investigate a particular house that I believed was a trafficking site. I still have a few contacts on the street who'd tipped me off. Finally, I showed up at the FBI field office and forced my way in to see Bando."

"I bet he didn't like that."

"His boss didn't. But he listened. After looking into my background more, he suggested I go in undercover. We saved three women and arrested one trafficker and two johns." Then he clarified, "Men who'd paid for the women's time."

"How many times have you done that? They see your face, right? Won't someone eventually figure out you're working with the FBI?"

"I go in, get my eyes on things, get evidence, and then Bando waits a day or so to go in. Most of the rings I deal with have plenty of high-end clients, so I don't stick out."

"But you came in while the arrest was happening this time. When I was inside. They saw your face and know you're involved with taking them down."

"Yes."

"So, you might not be able to help Agent Bando anymore."

"I can still help."

"But not by going undercover." She guessed Bando would do his best to keep it quiet, but word would likely spread in those circles, and once it did, none of the other traffickers would ever trust him. Bando wouldn't be able to risk using him.

He hesitated. "Probably not."

She turned to look at the fire. Her initial reaction was to feel horrible. Because of her, he was now hindered on how much he could help. But then she remembered his knife wounds and felt relieved that he'd likely now be safer.

A few minutes later, she got up to find something to make for dinner.

Meric's phone rang, and she looked over. He'd received a few calls, but only from Alfred. Apparently, he hadn't given this new phone number out to any other business contacts. The calls usually stopped by evening.

"Are you certain?" Meric sounded more tense than he usually did when he spoke to Alfred. He paused and listened. "You looked into his background? You're sure?" He listened again. "Thank you very much. I'll let you know our plans." He ended the call.

"Is something wrong?" she asked.

"No." He set the phone down on the table. "They caught him."

"The one targeting me?"

"Yes. He's in custody."

"They're sure it's him?"

"Bando said yes. They found the listing on the dark web, the one advertising the job of finding you and delivering you to a locker at a truck stop. Bando arranged a fake drop, and when the buyer came to pick up, they arrested him. He was already on the FBI watchlist for trafficking."

"Did he confess? Did he tell them why he did it all?"

"He confessed but wouldn't talk more than that and then requested a lawyer."

Liliana took a deep breath and plopped down on a kitchen chair. *It's over.* She prayed this would stop the dreams of Meric being hurt and killed.

Meric remained in his chair. His gaze was directed at his computer screen, but he seemed to be looking through it rather than at it.

Several minutes passed. Liliana wondered what was next. She'd been actively trying to free him, but now she wanted to stay with him awhile longer and do her best to help him heal, though she had no idea how to do that or how long it would take. If it was even possible.

"I have a deal I need to finish up in California," Meric said.

She looked over at him.

He paused. "Would you come with me?"

Relief flooded through her. "Yes."

◾ ▦ ◾

Meric led Liliana through LAX. She seemed to be getting better at handling crowds. When a woman bumped her in a crowded walkway, she didn't jump, or at least she hid it well. He'd booked first class seats by the window for Liliana. She'd never been on an airplane, and he wanted to make sure she didn't have to sit too close to any strangers and could enjoy the view. She'd watched the landscape and clouds out the window almost the whole trip. He'd caught himself watching her and had forced himself to stop.

They stood at the baggage claim for a few minutes. Meric picked up both bags off the carousel and then led her toward the car rental counter.

He still wasn't sure why he'd invited her to come. He should've sent her back to his penthouse in Houston and come to LA alone. But he couldn't quite convince himself to regret bringing her. He was thankful that she must still feel reasonably comfortable with him, even after he'd royally messed up by kissing her, taking advantage of her delicate mental state in that moment, or else she wouldn't have agreed to come.

When the man at the car rental counter reviewed the cost per day for the luxury rental he'd booked, Liliana's eyes grew slightly wider, just as they had when he'd bought their plane tickets. She'd obviously been working to understand American currency.

A few minutes later, they were in a white Jaguar SUV with cream leather interior.

The drive to the hotel was quiet, the only voice coming from the GPS app providing directions.

As they drove into Beverly Hills, she watched the buildings, the people. He'd chosen the hotel primarily for appearances. He didn't particularly care where he stayed, but the people he was doing this deal with would care. He'd learned that if he flaunted money and power, it helped the deals move a little more smoothly. As ridiculous as that was.

And he had to admit a part of him wanted to give Liliana the best, though as she looked out the window at Rodeo Drive and fidgeted, he worried this would be too much for her tastes.

He turned into the courtyard in front of the hotel. A valet was immediately there to open her door. He walked around the car to her. She was looking up at the eight-story Mediterranean façade of the hotel.

"Mr. Toledan, welcome to The Luxley Beverly Hills. We're so happy to have you and your wife as our guests." The man in a well-tailored suit motioned for them to follow. "Please."

Liliana glanced back at the car, perhaps wondering who would park the car and get the bags.

Meric murmured in Spanish, "It's okay."

The man in the suit introduced himself as the manager of the hotel, told them about the various amenities, and then led them up to the room. Liliana looked around a lot but said nothing.

In the room, a couple of maids were just finishing putting their clothes away. The manager had surely sent two maids thinking it would be a much larger job. Neither he nor Liliana had brought much and certainly nothing that required pressing or any great care. He handed each maid a large tip, and they left.

Liliana looked around the living and dining space, furnished in traditional, dark wood pieces. "Is anyone else here?"

"No. I'll give instructions not to service the room unless specifically requested."

She nodded. Then she tentatively walked farther into the space. "Does the couch fold out into the bed?"

"There's a separate bedroom." And kitchen and study and walk-in closet and marble bathroom.

She walked over to the window with a Juliet balcony and a view of the Hollywood Hills. She did seem to like the beautiful views. Perhaps she might enjoy this trip.

"I need to buy some clothes," he said. "I didn't bring anything appropriate for business meetings."

She looked at him over her shoulder and grinned. "Jeans and T-shirts aren't appropriate?"

"I wish. But for this particular group, definitely not. Rodeo Drive is just around the corner. I was going to go buy what I need. Would you like to come?"

"Sure." She walked back across the room, and he led her out the door.

Several employees greeted them as they went back through the hotel, and then they were out on the sidewalk.

"Does the entire staff memorize every guest's name?" Liliana asked.

"No."

"Oh."

They walked a few more steps.

"If you're uncomfortable and don't want to stay," he said, "you can go back to Houston."

She smiled, a bit forced. "No, I'm okay."

"This should only take a few days," he said. "A week at most."

Her smile turned more genuine. "I'm not in any rush." Then she added, "I'll help you pick out a nice suit."

As they turned onto Rodeo Drive, he noticed how she kept her gaze forward and didn't look around much, probably trying not to look as out of place as she felt.

At the first men's clothing store they came to, he walked inside. He asked Liliana's advice in choosing clothes for a few days.

He instructed them to make the needed alterations and deliver everything to the hotel by tomorrow morning. When the clerk said the total amount, Liliana let out a little cough.

When they headed back down the sidewalk, he noticed as she looked at a few women wearing more stylish clothes and then fidgeted with her shirt, something she rarely did. Was she uncomfortable about her own appearance? She wore a simple but flattering outfit—jeans and a white tunic, no makeup, and no hair product—and yet, she was the most beautiful woman within view.

As they walked past a ladies clothing store, he took her hand and led her inside. The place was decorated in creams and pale pinks and soft fabrics.

"I thought we were going back to the hotel."

A saleswoman walked up to them, and recognition lit her eyes. "How may I help you, Mr. Toledan?"

"Please pick out some items for my wife to try on."

The saleswoman smiled. "Absolutely." She motioned toward a small couch and then walked away to begin gathering pieces for Liliana to try.

Liliana whispered in Spanish, "What're you doing? I have plenty of clothes."

"I want to do this for you. Will you let me?"

She paused and then surprised him by saying, "All right."

"Just so we're clear," he said, still in Spanish, "I think you look perfect, but I can see you feel out of place."

"I just want to be sure not to embarrass you."

"You're not capable of embarrassing me." Surely, she realized her days of being anonymous were over. She wouldn't be able to hide as effectively here.

The saleswoman came back with several items. Liliana vetoed anything at all scanty and then followed the saleswoman to a dressing room.

"Don't look at the tags," he said to Liliana. He took a seat on the small couch not far from the dressing rooms.

While he waited, a few shoppers glanced at him. He ignored them.

As Liliana tried on everything, the saleswoman grabbed a few more things, and a while later, Liliana came out holding several items.

The saleswoman took them. "I'll ring these up."

Meric walked up to the counter. "I don't need to hear the total." He handed her his card. "And please remove the tags."

"Certainly." She charged the card, removed the tags, and then wrapped the items.

Meric took the bags and led Liliana out of the store. Several of the shoppers continued to glance their way. He hoped Liliana didn't notice that they were looking at her too.

On the way back down Rodeo Drive, Liliana kept her chin up and her gaze straight ahead, surely trying to better hide her discomfort.

▪ ▨ ▪

Liliana put the new clothes away. She was glad he hadn't let her see any of the prices. She was impressed at how well he'd read her discomfort. While she did want to look the part of Meric Toledan's wife, at least to a point, she resolved to be herself and not worry about being what other people expected.

A little while later, she went with him to pick up Alfred from the airport. On the drive back, Alfred went over the schedule with Meric.

"Initial meeting with all the players tomorrow at eleven a.m.," Alfred said from the back seat.

Meric nodded while making a turn.

"You said you'd pick up whatever attire you need—" Alfred continued.

Liliana looked around the seat at Alfred in the back. "He bought some clothes earlier. They'll be delivered to the hotel by the morning."

"Good." Alfred checkmarked something in his notebook. Then he looked back up at her. "Are you coming along?"

She drew her brows together. "To the meeting?"

"The other parties are trying to make it more of a gathering than a meeting. It's at one of the current owner's homes. They keep talking about a 'relaxed organic environment.'"

"What does that mean?"

"Pretentious in a hippie skirt," Meric said dryly.

Alfred snorted.

Meric added to Liliana, "Snotty and judgmental but pretending to be the kindest people in the world."

"Sounds fun," Liliana said with mock brightness. Then she looked at Meric. "It might make you seem more approachable for them to see you have a personal life."

He glanced at her, and in that one look she swore she could see what he was thinking—he had a pretend personal life.

She laid a hand on his bicep, and heat flooded up her arm, just as it had when he'd taken her hand earlier. "I'd like to come if you don't mind."

His gaze flickered to her hand. "It won't be very interesting."

"I want to see you in your natural habitat." She was pretty sure that was the right phrase.

"You mean some Hollywood heavy-hitter's house?"

"I mean a business setting."

"You can come if you'd like," he said. "But just remember you can leave whenever you want."

Back at the hotel, they had dinner with Alfred, and then Alfred said something about checking out the nightlife. She and Meric went back up to their room. Before she could even open the discussion, he grabbed spare blankets out of the closet and laid them out on the small couch in the living area. Again, she didn't argue, though she hated how far away he was—the study and dining room separated them. She figured he hadn't booked adjoining suites to avoid gossip about sleeping in a separate bed from his wife.

Meric handed the key fob to a valet, and he and Liliana, with Alfred trailing, headed up the front walk of a mansion. Liliana could think of no other appropriate word than mansion. It was white and modern and sprawling.

Meric wore one of his new suits, but instead of being his usual black, it was a lighter gray, and he wore no tie, just a white shirt with the top button undone. Liliana was glad for her new clothes—a silky white shirtdress, flowy white pants, and sandals. It covered well and still felt like her, but it was definitely more stylish and matched the quality of Meric's suit.

The double front doors opened as they approached, held by a pair of maids.

Liliana smiled at the maid closest. "Thank you."

The young girl glanced at her but made no comment, as if not used to being spoken to directly.

From the front door, the house was open and massive, and directly ahead was a panoramic view of the ocean through windows spanning ceiling to floor. The décor was all white and glass and metal—so much like Meric's home yet completely different. This was all straight lines and blank surfaces, none of the molding and fluffy couches of Meric's home.

"Meric Toledan. What a pleasure." A woman descended a floating staircase with glass railings. She was tall and thin, wearing a yellow sundress and no shoes. Her clothes looked ready for the beach, but her face was perfectly made up, definitely not ready for the water. Her dark hair was pulled back, emphasizing how precisely symmetrical her facial features were. She stopped in front of Meric. "We've so been looking forward to meeting you. We're going to have such a lovely day."

Meric's tone was perfectly polite but a little detached. "I'm sure we will." Then he added, "Mrs. Chauvelin, this is my wife, Liliana."

"I insist you call me Rebecca." She smiled just enough to show straight, white teeth but not so much as to wrinkle her perfect skin. She turned to Liliana. "The elusive young woman who finally snagged the most eligible bachelor in the country."

Liliana just smiled, not sure what to say.

Meric went on, "And this is my right hand, Alfred Hilliard."

"Welcome," Rebecca said. Then she turned and led them to the left. "We're all meeting for brunch in the dining room."

The dining room was another expansive room with the same views of the ocean. A servant led Alfred to one end of the table and Meric and Liliana to the other. Several other people were already there. Rebecca kissed the cheek of the man at the head of the table and then took the seat to his right. She led the conversation on various topics, all centered on the Hollywood culture. Liliana knew almost nothing about any of it and so remained quiet. As she listened, she determined that Rebecca was an actress, an extremely famous one, and her husband worked in the industry as well.

After the meal, they were all ushered out to the pool. Liliana chose a seat at a table under an umbrella.

"Bored yet?" Meric murmured, leaning close to her from behind.

"Ready to watch you work your magic." She could tell he was just as bored as her and ready to discuss something of substance.

A man came up to Meric. "I have some questions, if you don't mind."

Meric faced him squarely. "Of course."

Liliana listened to their conversation. Though she didn't understand all of it, she recognized that Meric had clear answers for all questions. At the seat next to her, Alfred took notes on his tablet.

"Mama!" A little boy, maybe four years old, came running out of the house and into Rebecca's arms.

"What're you doing out here, my wild man?"

"Nursie said I couldn't go swimming."

"Of course you can go swimming. And I see you already have your new trunks on."

Rebecca's husband—whose name Liliana had gathered was William Chauvelin—came over and took one of the four chairs at the table. He smiled at Liliana, she nodded a greeting at him, and they both watched as the little boy jumped into the pool with a big splash. She glanced over at Mr. Chauvelin briefly before returning her attention to the pool. There was something familiar about him—something she couldn't quite put her finger on—though she was positive she'd never seen him before.

Chapter
THIRTY-EIGHT

Liliana woke with a start. She'd hoped the dreams would stop now that the buyer had been caught. It must be residual stress. She got up. She was getting better at handling the fear the dreams caused, but she still felt the need to see Meric and be assured that he was all right.

She walked through the dark study and dining room. As she approached the back of the couch, she could see he wasn't there. For a second, fear gripped her throat with a taloned claw and squeezed.

She glanced around and saw him standing at the open doors of the Juliet balcony off the living room. He was looking through the darkness out to the Hollywood Hills. He wore no shirt, and he was gripping the wrought iron railing tightly enough to flex the muscles in his arms and back. The moonlight reflected off his skin and showed the cut of his jaw and his angular features, but his dark eyes were all shadow.

He was a beautiful man.

And not just physically. She was just starting to realize how tortured he was. And even with all the pain he carried around like a yoke, he risked his life to save innocents. To save her. He let no one see who he really was, always hiding behind his shield of ice. But she saw him.

She loved him.

She touched her fingers to her lips as the realization flooded her, filled every vein.

Then she turned and quickly moved back to the bedroom.

Emotion hit her like an ocean wave. She realized it'd been building for some time, since first meeting him, but she'd been too overwhelmed with grief and fear to recognize it. And now it took her over.

I love him.

She sank to her knees by the bed.

What now?

"Liliana?"

She looked up to see Meric in the doorway.

"Are you all right?" he asked.

She nodded. "Yes."

"Why are you on the floor? Are you hurt?" He didn't move closer.

As she looked at him, still bare-chested, heat filled her. She thought of their kiss, how it'd felt, how he'd tasted, how he'd touched her.

She stood.

If he took just one step closer, her self-control would evaporate.

He stayed in the doorway.

"I'm fine. I promise." She lay down in the bed, though she felt so warm she feared she would cause the sheets to catch fire.

Finally, he walked around the bed to the bathroom and closed the door. A minute later, he came back out. He paused to look at her. She desperately wanted him to stay, consummate the marriage, make it forever. But she knew he wouldn't feel it was out of love; he would feel that he'd abused her.

He left the room.

She knew he might never want her affection.

She lay there the rest of the night, trying not to shatter.

Liliana was quiet, even more than usual. Meric started to worry she was ill, though she said she was fine. He tried to focus on the property tour, but he knew he was missing details he would normally catch.

He glanced back at Alfred, who was walking just behind him and Liliana. "Please take excessive pictures."

"Yes, sir."

In the complex was an oceanfront hotel, a large spa, a restaurant that extended out onto the beach to the water's edge, and about fifty-thousand square feet of small shops, all of which were connected by a common area covered in gardens and shared a parking garage. They toured the hotel and spa, with Liliana saying nothing unless a question was specifically directed at her. And was it his imagination that she was trying to avoid looking at him? Worry that she was upset with him, with something he'd done, wiggled through his mind, but he reminded himself that she'd been fine all the way up until she'd gone to bed last night. Why had she been sitting on the floor when he'd come through to use the restroom at two in the morning?

The group—all the current owners of the various portions of the complex, their attorneys, a few miscellaneous people who appeared to be assistants, as well as a few security personnel—went into the restaurant both to tour and to have lunch.

Finally, Liliana quietly said to him, "There aren't very many people here."

Certainly not compared to the rest of the complex. He switched to Spanish—he was fairly certain no one in this group was fluent. "I own a very exclusive restaurant with several locations. I plan to completely redevelop this portion of the property and rebrand it. We've been receiving an overwhelming number of requests to open a location in Southern California. It should bring quite a bit more business to the complex."

"I figured you had a good plan." The confidence in her eyes as she looked at him affected him much more than it should.

Then she looked away.

The hostess led the group to a large table set up at the back of the restaurant overlooking the ocean.

"No, no, I'm sitting next to Liliana." Rebecca Chauvelin nudged a middle-aged man out of the way and took the chair next to Liliana. Meric took the chair on the other side of Liliana and motioned for Alfred to take the next.

* * *

"Who does your hair?" Rebecca asked Liliana.

"I'm not sure what you mean." She tried not to sound like an idiot.

Rebecca smiled. "Who cuts it, styles it, does whatever magic it takes to get it to look like that?"

"I wash it." She didn't want to say that her mother had always trimmed her hair—she still didn't like talking about her family with anyone. Except Meric.

"Wait, you *only* wash it?"

"And brush it."

Rebecca gave a little laugh.

Liliana folded her hands in her lap.

Rebecca touched Liliana's arm. "Oh, please don't be self-conscious. I'm just a little jealous. I have to do a lot more than wash my hair to get it to look like this."

"It's beautiful." Her hair was long, though not as long as Liliana's, and it was dark and wavy like hers.

"Nope, you're not forgiven." Rebecca grinned as she picked up the menu. A few seconds later, she set it down and addressed a woman across the table. "Why does this place not have Pavillon Blanc du Château Margaux?"

"I don't know," the woman answered. "I'll have to look into it."

Liliana assumed the woman was the current owner of the restaurant.

The waitress came by and took the drink orders.

"How are you enjoying our little town, Liliana?"

Liliana looked up and realized the man seated next to the restaurant owner was addressing her. "I haven't seen much of it yet, but it seems nice." Way over the top, but pretty.

"Well, we should rectify that." He smiled, and the corners of his eyes crinkled a bit. She guessed he was in his fifties, but he was dressed much younger, trendy but not ridiculous. She'd been trying to remember everyone's names—she was pretty sure he was Richard something-or-other, an actor.

"I'll have to see how much time Meric has for sightseeing."

"Of course."

There was more meaning hidden in those words, but she wasn't sure what exactly.

Rebecca leaned forward, and Liliana realized she was looking around her at Meric. Listening to the conversation he was having? She seemed to be watching him pretty closely, but not the other people he was talking to.

"Oh my gosh, it's Rebecca Chauvelin!"

One of the security personnel shifted to move closer to Rebecca, but he stopped when she held up her hand. She smiled over at a couple of young women approaching the table. One was blonde and the other had auburn hair.

"Can I get a picture?" the blonde asked Rebecca.

Rebecca's smile was gracious, warm. "Of course. Come here." She stood, and the blonde leaned in close to her and took a picture of them both with her phone.

Then Rebecca glanced over at the auburn-haired girl.

But that girl wasn't looking at her. "Mr. Toledan, I'm a huge fan."

He turned in his chair and looked at her. He didn't smile like Rebecca, but Liliana saw the effort he put forth to appear more friendly.

As the young woman got a full view of his face, she paused. "Um

. . . could I . . . I mean, would you mind if . . ." She swallowed and tucked her hair behind her ear. "Could I get a picture with you?"

Meric continued to try to be more social than was natural for him. She knew that wasn't his actual friendly tone, or at least that wasn't how he sounded with her when they were alone. "I'm sure there are several much more interesting people at this table who would be happy to take a picture."

The girl's smile wobbled. She didn't look upset, more like his response served only to make her more enamored. Finally, she blinked and turned to Rebecca. "Mrs. Chauvelin, could I get a picture?"

"Of course." Rebecca struck the same pose as she had with the blonde.

Both girls also asked for a picture with Richard, across the table, whom they addressed as Mr. Blake. Liliana was pretty sure those were the only two actors at the table. Rebecca's husband was some kind of producer or something. The woman who owned the restaurant was the daughter of a famous actor but apparently not well-known herself.

As both girls posed with Richard, one on either side of him with his arms around them both, Liliana noticed Rebecca look over at Meric again, a more prolonged gaze this time.

Then, just as suddenly, Rebecca's expression changed, and she returned her attention to Liliana with a smile. "You have to tell me all about Mexico. I have a part coming up, and I really want to understand the culture."

Liliana answered her questions. As they talked, Liliana noticed Rebecca's gaze flicker to Meric more than once. Was she attracted to him?

A waiter—or was he a busboy—came up to the table. "Excuse. Uh, who order de, uh, de Esprite?"

Everyone just looked at him, surely not understanding.

Meric asked him to repeat himself in Spanish.

The man looked relieved. "I need to know who ordered the

Sprite to drink. We're out. I need to know if 7-Up is all right instead." He still didn't pronounce Sprite correctly, but with the added context, it was simple to figure out.

Meric nodded and spoke to the table. The restaurant owner confirmed she was all right with 7-Up instead, and Meric relayed it.

"Thank you, señor." The man smiled broadly and left.

"Sorry about that," the restaurant owner said to Meric. "My Spanish is terrible. You sound very fluent. Where'd you learn?"

"My mother was from Mexico. She insisted I speak well in both languages."

Out of the corner of her eye, Liliana noticed Rebecca's attention snap to her husband across the table. Her husband looked over at her, shrugged, and went back to speaking with Richard.

Rebecca again looked at Meric.

THIRTY-NINE

After lunch, the group headed out to tour the shops, which was the part of the property Richard Blake owned. Most of the shops were small spaces packed with beautiful displays. Liliana let herself fall back so she wasn't in Meric's way. Or maybe it was because she felt worn out. It wasn't all the walking—this was nothing compared to how much she'd walked back home. This was more of an emotional exhaustion. She was constantly focused on not looking at him, pretending she didn't feel what she did.

Alfred had fallen back as well. "Everything good?" he asked.

"It's so crowded. Just giving Meric some room."

He nodded. Then he leaned closer and murmured, "I just watched Mr. Blake's last movie the other night. And now I've actually met him."

Liliana grinned. "Are you—what's the word I heard for this—starstruck?"

"I didn't think I would be, but it's surreal seeing someone in person you've seen so many times on the screen." Then he added, "But I'll die before letting Mr. Toledan know."

"Why?"

"Uh, obviously, I have to try to be as above-it-all as him. That man does not get ruffled. Ever."

She felt honored that she'd seen so much more of him, of who he really was, than anyone else saw. She grinned at Alfred. "Your secret is safe with me."

"Knew I could count on you." He cleared his throat and stood straighter. He looked like he was mimicking Meric.

She struggled against a laugh.

Meric looked over and made eye contact with Alfred, and Alfred moved through the people and displays to Meric.

"Trouble in paradise?" Richard Blake had moved over to stand where Alfred had been a moment ago.

"Excuse me?"

"Just making a friendly observation. Toledan treating you all right?"

"He treats me like a princess."

"You know an interesting fact about fairy tales—the princess is not often treated that well."

She forced a smile. "He gives me literally anything I want and is nothing but kind."

He pursed his lips while looking over at Meric.

Liliana hoped he went away.

"Why don't you let me show you around?" he asked.

Was he flirting?

She continued to force a smile. "Excuse me. I'd like to get back to Meric."

She slowly shifted through the crowd. Most people were browsing the store, which was mostly high-end tourist trinkets.

She picked up part of a conversation . . . "I wasn't looking to. But I guess it would be better for the property as a whole if there was one owner with a unified vision." It was the woman who owned the restaurant. "I've been struggling with parking and could never get the Chauvelins to loosen the parking garage regulations."

Liliana didn't want to eavesdrop, so she kept going. Meric was speaking with someone behind the counter, perhaps the owner of the business.

"Nothing serious. We had a couple of roof leaks, but Mr. Blake redid the roof a few years ago. No trouble since."

Meric nodded. "If a path was added from the condos at the next development over, do you think that might be a help to your business?"

The man's eyes lit up. "They have to walk along the road to get to us now. A proper path would be great."

Alfred jotted notes.

Meric shook hands with the shop owner. "Thank you for your time."

"Thank you for taking the time to ask my thoughts."

Meric turned to go. She fell into step with him.

"Everything all right?" he asked her.

"Of course."

"Anything catch your eye?"

She switched to Spanish. "Something caught my ear. I'll tell you later."

He lifted his chin slightly.

They moved to the next shop, a beachwear place, a little larger than most of the other shops, and Liliana again fell to the back. This time, she pretended to look around at the merchandise.

"You'd look fantastic in that. You should try it on." Richard Blake was back.

She'd been absently flipping through bathing suits. She moved on to sunglasses.

"Not nearly as interesting," he teased.

"Richard, might I ask you a few questions?" It was Meric's voice, coming from over by the counter.

Richard walked away.

She wondered if Meric had noticed her discomfort somehow. Probably not—he was very focused on what he was doing. She continued to pretend to browse.

Without someone to talk to and distract her thoughts, she kept replaying what had happened last night. She couldn't seem to control her thinking. She'd barely let herself look directly at Meric all day—she wasn't confident she could hide what she felt if she did. Maybe that was why Richard thought there was "trouble in paradise."

She sighed.

Chapter FORTY

"Are you sure?" Meric asked.

"I'm just going to hang out here and read," Liliana said.

"Call me if you need anything at all." Alfred had brought their usual cell phones with him when he'd come out to LA.

She nodded.

He hesitated but then headed out the door.

Then in the hall he paused again. He'd tried to find a way to talk to her last night, but she'd been keeping him at a distance. That was good, right?

He pressed the button for the elevator.

▪ ▪ ▪

Liliana sat on the couch, where Meric had slept again last night. She could faintly smell him on the blanket and pillow.

She'd hoped a night of rest would help, but if anything, she felt worse.

She'd kept him at a careful distance, telling herself it was the right thing to do, but a part of her kept hoping he'd break down her barriers. He hadn't. He'd seemed perfectly comfortable with the distance, just like always.

Then she stood and walked to the glass doors overlooking the courtyard. *There is something a lot more important than how I feel about him.* He needed to heal. He needed to understand he was not his father. She straightened her shoulders and refocused on why she'd come with him on this trip—to try to help him. He was the most important person in the world to her. She would put him first and do anything she could to help him understand he deserved to find someone he could love and who would love him back.

No matter how much she was hurting.

And then she would set him free, just as she'd planned all along.

She stood there, not really seeing the courtyard, and pounded her emotions into submission with a sledgehammer. Meric came first. Meric would always come first for her.

A knock at the door.

She blinked and turned away from the window. Maybe it was the hotel cleaning service? She walked over to the door and looked out the peephole.

Why is Rebecca here? The gossip rags very possibly knew where Meric was staying, which meant everyone knew, but why would famous Rebecca come see her?

She opened the door. "Is something wrong?"

Rebecca grinned. "That's an awful nice greeting."

Liliana realized she was still a bit on edge from everything that'd happened. She wasn't sure if she'd ever feel truly at ease again. She forced a smile. "Why aren't you at the meeting this morning?"

Rebecca breezed into the room. "I'm bored with all the numbers and negotiations. I want a day of fun. And who better to have fun with than my new friend Liliana?" Then she added, "Besides, maybe I can pick your brain about Mexico some more."

Liliana wasn't sure what Rebecca meant by fun, but she suspected it was different from her definition. Rebecca's idea of a good time probably didn't involve sitting in a corner reading. "I'll tell you whatever you want to know about Mexico, but keep in mind I've never been to any of the big cities. I'm sure there're some pretty big cultural differences."

"Really?"

"Is the culture in Beverly Hills different than in rural Alabama?" They'd driven through Alabama on their way to the cabin—it was *very* different from southern California.

Rebecca held up her index finger. "Point taken." Then she pivoted and took in the hotel suite. "I haven't been to the Luxley before. This is nice."

Coming from Rebecca, that compliment was probably a big deal. Liliana thought it was pretty but way too much space. Who needed a formal dining room at a hotel?

Then Rebecca looked at the couch, at Meric's blanket and pillow. Liliana thought about saying she'd taken a nap on the couch, but she didn't want to lie. She waited for Rebecca to comment.

Rebecca faced Liliana and propped her hands on her hips. "Is the spa nice?"

"I don't know."

Rebecca raised her brows. "You haven't been yet? Wasn't your flight to get here long?"

Liliana didn't see what one had to do with the other.

Rebecca glanced at the couch again and then meandered over to the glass doors. "I need refreshing after long flights like that."

Did a shower and a good night's sleep not count?

Rebecca swiveled on her spikey heels and faced Liliana. "Spa. My treat. No debating."

Liliana paused before answering. She wasn't sure she really wanted to go to a spa. Would she be expected to be in some state of undress? She would not be comfortable with that. But then she also didn't want to offend someone from Meric's deal, someone Liliana suspected had a lot of sway with the other parties in the deal. "Okay."

"But first." Rebecca snagged Liliana's hand and pulled her over to the couch.

The sudden touch bothered Liliana, but she did her best to

hide it. She sat next to Rebecca and tucked Meric's pillow a bit more to the side.

"I hope you don't mind some unsolicited advice," Rebecca said. "You're a really nice person, and I like to try to look out for nice people."

Liliana waited.

"It is so hard to find genuine friends. Especially in LA," Rebecca said. "If you are one thing, it's genuine."

"Thank you." Liliana didn't know where she was going with this.

"I just want to say you should never give up on finding a good marriage."

Liliana said nothing but braced herself. *She's figured out the marriage isn't real.* Who would she tell? Meric didn't need to deal with a bunch of journalists writing more garbage about him—they would inevitably make him the villain. And that would do nothing but reinforce his own view of himself as a barely controlled predator.

"When you have a good marriage, everything just falls into place. William and I work perfectly together. I'm the yin to his yang. I accept all his eccentricities. And having a child with him is—well, it's amazing. I would do *anything* for my son."

Liliana latched on to the motherhood aspect of her statement, anything to get off the topic of marriage. "That's admirable. I hope to have children someday." Though she knew her marriage to Meric wasn't likely to last, and she felt in her gut she would never be able to love anyone else, and she would, therefore, probably never have children. But she still dreamed.

"I mean it. Literally anything. I would kill for that boy."

"Every mother should defend her child."

Rebecca raised her brows so high her forehead wrinkled—the first sign of even the hint of a wrinkle on her face. "You agree, then?"

"Of course." Who in the world would possibly disagree with defending one's child?

Rebecca's smile slowly spread. It was different from her usual light, airy smile—kind of determined somehow—and Liliana wasn't sure what to make of it.

Rebecca jumped up. "Let's go. Off to the spa."

"Don't we need to make an appointment?"

Rebecca lifted her chin. "I am Rebecca Chauvelin. I don't make appointments." She swept toward the door.

Liliana assumed she was teasing. She grabbed her phone, along with the room key and some cash Meric had given her and followed Rebecca. She would've liked to change out of her simple jeans and long-sleeved T-shirt and into one of the nicer outfits, but Rebecca was already out the door.

Rebecca had been correct—they hadn't needed an appointment, but Liliana wasn't sure if that was because of Rebecca's fame or Meric's wealth. Apparently, he'd given instructions to the hotel manager that Liliana was to be given anything she wanted and to charge it all to the room.

Rebecca tried to talk Liliana into a massage, but she refused as politely as possible. But she did talk her into getting a facial, having her hair done, and then getting pedicures and manicures.

"I don't know. If I were you, I think I'd want a self-sponsored green card, not depend on someone else to be able to stay here. There are ways to do that."

Sitting at a manicurist's station, Liliana looked over at Rebecca. The comment had come out of nowhere.

"I could help you with that," Rebecca added. "If you want."

Liliana wasn't sure how to respond. Before leaving Houston, that was exactly what she'd been focused on—gaining independence. While she certainly didn't want to be completely reliant on anyone else, her goals had shifted a bit. She still wanted to be strong, to be able to stand on her own, but she now also wanted a partnership—two people who are perfectly able to be independent but choose to lean on each other.

"You could move here," Rebecca continued. "That would be so fun. William will find you a really good position somewhere, and you can have your own little house."

Liliana struggled to find some way to respond.

"Oh dear, I see I've overstepped," Rebecca said. "Don't mind me—I just get wrapped up in my ideas." Then she added with a grin, "Me and my good ideas."

Rebecca's manicurist asked Rebecca about the design of her nails, and Rebecca turned to her.

Liliana's attention shifted back to the manicurist painting her nails with clear polish. The woman had her head bowed close to her nails. Liliana suspected she didn't speak great English.

Liliana had read about self-sponsored green cards, and if she remembered correctly, there was no way she'd qualify. They required extraordinary skill in a desirable field or money to invest in American enterprise.

Liliana's phone beeped, and she pulled it from her pocket, careful not to mess up the polish. Meric had texted. "I'm back at the hotel. Are you hungry?"

Liliana set her phone on the table and texted one-handed. "I'm with Rebecca at the hotel spa. I think we'll be done soon."

Rebecca leaned over and read the screen. "Nope. I'm taking you for a bit of shopping first."

"Meric already took me." She smiled, hoping to get out of it without offending her.

"You don't even have a bag. How can you survive without a proper purse? I'm not taking no for an answer."

She texted Meric, "Rebecca wants to go shopping."

He texted back, "Okay. I'm going to find the gym."

"See," Rebecca said. "He can entertain himself for a while."

Liliana held in a sigh. It wasn't that the day had been all that bad, just not what she would choose.

A little while later, Rebecca's driver took them the short distance to Rodeo Drive.

■ ■ ■

Meric had hoped to take Liliana for a nice meal, maybe have a chance to talk a bit and make sure she was all right. He didn't feel on his game after the morning meetings and needed a mental break before returning emails and reviewing the final edits on the purchase contract. Perhaps his visit to the gym would help him blow off some steam and feel sharp again.

He changed into loose jeans and a T-shirt and then headed back down to find the gym.

The gym consisted mostly of treadmills and elliptical machines, but in the corner hung a heavy bag. He was a little surprised to see it at a place like this.

Thankfully, the room was empty. Most guests probably got their workouts in during the morning. He tucked his phone and room key in his back pocket and started with a jab, cross, hook combo. His fists pounded the canvas of the bag, and the chain connected to the ceiling rattled.

It'd been too many days since he'd hit something.

He felt like his concern for Liliana poured out through his fists, his sweat. He couldn't stop worrying about her, and yet he berated himself for thinking about her so much. She was healing and claiming her independence—that was a good thing, exactly what he'd hoped to help her gain.

He heard someone else walk into the room, but he ignored them.

And then someone moved closer. Too close . . .

He ducked just in time to miss getting punched across the jaw.

Chapter
FORTY-ONE

Meric backed up to give himself room to assess the situation. Who in the world would be attacking him *here*?

There were five men, all wearing suits—and ski masks. They were probably wearing suits to blend in with the clientele at this hotel, and he guessed they'd put the masks on just before entering the gym.

The lead man pulled out a knife.

Any fleeting thoughts that Meric had about someone simply wanting to rough him up because they'd taken the media stories too seriously evaporated. Could they have been sent by one of the many traffickers he'd helped arrest?

The man lunged at Meric. Meric slid back, parried the man's hand to the side, knocking him off-balance, and slammed his foot down on the man's knee. He collapsed. One down.

Meric held his hands out toward the other four men. "What's this about?"

One of them shrugged. "A job."

"What's the job entail?"

"Make it look like an accident if possible, but get it done one way or another."

This is a hit. And there were still four more men he needed to deal with.

"I can tell you one thing," Meric said. "No way you're making anything look like an accident."

The same one shrugged again.

Meric exploded forward, toward the one on his left, while shifting to the side to keep the others between him and the man. He rammed his fist into the man's face, and he crumpled to the ground. Two down.

Then he moved toward the next one, but the one on the right was already reacting and grabbed him from behind in a bear hug. "Knock him out," the one behind him said to the others.

Meric threw his head back and cartilage crunched. He felt wetness on the back of his head, surely from the man's nose breaking. The man let go.

One of the others was already reaching for him, but he pushed him back with a thrusting front kick to the hip. Then he threw a wild hammer fist at the other one who was also coming at him. It connected, but he didn't see where exactly. He was already looking over his shoulder and ramming a back kick at the groin of the man behind him. He dropped. Three down.

The man he'd pushed away came barreling at him. He was big—not easy to stop. So Meric didn't try. He stepped to the side and pushed the man to keep his inertia going straight into the wall. The thud reverberated around the room. Four down.

Meric turned to face the final man.

The man started backing up.

Meric moved toward him, glaring like a lion hunting.

"Who sent you?" he growled.

The man glanced at the door behind him.

"We're not done playing yet," Meric said. "You started this game. Time to finish."

The man turned and ran.

Meric lunged and grabbed the back of his jacket in both fists. Then he shoved him face-first against the wall. Another thud.

Meric growled in the man's ear. "Who sent you?"

No answer.

Meric slammed him against the wall again. "Who?!"

The door opened, and a security guard rushed in. He aimed his gun at Meric. "Freeze!"

Meric backed away and held his hands up.

The guard's gaze darted from him to the man still pressed to the wall and then over to the other man Meric had rammed into a wall. He was possibly unconscious but still standing due to his head being half-buried in the drywall.

Meric said calmly, "I'm Meric Toledan, a guest here. These men attacked me."

The guard glanced around again. "All five of them?"

"Yes."

The guard stared at him. He'd probably never had to deal with something like this.

"Please call the manager," Meric said. "I'll answer any questions you like."

The guard hesitated, and then he took out his phone.

Meric hoped he didn't have to tell Liliana about this. It might upset her and make her feel unsafe. But as his adrenaline started to wane, pain seared through his body. He sighed. His stitches from the knife wound had broken. He glanced down to see blood soaking through his light gray T-shirt. Great.

The manager, a middle-aged man with hair graying at the temples, rushed into the room. It took him a few seconds to take in the scene.

Then he turned to the guard and pushed his hand down, the one still holding his gun on Meric. "Put that down. This is Mr. Toledan, a distinguished guest."

The man who'd been pressed against the wall, apparently still conscious, turned and grabbed the manager in a headlock.

The manager's eyes grew wide with fear.

The attacker started dragging the manager toward the door, using him as a shield.

The guard aimed his gun. But Meric pushed it back down as he moved forward, following the manager.

"Back off," the attacker said.

"You're not getting out of here," Meric said.

The attacker cursed at him.

Meric drew slowly closer.

"Back off!"

Meric was close now. The manager stared at him with wide eyes.

The attacker shifted his head, and Meric took the opportunity to slam his fist into the man's nose. Blood splattered onto the side of the manager's face.

The attacker stumbled back and fell. Meric caught the manager so he wouldn't fall with him.

The manager stared at Meric and then at the man on the ground.

"I'll stay here until the police arrive," Meric said.

The manager nodded.

Meric turned to the guard. "You might want to go ahead and call them."

The guard looked at his phone as if just realizing it was still in his hand. He dialed.

Meric sighed again. He wanted to get out of here, but he didn't feel comfortable leaving the manager and the guard alone with these five men who could possibly wake at any moment.

Before the police arrived, Meric called Bando. Perhaps he could help keep the situation under control and out of the news.

▪ ▦ ▪

Finally, Liliana walked into the hotel room. She carried just the one shopping bag. Rebecca had said the trip wasn't ending until Liliana owned a proper purse, so Liliana had broken down and bought what Rebecca had called a wristlet. Rebecca had said it hardly counted but she'd accept it this time.

Liliana walked through the living and dining rooms to the study just outside the bedroom, expecting to see Meric working on his computer.

He wasn't there.

She supposed he might have gone to dinner alone. She wouldn't blame him, but she would be disappointed to lose the one opportunity to spend any time with him today.

She heard a sound from the direction of the bathroom. As she passed through the bedroom, she dropped her bag on the bed, and then walked through the open double doors into the bathroom.

Meric was standing at the vanity closest to the window. Shirtless. Heat started to rise up her neck. Until she realized what he was doing.

"What happened?" she asked.

He glanced at her and then went back to stitching his side. "It came open. I'm just fixing it."

"Did you work out too hard or something?"

He pulled the needle through his skin. Other than a tight jaw, he gave no indication of pain. He didn't answer her. She knew him well enough to know he preferred not to lie if he could help it, which was sometimes why he simply didn't answer questions. If it were as simple as an accident while he worked out, he'd have no reason not to tell her. Something else had happened.

She moved closer and lightly touched his hand, stopping him mid-stitch. "What happened?"

"It's nothing I can't handle." He tried to step back, but he stopped when she rested her other hand on his bicep. He met her gaze.

She thought she saw something in his eyes. Whatever it was made her feel jittery, in a pleasant way. Like when he'd kissed her. He looked away.

"I know perfectly well you can handle anything," she said. "That doesn't mean I don't want to know about it."

He didn't respond.

She carefully took the needle from his hand. "There's no way you can see properly," she said. "Tell me what to do."

"The bleeding hasn't stopped yet."

"Has blood ever bothered me before?"

He sighed, but then he said, "Just try to match the other stitches."

She lowered herself to see better and carefully pulled the needle through his skin. He didn't flinch, but his stomach tightened a bit.

The wound, which had begun healing, was now completely ripped back open, edges jagged and bleeding, though slowly.

After completing a few stitches, she looked up at him. He was watching her closely.

"How should I tie it off?" she asked.

"I can do that part." He took the needle from her and stepped back. His body flexed as he twisted to see the wound.

Once he'd tied it, she picked up the tiny scissors that were sitting on the counter and snipped the thread. Then she took the needle. "Is this from a sewing kit?"

"It did the job." He shifted to leave the room.

She stood in front of him. "What happened?"

He paused before making eye contact. "Do you trust me?"

Her voice was quiet, clear. "Yes."

He hesitated. Perhaps he hadn't expected her to answer so quickly, easily. "I ask that you let me deal with this."

"You're trying to protect me."

"Yes."

"Keeping me in the dark is not the way to protect me. You already know that."

He sighed. "You're finally starting to heal. I don't want to take that away from you."

"You'll only take it away if you shut me out." Then she added, "Someone hurt you. Worrying about you, wondering every second if you're okay, envisioning the worst possible scenarios—it'll eat me alive." And she couldn't help him if she didn't know what was going on.

He stepped back and leaned against the wall next to the tub. He rested his head back and looked up at the ceiling. This angle accentuated the precise line of his jaw, the strength of his neck, even the lovely curve at the base of his throat. But she didn't let herself admire more than that. If he saw how attracted she was to him, he might push her away. Knowing the right way to handle him was so difficult, and she couldn't afford to fail.

He lifted his head off the wall and looked at her. "I went to the gym. They have a heavy bag, shockingly."

"Good." She had a feeling hitting the bag helped him mentally, emotionally. It was a way to get all the self-hatred out.

"Several men attacked me."

She took a couple of seconds to make sure her voice was level. "How many?"

"Five."

"Did they get away, or were they arrested?"

"Arrested. I presume anyway, after they gained consciousness."

"You fought them off by yourself?"

"Yes. I think they weren't properly prepared."

"They thought the rich guy was a wimp." A part of her wanted to smile with pride at him, but she held that back. "What did they want?"

"It was just a job for them."

"Who hired them and why?"

He shook his head. "I don't know. I don't think they know the why for sure. I doubt they even know the who."

"Do you think it could be someone who believes all the things people say about you?"

"It's possible. I have no way of knowing for sure."

"Whoever it was must know you well enough to have felt hiring five men was warranted. It could be one of the traffickers you've helped arrest."

"Maybe."

"Or someone who hasn't yet been arrested. Have you been working on anyone in particular?"

"Yes."

"The one whose thugs stabbed you."

He hesitated. "If I had to guess."

She nodded once. "Are you hurt anywhere else?"

"No. I'm good."

"You should put some antiseptic and a clean dressing on that."

He nodded, and then his expression turned more serious. "I have a favor to ask."

She waited.

"I'd prefer you not be alone the rest of our trip. Would you mind staying with me?"

"Sure."

"You won't mind too much?"

She smiled a little. "Not at all." Then she added, "That means I won't get dragged on more shopping trips."

"Did you buy anything?"

"Rebecca said I had to get a proper purse."

"I hadn't thought about that."

"I should hope not. They'd have to come take your machismo card away."

The corner of his mouth pulled in. The smile even made it to his eyes. "Show me."

"You can't possibly care."

He walked past her to the bedroom, picked up the bag off the bed, and took the wristlet out. It was a pale blue textile—some designer she'd never heard of but had to be quality, based on the price. "You don't want something bigger?"

"What would I put in it?"

"What do other women put in their bags?"

"Um, I have no idea. Makeup, maybe?"

"I guess you don't need a bigger bag, then. You definitely don't need makeup."

Before she could think of how to respond, he set the wristlet on the bed. "I'm glad you bought something nice."

She took his hand and led him back to the bathroom. "Antiseptic and a proper dressing. Do we have any?"

He followed obediently and didn't pull away from her. "The manager sent something up."

She found the paper bag on the counter. "The manager knows about the attack? Does anyone else know?"

"Just a security guard. The manager agreed to keep it quiet. Not good for business."

"Did you tell Agent Bando?"

He nodded.

She found antiseptic ointment in the bag. He held his hand out for it.

"We don't need you twisting and breaking my beautiful stitches." She knelt next to him and carefully dabbed the ointment on the wound. Then she applied some clean gauze and taped it on with medical tape. She looked up at him. "Feel all right?"

He was looking at her again, not the wound. "Thank you, Liliana." His voice had lost its lightness.

She liked it when he said her name.

As she stood, she tried not to look at his bare chest, strong arms, flat stomach . . .

"Are you all right?"

She nodded, then turned and cleaned up the supplies.

He moved closer, just behind her. "Something's been off with you."

She looked at him in the mirror. "I'm fine, I promise."

"Whatever it is, you can tell me."

She forced a small smile. "You already know my secrets."

"I'm here for you. Whatever you need. Anything."

Her smile turned more genuine. "I know." She swore she could feel his body heat reaching out, enveloping her, filling her head like alcohol.

She turned to face him, focused on his dark eyes. "That goes both ways, you know. I'm always here for you."

His tone was muted. "Thank you."

Something in the air between them changed.

He shifted slightly closer, still looking at her in that way of his. She was sure of it this time—there was something in his eyes. She wanted to reach out to him; he was so close. That something in his eyes seemed to intensify. Was he going to kiss her?

His gaze dropped away from her, and then he walked out of the room.

She rested back on the stone counter and caught her breath.

Chapter FORTY-TWO

In the morning, Meric was kind as always but distant. As usual. They got in the car, and he drove them back to the Chauvelins' house. He said he was hoping to tie up the last details today or tomorrow, and then they could go home.

An older woman dressed in a black dress and white apron answered the door. She led them to a huge sunken living room overlooking the ocean, right on the edge of the cliff. The wall of two-story windows bowed out toward the water.

"Whatever you say, Rebecca," they heard William Chauvelin mutter as they entered the room.

Rebecca was looking at him with a fiery glare, but he looked back at her with such cold Liliana swore the temperature in the room dropped ten degrees.

Meric cleared his throat.

Rebecca turned and smiled, all fire gone. Liliana knew she was an acclaimed actress, but the change was startling.

"There you are," Rebecca said. "And your new bag looks so cute with that outfit."

"Thank you." Liliana wasn't sure how to behave after that scene.

William Chauvelin walked out of the room. He gave no indication of anger, not even discomfort.

"Please have a seat," Rebecca said. "We're just waiting for the others to arrive."

Meric waited for Liliana to sit on one of the sofas, and then he sat next to her, a good foot between them.

"If you'll just give me a moment," Rebecca said. "I'll have refreshments brought in." She left the room.

Liliana murmured to Meric, "That was uncomfortable."

Meric glanced back toward the wide doorway, where they'd both exited. "Very."

They waited a few minutes. Meric watched the ocean out the window, expression as impassive as ever. He didn't talk to her, didn't even look at her.

Liliana heard a small sound and looked back at the doorway just in time to see the woman who'd let them into the house walk by with her hand over her mouth. A small sob escaped as she rushed by.

"Did they fire her?" Liliana whispered.

Meric raised his brow slightly. "We weren't supposed to see their little tiff."

"Poor woman."

Rebecca had been so nice—Liliana had a hard time believing she'd fire the woman for something that was hardly her fault. But then she was a very good actress. It could've been William, but he hadn't seemed that perturbed. Was he a good actor too?

Liliana's head hurt.

She said a little prayer for the woman to find a new job quickly and tried to put it out of her head.

Rebecca came back with a tray of tea and coffee and set it on the low table in front of them.

Richard Blake walked into the room, followed by a young man in a button-down shirt and fitted vest. It reminded her of something Alfred would wear. Richard sat in the armchair closest to Liliana. Then a middle-aged man dressed in a suit and holding a briefcase came in and stood several feet behind Richard.

Liliana asked Meric, "Is Alfred coming?"

"I told him to take the day for sightseeing. I shouldn't need him."

"What about a lawyer?" she asked.

"My legal team has reviewed each draft of the contract, but I prefer to handle the final details myself."

"Brave man," Richard said.

Liliana got the feeling he didn't necessarily mean that in a good way, maybe an underhanded insult. Meric gave no reaction.

Everyone else arrived over the next few minutes, all with additional people following them like an entourage.

And then contract discussions started. Liliana tried to understand, but she didn't know several of the terms and she wasn't about to interrupt Meric to ask him to translate or explain. Instead, she found herself paying attention to the interactions of the people.

The Chauvelins stayed on opposite sides of the room from each other, and then she noticed Rebecca shooting glares at Meric. She'd assumed her tiff with her husband was something unrelated to the deal, but why would she be glaring at Meric?

Was something else going on?

Then she remembered how Rebecca had watched Meric so closely at the restaurant the other day, and how William had shrugged at her after the exchange with the Spanish-speaking staff person.

She wanted to figure out what was going on, if it was related to the deal, before Meric signed the final papers.

Richard called for a break, and everyone stood, stretched their legs, got some coffee, or went to find a restroom.

Liliana scooted closer to Meric and murmured in Spanish, quiet enough so that no one should be able to understand, even if they did know some Spanish. "Have you noticed our hostess?"

"Apparently she's decided she doesn't like me. Not uncommon."

"I think it's more than simply believing stupid stories. I think there's something more going on."

He turned to face her properly.

"She was watching you at lunch the other day, too, but it was different. I thought maybe she was attracted to you, or maybe just curious. Something's changed since then."

"Any idea as to what?"

"Not yet. Can you stall the talks a little?"

He nodded.

"Do you mind?"

"Not at all. I don't like going into a deal not knowing all the angles."

"I'm going to mingle with the assistants and lawyers, see if I can get anything out of them." She stood and meandered toward the windows, where one of the lawyers was standing. She struck up a conversation. She wasn't naturally that good at small talk, but she tried to mimic how Rebecca engaged people. It seemed to work pretty well.

She moved through that lawyer and a few others, and then came to Richard Blake's assistant.

"Have you watched Mr. Blake's movies?" he asked her.

"I'm sorry to say I haven't." She lowered her voice. "To be honest, I'd never heard of him before this week. But that's not surprising since I've only recently moved to America."

"Your English is good. I do hear your accent—Mexico, right?"

"Yes. A rural area not far from Arriaga. It's the south—"

"Southwestern coast." He grinned.

"How'd you know that?"

"Mr. Blake has a house on the ocean not far from there."

"Really?" What were the chances? It was the poorest state in the country and far from the US. Why would he have a house there?

"Yeah, it's really nice. Right on the ocean. As big as this place." He indicated the house they were in with his hand. "Maybe bigger. Lots of land too."

A thought exploded in her head. *It can't be.* "Modern like this?" she asked.

"No. Very traditional. Tile roof, red clay floors, wooden old-world furnishings, and you should see the tile in the master bath. The whole room is done in this blue and white tile. But it's all one continuous design."

Liliana's heart began to pound. "What kind of design?"

"It's like an old-time marketplace. Not one tile is the same, like some huge mural wrapping all the way around the room, behind the sinks, in the shower, around the tub. It's so cool. Every time we go there, I try to find a way to check out the room, try to see if there's some larger story in the mural."

There was a larger story. Liliana had found it when she'd helped her mother scrub that room. It was the house her mother had cleaned all those years.

Her mind scattered, scouring every corner to find a connection, understanding, something.

"It sounds amazing," she said. "I wish I could see it."

He shrugged. "Maybe Mr. Blake will let Mr. Toledan vacation there. He lets certain friends use it."

"I'll have to tell Meric to make friends with Richard."

Richard walked back into the room and poured himself a cup of coffee.

She said to the assistant, "I think I'll just go start working on that."

He grinned. "Good luck."

Richard returned to the armchair. Meric had wandered off to speak with the woman who owned the restaurant portion of the property.

Liliana took her seat on the couch. "Ready for these talks to be over?"

He pursed his lips. "I don't mind negotiations, as long as I get to gouge someone. But this one is taking a rather long time. Too much socializing mixed in."

He was the one who'd suggested the break—he didn't seem to mind the socializing. "So, what movie of yours must I absolutely see?"

His eyes lit up, and he sat forward and set his coffee on the table. And then he broke into a long ramble about all the movies he'd been in. Liliana tried to nudge the conversation on to something else, but it kept coming back to his movies, along with some mean gossip about other Hollywood elites. The more he talked, the more she realized his career and reputation were the only things he cared about. She came to think that crack about gouging someone in the negotiations was less about monetary gouging and more about reputation and image.

In the end, she found him rather boring and was thankful when Meric came back.

William called for everyone to return, and they all found their seats. As they continued discussions, Meric stopped at a particular line in the contract. It sounded like a simple section, but he was adamant about changing something. She was sure he was simply using this to stall.

She stood and walked out of the room, headed for the hall that had been indicated as the direction of the closest restroom. But instead of using the restroom, she peeked in all the doors—a closet, a guest room, the common restroom . . . The hall turned, moving closer to the ocean side of the house. She came to an office and slipped into the room. She would not usually do something like this, but she was determined to figure out what was going on with the Chauvelins and how it involved Meric.

There were huge French doors leading out to another patio, and in front of that was a large desk and a seating area to one side. The white walls were covered in paintings that were just splashes of paint on canvas.

In the hall, she heard voices. She ran across the room and hid behind the desk. The voices passed—probably servants.

She started opening desk drawers—pens and pencils, bank paperwork, a few files, an iPad.

At the middle drawer, she stopped.

There was a document regarding a property with a Houston

address. She didn't recognize the address. It could be nothing. She already knew the Chauvelins invested in property—that was the whole reason she and Meric were here in the first place.

But something told her not to ignore it. She took her phone out and did an internet search for the address. In the first page of search results popped up a picture. It wasn't a commercial property but some kind of estate.

A wild thought entered her head, but it was surely nothing.

Just in case, she snapped a picture of the document. Meric would understand what the document was for exactly, and she wondered if he would have some idea of the address.

As she walked back into the room where everyone was still talking about the point Meric was arguing, she pasted on a bland expression, as if bored by the negotiations. She sat next to Meric and showed him the picture on her phone of the document, zoomed in to the address.

Though he gave no outward indication of surprise, she could see in his eyes he recognized the address.

Chapter FORTY-THREE

Liliana put her phone back in her bag, and Meric took his phone out and texted Agent Bando, all while still arguing his point with the others about the contract. He held the phone so that Liliana could see the screen.

> We may have a situation.

I'm in LA. Is it related to the incident last night?

> I'm not sure. Please look into William Chauvelin ASAP.

The producer?

> Yes. We're in a possibly delicate situation. Will let you know what information I find.

You're with Liliana? Are you safe?

> In a meeting with multiple others. We're safe.

Richard's voice rose. "Are you even paying attention?" Meric had kept up perfectly with the conversation, but apparently Richard didn't like that he'd been texting at the same time.

Meric handed his phone to Liliana and looked at Richard with his usual detached expression. The discussion continued.

Where are you?

> It's Liliana. Meric is stalling and gave me the
> phone. We're at Chauvelin's house on the
> ocean.

She gave the part of the address that she remembered from listening to the phone navigation.

Bando had a few more questions, which she answered succinctly, while hoping her written English got her meaning across properly. Then she cut off the conversation to make sure she didn't draw attention to herself.

Meric let go of the point he was arguing, to the visible relief of several people. As a couple of the lawyers discussed the next portion of the contract, Meric leaned closer to Liliana and whispered in her ear, "May I see that picture again?"

She handed him her phone. He quickly read the document and handed the phone back to her.

She murmured in Spanish, "You know the property?"

"It's related to what you helped me with last night."

His stitches—the knife wound. She focused all her effort on not looking surprised or upset. He'd been on assignment for Bando when he'd been injured—that explained his immediately texting Bando. The Houston estate was somehow connected to that. Was that where he'd been hurt? Did William Chauvelin own the estate? Why else would he have a legal document about it?

Could William be involved in trafficking?

Liliana shifted to get up, but Meric grabbed her hand. He whispered in her ear, "Please don't leave my sight."

She stayed put, though the urge to do something raced through her veins.

A few minutes later, Meric latched on to what appeared to be another minor point. After fifteen minutes of negotiation, Richard called for another break.

"Let's go look at the view," Meric said to Liliana.

"It's so pretty." She stood up when he did, and they walked over to the windows. Then Meric motioned toward the doorway to the next room. They walked over. There was a grand piano in the middle of the room and not much else, except that it had access to an outside patio that led to the pool area. They went outside and stood at the railing, as if admiring the view.

Though they were alone, Liliana was still careful to keep her voice muted. "William Chauvelin owns the estate in Houston where you were attacked?"

"It looks that way. I was supposed to meet with the major buyer I've been tracking for months, but he didn't show and his people attempted to hold me prisoner instead."

"Do you think William is the buyer?"

"We know he has a lot of power and money. He fits."

"Does he know who you are? How is it possible you end up in this deal together?"

"If he is the trafficker I've been targeting, he would certainly know I was the one he was supposed to meet with at the estate, but he would have no way of knowing I'm working with the FBI. He would likely see me as competition." Then he added, "He's the one who initiated this deal."

Panic threatened to strangle her. "Then you need to get out of here."

"This is too good an opportunity. With all these Hollywood elites and lawyers, he can't possibly do anything, nor do I have any idea what his goal is. I need to find a way to corner him."

All she wanted to do was get him out of here. But then she reminded herself that if they could get William arrested, Meric would be safer. "I should sneak around the house some more. I'll find something."

"No," he said. His voice was imploring. "Please don't leave my sight."

"His attention is on you, not me. I can help."

He rested his hand on her cheek. "Please."

The warmth of his touch distracted her for a second. She forced her mind to work. "But what about Rebecca? What is her part in all this?" She paused, as a memory surfaced. Something Rebecca said.

"What?" Meric asked.

"I thought it was a little weird at the time, but she offered to help me get a green card and said William could easily find me a job."

Anger flashed in Meric's eyes.

"But Bando caught the person targeting me," Liliana said.

His voice was hard and low. "Bando caught the man who showed up for the fake drop."

"But didn't he confess?"

"He could've been threatened to confess. Or paid off. Any number of things." He took Liliana's hand and started leading her toward the door. "You need to get out of here. Now."

"No." She stopped.

"You're not safe."

"No less safe than you are. Like you said, we won't get an opportunity like this again."

"Please, Liliana."

"I'm not leaving, but I promise to stay in your sight." Mostly so she could make sure he was safe.

Liliana noticed through the glass that Richard Blake's assistant had wandered into the room with the piano. And it clicked into place—that was the connection. Richard must have allowed William to vacation at his Mexico house, and William had somehow seen her. She was sure she'd never met him—she never helped her mother when anyone was staying at the house. But her mother had kept a family picture in the little room she'd stayed in. Liliana also looked a lot like her mother—perhaps he'd gotten obsessed with finding a younger version of her. That made sense to Liliana. Her mother had been a beautiful person.

A wave of rage rolled over her as she realized the man possibly responsible for the deaths of her family was in the next room.

Liliana kept Meric's hand and led him back over to the railing. "Why would Rebecca be glaring at you?" she asked.

The muscles in his jaw worked. Then he looked out over the ocean. Finally, he said, "I would think she'd be glaring at you if she had any idea of what's going on. She seems like the jealous type."

"Could William have tricked her into talking me into getting a green card and leaving you?"

"It's possible." Then he added, "Will you please consider leaving? I'll make an excuse that you're ill."

She let her rage show in her eyes. "That man killed my mom, my dad, and my little sister."

He met her gaze. Several moments passed.

He rested his hands on either side of her face. "We'll get them justice. I promise."

Then he let her go, took out his phone, and made a call.

■ ▦ ■

Meric walked up to William Chauvelin, who was in conversation with Richard Blake.

"May I speak to you for a moment?" Meric asked William. "I wanted to get your thoughts on paragraph twenty-five."

Richard Blake rolled his eyes.

"All right," William said.

Meric glanced at Richard and added, "Privately." He headed toward the doorway to the music room, and William followed to the now-empty room.

They discussed paragraph twenty-five of the contract. Meric tried to get a better read on the man, but it was extremely difficult. Meric understood why people got so annoyed with him in negotiations—he knew he was also very difficult to read.

"I'm hoping to get this finished up today," Meric said. "My wife has been feeling ill." Perhaps he could get a reaction by talking about Liliana.

"Poor thing."

Meric watched him closely as he made his next comment. "Hopefully she's not pregnant. That would be inconvenient right now." Meric knew the buyer he'd been tracking had an obsession with virginity.

And there it was—the slight curl of his lip and a flash of anger in his eyes. And then it was gone. "Are you trying for kids?"

"Not trying, per se, but not exactly working against it either."

William nodded, nothing in his expression but cool detachment.

Liliana walked into the music room. "Meric, one of the lawyers is looking for you."

He made eye contact with her and nodded once, indicating he thought they were on the right trail. It took all of his strength to walk out of that room, to leave Liliana there with that monster. But he trusted her, that she would make her plan work as they'd discussed.

▦ ▦ ▦

"Looks like the talks are getting close to being wrapped up," Liliana said.

"Yes. It looks like everything will work out very nicely. It's satisfying when something you've worked on for so long comes together." He had gray hair at his temples. He must be several years older than Rebecca.

"I'm sure it is." She smiled. "But are we talking about the property or are we talking about your deal in Mexico?"

"I'm sorry—what do you mean?"

"Your deal in Mexico." She kept smiling. "That was a total mess, wasn't it?"

"I'm afraid I don't have any properties in Mexico."

"No real estate, that's true. But you have connections with certain, shall we call them, aggressive individuals. I wonder if you work with multiple cartels or just the one." She moved a casual step closer, still leaving several feet between them, and lowered

313

her voice. "How insane has it been driving you? Knowing that using the same supply route all the time is what put me directly in Meric's path?"

He didn't respond.

"Oh, you hadn't realized that," Liliana said. "I apologize—it's rude to point out other people's stupidity."

He lifted his chin.

She could see she was starting to get to him. Just like Meric, his emotions were difficult to see, but also just like Meric, she could read the subtleties in his expression.

Just like Meric . . .

She pushed that thought to the side. She had to focus on the immediate issue.

"I suspect I know what's really been eating at you." She paused, both to frustrate him and to see if she could get something out of him they could use, anything. "Knowing he married me. Imagining our intimacies."

Rage flickered in his eyes.

"You'd bought yourself a virgin," she said. "And you never got delivery. Is that why Josh and Carl didn't make it, as a punishment, or was that just to cover your tracks?"

He glanced at both doorways and took a step closer to her.

She forced herself to remain still.

He barely growled the words. "The smartest actions have multiple benefits."

"Like how I married Meric. I got money, protection, and I made myself less desirable to you all at the same time."

"Less desirable is not what you want to be."

"What does less desirable get me?"

He'd started to lean closer to her but straightened. "What are you hoping to get from this conversation? You're in *my* home. You're unprotected here."

"You're not about to touch me with all these people around."

"You think I don't know exactly where you are at all times?"

"Obviously not, or else I'd be captured by now, wouldn't I?"

He leaned closer again. "What are you trying to accomplish? You may think you have protection with Toledan, but that's nothing more than an illusion. I lured him here, brought him into my home—made him fulfill the delivery Carl failed to complete—and he had no idea."

"Maybe I'll let Rebecca in on your little secret."

He laughed under his breath.

And then Liliana remembered something Rebecca had said about accepting her husband's "eccentricities."

"She knows," Liliana said.

"She doesn't care what I do, as long as I make sure she's the top actress in Hollywood and our son is given everything. That's all she needs. And she makes me look like the loving family man. The perfect wife."

"What does being less desirable get me?" she asked again.

He shifted even closer, in her face. She stood her ground. "You would've gotten a better position—better food, regular bathing, nice clothes. But not now. The used ones don't get any of that."

"But they get used just as much."

"More. Now I'll rent you out to anyone who'll pay. You're beautiful, so plenty of men will pay."

Rage filled her veins, made her muscles tighten. She met his cold gaze.

The doorbell rang.

"Don't you want to see who that is?" she asked.

He gave no response, but she could see his mind working behind his eyes.

She took her phone out of her front pocket. The bottom end, where the receiver was, had been just hanging out of her pocket. She showed him the screen, the still-active call.

His eyes widened. "You little—" He reached for her throat.

She brought her arms up between his and slammed his hands to the side.

315

And then Meric was there and pulled William into a choke hold from behind. He growled in William's ear. "How does it feel to be bested by her?"

William spat unintelligible curses.

Bando and several agents entered the room. "William Chauvelin, you're under arrest for multiple counts of human trafficking and the hired murder of Carl Walsh and Joshua McConnell. You have the right to remain silent . . ."

William flailed and cursed but couldn't get out of Meric's grip.

The others, all the people involved in the deal, as well as several servants, rushed into the room, or at least watched from doorways.

"William!" Rebecca screeched. "What's going on? Why are you arresting my husband? He hasn't done anything."

Richard held his phone up, obviously recording the scene.

Bando took William from Meric to put handcuffs on him. William struggled, and Bando slammed him against the grand piano.

"Stop it!" Rebecca yelled.

Liliana walked up to her. "How did you know?"

"How'd I know what?" She looked back over at Bando. "You're hurting him. Don't you know who he is? Stop!"

"How'd you know about Meric?" Liliana demanded.

Rebecca's attention shifted back to Liliana. "This doesn't change anything."

"With William gone, will your career suffer?" Then Liliana added, trying to find any angle that would enrage Rebecca, get her talking, "What about your son? Who gets all of William's property? Your son . . . Or William's older son? His *first* son." She had no idea whose name any of the property was in or what the legal implications of his going to prison were, but she was counting on Rebecca being in too much of a distressed state to think clearly.

Rebecca screeched, "My son will not be second to anyone!"

She'd obviously hit a nerve and pushed harder. "How'd you

know?" Liliana yelled back. "You noticed the similarities, didn't you? And then you found out his mother was from Mexico—William's favorite hunting grounds."

"My son is not second to anyone. He is first in line!"

"Is that why you sent those men to kill Meric? To take him out of line? Or was it because Meric was such a pain and kept getting in the way?" She'd seen Meric's text to Liliana that day at the spa, that he was going to the gym—she'd known where to send the attackers. No one else would've known that.

"He had to go down! He was causing so much trouble, making William's life difficult, distracting him. William just wanted what he'd bought and paid for, but Meric kept messing everything up." She grabbed Liliana by the shirt.

Liliana punched her square in the face, and Rebecca stumbled back, holding her nose.

"That's for hurting my husband," Liliana said.

Everyone stared at Rebecca as she wailed in pain.

One of the FBI agents came up to her. "Rebecca Chauvelin, you're under arrest for the attempted murder of Meric Toledan."

"And maybe for accessory to human trafficking," Agent Bando added. "We'll see how many charges we can make stick."

The other FBI agent handcuffed Rebecca. He led her toward the door, and another agent followed with William.

Liliana was thankful their son didn't see any of this. She worried about him losing both of his parents so abruptly, but surely, it was better for him to be raised by someone else. She just hoped he could live down the legacy of his parents.

Bando instructed everyone to stay where they were, that they would be questioned.

Liliana walked over to Meric.

Meric stared at the doorway, where William had just been escorted out, and then he stared at Liliana. "He's my father."

FORTY-FOUR

Meric closed his eyes for a few seconds, like restarting a computer. Then he looked at Liliana and asked, "Are you all right?"

Her whole body felt like it was vibrating with energy—anger, fear, confusion, determination. "I'm fine. Are you all right?"

He took her hand in his, the one stained with Rebecca's blood. "Are you hurt anywhere?" He touched her neck lightly with his fingertips. "Did he hurt you?"

"I'm not hurt." She rested her hands on either side of his face. "Are you all right?"

"I don't know." He turned and walked out onto the patio. He gripped the railing so hard the tendons in his hands popped out.

She followed and rested her hand on his back, gave him a minute to try to process.

Finally, while still faced away from her, he said, "I'm sorry."

"You are not responsible for anything that monster did. You stopped him. If not for you, he'd have gone on for years longer, hurt so many more people." She moved closer and tried to catch his gaze, but he wouldn't look at her.

"I admit," she said. "I saw similarities. You have his jaw line and build. There are certain subtle mannerisms. You both don't show emotion. You're very difficult to read and have a natural coldness about you."

His jaw clenched.

"But I see past the cold," she said. "I always have."

Silence.

She knew what that silence meant—he was going to pull away, completely this time. For her protection.

"You care about people, Meric. You put others first. You truly believe it's the right thing to do. You make that choice no matter how much you suffer being alone. You are not your father, Meric. You are the man you've chosen to be."

He shook his head and looked away.

She took a deep, slow breath and prayed the gamble she was about to make paid off. "I know this," she said, "because I could never love a man like him. But I love you."

His gaze snapped to her.

"I'm not asking for anything," she said. "I don't want money or anything else. I won't even ask you to stay married to me. All I want . . ." She paused to steady her voice. "All I want is for you to forgive yourself, to allow yourself to be happy." A tear fell down her cheek. "Please, Meric."

Silence.

The breeze played with her hair, and the falling sun peeked through the clouds.

The door to the patio opened, and then Bando's voice broke the silence. "Meric, I need to take your statement." He paused. "Is everything all right?"

Liliana wiped her cheek and turned to face Bando. "I'll leave you alone. I'm sure you have a lot to go over." She walked past him into the house.

◼ ▓ ◼

Meric wasn't sure what to do. It'd always seemed so simple, knowing the right thing to do. Now, everything was jumbled in his head. It was disconcerting and alien to him.

Bando asked again if he was all right.

Meric could not remember anyone ever asking him that, other

than his mother when he was a child and Liliana. He pulled his emotions back and pushed his usual detached façade forward. He answered all of Bando's questions.

Finally, they were able to leave. He'd hoped he'd feel better, more clearheaded after getting out of that house, but he didn't. He opened the car door for Liliana and then got in behind the wheel.

Their drive was quiet.

As was the elevator ride up to the hotel room.

He sat on the couch, and she walked to another part of the suite.

Then she came back and sat next to him. "You should eat." She held out a pear to him, probably taken from the fruit basket in the suite's kitchen. How did she know he preferred pears to apples or any of the other fruit in the basket?

She took his hand and placed the pear in it. "Please eat."

He looked over at her, at those beautiful, dark eyes. He saw something more there than he'd seen before.

"Are you—"

"Don't think about me. I don't want you to feel any kind of responsibility or obligation. I don't want you to worry about anything," she said. "Think about letting go of everything that's hurt you for so long. Let yourself heal. You've tried so hard to give me the opportunity to heal; I want to help you with the same thing." She rested her hand on his cheek for just a moment, and her nails lightly brushed his skin as she pulled away.

She stood and walked out of the room. He watched her walk away from him.

■ ▩ ■

It was late when a text dinged on Liliana's phone. It was Agent Bando texting both her and Meric: "Rebecca is talking. She was trying to get Liliana to leave Meric and take a job William 'found' for her to get a green card. If that didn't work, he was going to have her create an opportunity to abduct Liliana. She tried making a deal by alleging Meric is a trafficker, and she has evidence of such. Part of William's plan was to anonymously provide evidence to law enforcement to take Meric down, once he had Liliana in his custody. Rebecca was not happy when I informed her all this evidence was from his undercover work with the FBI. Her spluttering reaction was classic. I wish I could show you the video."

She texted back her sincere thanks. Meric didn't respond.

She left Meric alone but peeked around the corner to check on him several times. He sat on the couch for hours, well into the night. He didn't speak, barely moved.

At a little after four in the morning, she checked on him again. He was gone.

She checked the kitchen and the small balconies, but he wasn't there. She looked for a note on all the tables. Nothing.

She took a deep breath and swallowed. Then she walked back through the bedroom to the closet and started packing.

She'd told him how she felt and made herself available, and she took his leaving, without even speaking to her or leaving a note, as an indication of how he felt—he felt some degree of attraction but nothing more. She'd promised him she didn't expect anything from him, and she'd keep her promise. She refused to make him feel trapped or pressured. She had no idea where she'd go, what would happen next, but she'd done what she could. She just prayed Meric found a way to heal.

She felt sluggish, but she kept moving.

She wiped her eyes again and looked in the bathroom mirror. Her eyes were puffy and red. The last thing Meric needed was a story in a tabloid about how his wife had left their hotel in such a mess. They'd turn it on him somehow.

After she was done packing, she tossed her bag on the bed and sat down. Then she knelt on the floor and prayed—for strength, for understanding, and especially for Meric.

Her tears stopped, and her eyes started to feel less puffy.

She glanced at the clock on her phone and was surprised to

see that it was after nine. And Meric hadn't returned, called, or even texted.

She stood, picked up her luggage, and headed for the door. Maybe Agent Bando would let her stay in the house where Jessa and Victoria were. But she had to figure out how to get back to Texas.

Out in the hall, she pressed the button for the elevator.

The doors opened, and there was Alfred on the elevator.

"Mrs. Toledan. I was just coming to see you." He glanced at her suitcase. "Where're you going?"

She tried to force a smile, tried to come up with some answer. But she couldn't think of anything and just stepped into the elevator.

Alfred hit the button for the lobby.

As they walked through the lobby and approached the doors to the outside, she heard voices, lots of voices. There were people outside—looked like reporters. Surely, they'd heard something had happened to the Chauvelins and had found out Meric had been there. They were probably already blaming him for something.

Alfred took her arm. "You don't have to talk to them. Just stay with me."

She didn't have many other options.

Hotel security helped clear the way, and Alfred opened the door of a taxi for her. The driver put her bag in the trunk. Why was Alfred here, ready with a cab? Maybe Meric had already put into motion her departure? That would make sense. He wouldn't just leave her—he would at least set up transportation.

But then Alfred got in the taxi with her. Maybe he'd been assigned the task of putting her on a plane?

"Where are we going?" she asked Alfred, as they pulled away from the hotel.

"Mr. Toledan asked me to escort you."

"To where?"

"I'm just supposed to escort you."

"Come on, Alfred."

"I honestly have absolutely no idea. Mr. Toledan set up the cab."

"You know everything he does."

"Not when it comes to you." He smiled a little, but confusion made it wobbly.

Liliana sighed and sat back.

A short while later, they pulled to a stop along a curb. The street was tree-lined and pretty, but she saw no reason why Meric would have them brought here.

She turned to Alfred.

He shrugged.

She got out of the car and stood on the sidewalk so she could get a better look around. There were pretty homes, a park on the corner, and a large white stucco building—more of a complex, really—on the other corner.

She turned to the cab driver in the hopes he had some kind of information. Anything.

The driver had gotten out and was standing by the car door. "Mr. Toledan asked me to wait here."

"Wait for what?"

He shrugged. "He paid me enough to cover my fares for more than a day. I didn't ask a lot of questions."

She looked around again.

And then she saw him.

He was in the park across the street, watching them. She glanced both ways and crossed the road toward him.

"What's going on?" she asked.

"I need to know—are you sure you meant what you said?"

She met his gaze. "Yes," she said. "I love you."

Something changed in his eyes, but he quickly glanced away, looking across the street.

"I don't want you to think that means I expect anything from you," she said. "I told you because I want you to understand how I see you. I see who you really are, and I want you to see it too."

He turned back to her. "Do you remember that first morning, after you'd showered, and I retreated back to my room?"

She nodded. She remembered how she'd felt she'd done something wrong.

"I'd known you were beautiful, but seeing you like that, finally fully seeing you, I was overwhelmed—your silky skin, thick satin hair, your grace. I wasn't sure how to handle it."

She didn't know how to respond. He'd admitted to being attracted, and she was as well, but she wanted more. Though she was not going to ask for anything.

He continued, "Over time, I realized there was more to it. It finally hit me the night I pushed you to get upset, get it all out. You remember?"

"It was what I needed."

"You let me hug you, and the feel between us changed. I hated walking away from you. It was torture. But I had to protect you. I couldn't let that moment of healing be marred by my attraction."

"It wasn't—"

"As I stood there at my balcony railing, I realized there was a reason you were so much more difficult for me than any other woman. There was a reason I didn't call Bando when we met and try to find another option. There was a reason I suggested getting married as a solution. It was about more than protecting you. I was attracted to more than your physical beauty. I was attracted to your strength, how you can be so broken and still have a kind soul. I stayed away to protect you from a monster like me."

"Meric—"

"I've been in love with you from the beginning."

She had no words.

Everything he'd done, every single action, all the hours he'd stayed away, all of it was to protect her? Not just from his attraction, but from how deeply he felt about her?

She went back through all their interactions and tried to understand.

Every time he'd pulled away, it was him controlling himself, the situation. Had he been hurting all this time?

She closed the distance between them with two steps and wrapped her arms around him. He held her tightly, a hand in her hair.

They stood there in silence.

Children laughed in the distance. The breeze ruffled her hair.

Meric murmured in her ear, "I will remember." He paused. "I will remember how you sacrifice yourself for strangers. I will remember how you fight. I will remember how you never let me push you away, how you fought for me." He touched her neck with his fingertips, and they tremored slightly. "I will remember how you make me feel. I'd thought I wasn't capable of deep emotion. I'd thought I was dead inside." He stood straighter and met her eyes.

Her heart threatened to beat out of her chest. *Is he saying goodbye?*

He whispered, "I love you." And then he lightly touched his lips to hers.

The kiss quickly deepened, and he pulled her tightly to him.

She felt lost. There were no solid thoughts in her head, just how this felt—the softness of his lips, the strength of his arms around her and his body against hers, his taste.

Then he stepped back. He ran his hands through his hair.

"Meric . . . I didn't think . . . I didn't want you to feel obligated to me when you couldn't return my feelings."

And then he smiled. An actual smile. He even had a dimple in one cheek. "I'm getting ahead of myself."

"Ahead of yourself?"

"We need to do things in the right order."

"What do you mean?"

His expression sobered, though the smile remained in his eyes, and he knelt on the grass. He looked up at her. "Liliana, will you marry me?"

"Um . . . we're already married."

325

"In the eyes of the law, yes, but I want you to have a real wedding. In a church."

She glanced back at the complex across the street. She could see better from this angle—could see the tall, square bell tower.

"I want to marry you before God," he added.

She rested her hands on his cheeks. "Yes." She grinned. "Yes."

His dimple showed itself again. He stood, took her hand, and led her across the grass.

Before they could get across the street, two cars, closely followed by a van, zoomed to a stop at the curb. Cameras flashed, and reporters yelled questions at him. They must have followed the cab. Or maybe someone had seen them in the park and tipped off the press?

They yelled a bunch of questions about the Chauvelins. Liliana worried it would dampen Meric's spirits, but he kept moving forward.

It wasn't until one of them asked, "Mr. Toledan, what are you doing here?"

He paused and looked over. "I'm marrying my wife."

More flashes and more questions.

Alfred had followed and now stood at the door to stop the reporters.

Meric and Liliana walked into the church together, into the sanctuary with tall, wood-beamed ceilings, and up the aisle toward a reverend waiting at the altar. They stood there together, before God, and held hands.

KEEP READING FOR
A SNEAK PEEK

at Melissa Koslin's Other Breathtaking
Romantic Suspense, *Never Miss*

"Sarah Jeane Rogers," she muttered. "Elizabeth Jeane Jones." Which ID to use this time? "Eenie meenie minie moe . . ." She held up the license in her right hand. "Sarah Jeane Rogers it is."

She took the license with the name Mary Jeane Smith out of her wallet and replaced it with a license with the name Sarah Jeane Rogers. She finished cleaning out her wallet and put Mary Jeane Smith away in the safe, closed the door, and checked that it was securely locked.

She walked out of the shadowed storage space, empty except for the small but heavy safe bolted to the concrete floor. The space was a little bigger than her last storage unit, but it'd been the smallest available and she didn't want to go searching all over LA in this heat and traffic for a better deal. She'd enjoyed Montana much more, but she knew better than to stick around anywhere too long. And they wouldn't likely spend much time looking for her in a place like this—crowded and hot, two of her least favorite things.

She pulled the overhead storage unit door closed with a clatter and locked it.

Inside the car, Mac had his paws up on the window and was watching her. She made a shooing motion, and he scooted back over to the passenger seat, still watching her as she unlocked the car with her spare key and got in.

"What?" she said. "I left the car running. You were fine."

He sat down on his seat and curled his fluffy tail around himself.

She tossed her drill on the back seat floor next to the case for her McMillan TAC-50 rifle, took a drink from the water bottle in the console, opened the apartment guide she'd picked up, and started scanning for studio apartments.

Mac got up on his hind legs and pawed the passenger window.

"You want to hear and smell what's going on? All right, just a few inches." She pressed the button to lower the passenger window. She kept waiting for that button to stop working too, like most of the buttons in this old Chevy Blazer. Mac stretched his long body to stuff his nose out the window. She smiled as he sashayed his tail contentedly.

People were gathering at the end of the block of blue roll-up doors. She'd seen a poster in the office about abandoned storage unit auctions today. She decided to stay a little longer until she figured out which apartments she would look at and allow Mac to enjoy watching the people.

She caught a glimpse in her rearview mirror just as Mac's tail stopped and his fur went up. There was a man walking up from behind the car. The man walked around the passenger side of the car, surely headed toward the auction.

A low growl sounded from Mac's throat.

The man stopped and looked at Mac, less in a shocked way but more like he was intellectually curious. "Is that a dog or a cat?"

"He's a Maine coon. He won't hurt you." *Unless you do something stupid.*

"A what?"

"It's a kind of cat."

He looked from Mac to her, made eye contact.

She started to think he was going to say something, do something. She felt his focused attention on her like the weight of a piano. Then his expression cooled, kind of detached, and he walked away.

She turned back to her apartment guide, not sure what to make of him. Mac purred, and she stroked his fluffy orange fur.

Then she looked out the windshield at the man, now standing at the back of a small crowd. He stood straight with his arms crossed and interacted with no one. There was something there, something a little different about him somehow, but she couldn't quite put her finger on it. Or was it just that he stayed back away from the other people that made him stand out to her? He was pretty standard-looking—tall, dark hair, jeans and T-shirt. Well, *standard* wasn't the right word . . . Around here, the lack of man bun made him seem unique. She laughed and went back to her apartment guide.

She started making calls to a few of the apartments to ask some key questions, the ones she didn't like to ask in person because people looked at her like she was a crazy paranoid.

Then the group of people moved down the row of storage units, closer to her. Mac changed to paws on the dash so he could look out the windshield at the people.

"Just a few more minutes, buddy." She dialed the next number. She wasn't having much luck so far finding a place that met her requirements.

A man wearing work pants and a T-shirt with the name of the storage facility on it cut the lock on the unit where the crowd was gathered. He lifted, and the roll-up door rumbled up on its track. An older man, surely the auctioneer, started giving statistics about the unit while all the people craned to get a look inside. Once everyone had taken a look, the auction started.

The man from before remained behind the rest of the crowd. He made a bid a hundred dollars higher than what the auctioneer called for, and several people turned and glared at him. He adjusted his rectangular glasses, re-crossed his arms, and remained focused straight ahead.

She realized she'd stopped apartment hunting and was just watching him. She didn't like to admit to herself when she found a man attractive, but that wasn't what really had her attention. She narrowed her eyes. *He knows something—he knows there's something of value in that unit that the others don't see.* Or was he just stupid?

No . . . he definitely wasn't stupid.

She crossed her arms and studied him.

A few seconds later, the auctioneer announced that the man had won the auction. The crowd started to disperse, except the man who'd won. He walked up to the auctioneer, surely to finish the transaction.

A glint from across the way caught her eye.

She turned back to the man. The auctioneer shifted around to the other side of him and drew him a couple of feet over.

She put her Blazer in gear, in reverse, and eased on the gas, wondering if the man had any idea he was about to die.

*　　　*　　　*

"Cash only."

"Of course," Lyndon said. As if he didn't know the auction had to be paid in cash.

The beat-up Blazer that he'd walked past earlier started backing up. He'd wondered why she'd sat there for so long.

The auctioneer—Walter—thumbed through his papers. "And there is the matter of the auction fee."

"Yes, of course." Lyndon had his hand on his cash in his pocket. "How much is the total?" He already knew the answer, of course, but thought it might be rude not to wait for Walter to calculate the simple figure.

The Blazer drove forward now, slowly around them, rather close to the line of storage units on the opposite side of the drive lane.

"And you'll need to have the unit emptied within forty-eight hours," Walter said.

Lyndon did his best to keep annoyance out of his tone. "What was the total?"

The door to the Blazer opened, and the young woman with the odd cat got out and opened the back door as well. Then she jogged toward him, and her long dark braid bounced on her shoulder. "Hey, can I ask you something?"

Lyndon watched her approach—though he knew he shouldn't—even while Walter talked to him. She looked like she had Native American blood in her veins. He saw it mostly in her eyes—large and dark, framed with long lashes.

"You bought that unit, right? Can I buy something from there off you?"

Walter rested a hand on her arm and attempted to guide her to the side. "We're almost done here. Then you can talk business all you like."

But she didn't move. Rather, she appeared to brace herself, which seemed at odds with her casual tone.

Walter gave up on her and put his arm around Lyndon's shoulders to guide him away. While Lyndon didn't particularly care for being touched, he moved with Walter. He was curious to know what she wanted, curious about her in general if he was being honest with himself, but he would not let himself feel this kind of intense interest.

The woman pushed him to the side.

Before he could get angry, he heard something hit the wall behind him. He looked over and saw a . . . Was that a bullet hole in the block?

The woman had taken his hand and was already dragging him toward her vehicle. He followed.

"Get in," she ordered.

He obeyed, and almost tripped on the long case that was on her back seat floor. She jumped in the driver's seat and tore down the narrow drive lane.

"What's going on?" he asked.

"Someone just tried to kill you. A sniper on the building opposite."

"What?" He paused to allow his thoughts to catch up to reality. "No, they had to have been aiming at something else."

"You mean the auctioneer who was nudging you into position? Don't think so." She turned out of the storage facility and merged with traffic, driving at the same speed as the other cars. Her voice didn't waver, her hands didn't shake, she didn't even appear to be sweating. And that odd cat lay on the front seat, curled up as if nothing out of the ordinary had just happened.

"Who in the world are you?" he asked.

"No one important." She made another turn.

"How did you know what was going to happen?"

She said nothing.

"Okay," he said. "Then let's go with, who are you and why did you do that?"

Again nothing.

"Are you going to tell me anything?"

"I don't know anything to tell you. Other than you really got on someone's bad side. You need to figure out what you did and remedy the situation."

"I haven't done anything that could possibly warrant being shot at." Unless . . . his theory had some merit. But no one else even knew about it.

"I don't know what to tell you other than figure it out." She stopped the car.

"You're not even going to tell me who you are?"

"This is where you exit the car."

He didn't move.

She shifted and took something out of her waistband, and she turned and aimed a semiautomatic handgun at him. "Out."

He hesitated for a second, confused, a feeling to which he was not at all accustomed. Then he looked more closely at the gun—a Glock 19. "There's no magazine in that gun."

"You wanna bet I don't have a bullet in the chamber?"

He lifted his chin. "You won't pull the trigger anyway."

She raised an eyebrow, and as he looked into her dark eyes, he considered changing his opinion about her killer instincts. Her eyes were deep, but not in a romantic way—more like she'd seen terrible things no one should have seen, carried memories she longed to forget.

He focused on a calm voice, and it came out almost gentle, which he hadn't heard in his own voice in years. "Please tell me who you are and how you knew that was going to happen."

Some of the cold in her eyes faded, and she lowered the gun. "Please just go. Trust me—it's for your own good."

"What do you mean 'for my own good'? Someone just shot at me, and you put yourself in the way of the bullet."

"They weren't going to shoot until they had a good line of sight."

"How do you know that?"

"Because that's how it's done. You lie in wait until you have a clean shot. If not, it gets messy real fast."

He felt his expression twist in frustration. "Who are you?"

She sighed, and he heard years of wariness in that quiet exhale, more years than her smooth skin seemed to hint at. All the cold finally melted out of her eyes, and he saw kindness looking back at him.

He could do nothing but stare back at her, at those dark eyes that now looked like the night sky, vast and beautiful, and so far away.

Her voice came out in a murmur. "Please."

He felt a strange instinct to stay. "You just put yourself in the middle of this. Whatever this is. Maybe we shouldn't separate."

"I'm sorry I can't explain, but no."

"I don't want you being hurt because of me."

"Trust me, you're better off alone."

"I'm worried about you, not—"

Her voice was still soft. "Please trust me."

He hesitated, still staring back at her.

Then he opened the car door and stepped out. He'd barely shut the door when she punched the gas and left him standing there. He watched her car disappear around a corner, irrationally unable to look away.

■ ▓ ■

Lyndon climbed the stairs to his apartment. His heart had stopped pounding, but his mind continued to race, which made his head feel like it was splitting in half with pain. He couldn't quite believe that she was right—that someone wanted him dead. And instead of focusing on the immediate issue, his mind kept turning back to her . . .

Lyndon rubbed his hands over his face. *I'm losing my mind.*

His neighbor's door opened, and a middle-aged man with a dark mustache stepped into the hall. "You're home early," Mr. Porchesky said to Lyndon with a smirk.

Lyndon felt his patience running thin. He continued walking.

"When are you going to get a real job?" Mr. Porchesky muttered.

"When my endeavors stop providing the income I need."

"*Endeavors*," Porchesky scoffed.

Lyndon suspected his neighbors thought he did something illegal. He'd never bothered telling any of them that he had three PhDs plus a master's in cybersecurity.

"Good afternoon." Lyndon unlocked his apartment door, walked inside, and locked the door.

He looked around, making sure he didn't see something different from what he'd left this morning, but everything was the same as always—his desk and other makeshift work surfaces took up most of the living room, with one little corner reserved for his business of reselling items of value from abandoned storage units, the one armchair in the corner, and bookshelves covering every other wall. Everything appeared to be in the same order in which he'd left it.

And yet something felt very different.

He headed to the kitchen and filled a glass with water. That just made him think of the water bottle in her console, which made him think of the way she'd turned and aimed a gun at him.

Then he thought about how she'd looked at him in the end, the kindness.

He sighed.

He was accustomed to being able to see angles others could not, but just now he couldn't see any of the angles—neither that shooter firing at him from atop a building nor the woman who'd first saved his life and then threatened it. Though he felt certain she wouldn't have actually fired at him. Why save his life just to take it herself?

When did my thoughts turn to such things?

His morning had started off so normally. He'd gotten up at his usual time of five a.m., and he'd worked on his research for several hours. He was waiting to hear back from Dr. Grant about his thoughts on his most recent email, so he'd been focusing on the one wild theory he'd developed. He wasn't one for wild theories, but this one was feeling more and more logical as he continued digging.

No one else even knew about this theory.

Something didn't fit. Maybe someone had mistaken him for someone else? Or perhaps the shooter was some lunatic. But if he was one of those shooters who stole headlines from time to time, he'd have shot up the crowd at the auction rather than wait for everyone to leave.

And the woman . . .

She'd said the auctioneer had been positioning him. As he thought back through the event, he had to admit that seemed accurate.

That was a place he could start—the auctioneer.

He walked over to his computer and sat down. He researched Walter's name and the name of his auction company.

After about an hour, Lyndon clicked on his desk lamp and set his glasses down with a clatter. He'd found nothing of great interest. Walter had what appeared to be a perfectly average family—a daughter and two grandchildren in Garden Grove. His business brought in decent money, but nothing terribly noteworthy. Lyndon found nothing that might possibly explain his behavior today. Perhaps he was nothing but a pawn? Being blackmailed? Based on the research, that seemed like the most rational explanation.

Another idea came into his mind like the slide of a gun snapping a bullet into place. She'd said to figure it out. If there was one thing he was good at, it was figuring things out. But he had nowhere to start—other than with her. He'd noticed several things during the brief time he'd been able to observe her, some things that seemed to nudge him in her direction, no matter how much he felt the need to fight against it. He put in his earbuds, blasted "Iron Man" by Black Sabbath, typed the first search—her license plate number—into the computer, and began piecing together her mystery. Or rather, discovering exactly how deep her mystery went.

Melissa Koslin is a fourth-degree black belt in and certified instructor of Songahm Taekwondo. In her day job as a commercial property manager, she secretly notes personal quirks and funny situations, ready to tweak them into colorful additions for her books. She and Corey, her husband of twenty years, live in Florida, where they do their best not to melt in the sun.

SHE SAVED HIS LIFE.
NOW THEY'RE IN A RACE TO STOP
A DEADLY ATTACK.

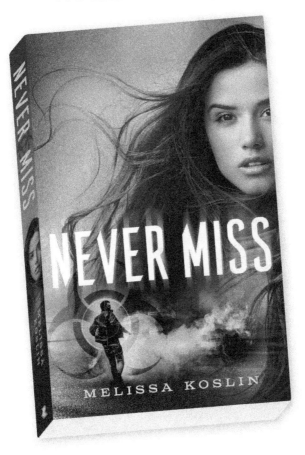

Former CIA sniper Kadance Tolle possesses a special set of skills and a rare pedigree. She comes from a family of assassins, and by saving Lyndon Vaile's life, she risks being found by them. Despite the danger, Kadance feels compelled to help Lyndon discover who is after him and his incendiary research, which indicates that the Ebola virus is man-made and about to be weaponized.

Я Revell
a division of Baker Publishing Group
www.RevellBooks.com

MEET
MELISSA

Find Melissa online at
MelissaKoslin.com
and on social media at

LET'S TALK
ABOUT BOOKS

Beyond the Book

Visit our Facebook page, where you can join our online book club, Beyond the Book, to discuss your favorite stories with Revell authors and other readers like you!

facebook.com/groups/RevellBeyondtheBook

Revell Roundup

Subscribe to our specially curated weekly newsletter to keep up with your favorite authors, find out about our latest releases, and get other exclusive news!

bakerpublishinggroup.com/revell/newsletters-signup